SOUTH BEACH SHAKEDOWN

ALSO BY DON BRUNS

Barbados Heat

Jamaica Blue

A Merry Band of Murderers
(editor & contributor)

Death Dines In
(contributor)

SOUTH BEACH SHAKEDOWN

A NOVEL

DON BRUNS

Oceanview Publishing

IPSWICH, MASSACHUSETTS

ISBN 10: 1-933515-02-3
ISBN 13: 978-1-933515-02-1

Published in the United States by Oceanview Publishing,
Ipswich, Massachusetts
www.oceanviewpub.com

Distributed by Midpoint Trade Books
www.midpointtradebooks.com

10 9 8 7 6 5 4 3 2 1

PRINTED IN THE UNITED STATES OF AMERICA

This book is dedicated to Jim Gideon, Anne (Pike) Gideon, Tom Biddle, and my brother, Dave Bruns, and his wife, LouAnn Frey. I stole their names. They are much nicer people than their fictional personae.

ACKNOWLEDGMENTS

I need to thank my buddy, Jim Gideon, who is an inspiration on so many levels. I love ya, man! To my, friend Mike Trump, and my reading pals, Jay Waggoner and Don Witter, thanks for the support. Bob and Pat thanks for an extraordinary interest in the project. Felix at Mango's Tropical Cafe on South Beach, thank you for your enthusiasm and the drink recipe. Thank you Deb at Circle Books. Thanks to the staff at the Grand Condominiums and DoubleTree Hotel on Biscayne Bay, to the waitstaff at the News Café, Nikki Beach, Larios, Opium, The Sky Bar, and Mango's — all on South Beach. Thanks to the Gold Rush in Miami, Mike's Bar at the Venetian, and the Sea Line Marina. Here's to the Redhead Lounge in Chicago, and a special shout to Tom Biddle, my friend who has turned his condo over to Gideon Pike for the remainder of this novel. Thanks to Sue Grafton who helped make this all possible, my wife, Linda, and Mark Mcgrath from Suger Ray, and finally, thanks to my brother, Dave, who has been a source of inspiration, encouragement, critical analysis, and enthusiasm. I'm thankful for everyone who is in my corner.

SOUTH BEACH SHAKEDOWN

Courtesy of Mango's Tropical Cafe, South Beach

1¼ ounces of Captain Morgan's Parrot Bay Coconut Rum
1¼ ounces of Ron Zacapa Centenario Rum
¾ ounce Amaretto

Fill a 15 ounce Hurricane Glass with ice. Add the above ingredients, and fill with pineapple juice and a splash of grenadine.

Garnish with a slice of pineapple, a Maraschino cherry, and an umbrella.

SOUTH BEACH SHAKEDOWN

CHAPTER ONE

He wished he were invisible. Not the kind of invisibility where no one could see you, but the kind where no one noticed you. Where you could walk through a crowd and no one would look. Head down, an anonymous face in the crowd. His kingdom for invisibility, right now, at this very moment. Instead, he was very visible. He was the center of attention as the Asian man in front of him spoke.

"Gideon, Gideon," Jimmy Shinn shook his head. "After we covered up for you? After what we did? And all we're asking is that you sign the contract. Another ten years, Gideon, for the publishing rights. And the recording rights next year. Be a player." The corners of his mouth turned up, but the capped teeth stayed clenched together.

Gideon Pike cowered under the dark-skinned Korean's gaze. The consequences. He had to weigh the consequences. He looked up at the man through thick, pop-bottle glasses, watching his facial expression. If he didn't sign, he knew what was in store. And eventually, Jimmy Shinn always seemed to get his way.

"The contract, Gideon."

"Let me think about it." He folded his hands defiantly on the kitchen table. He wished he were invisible.

"Sure. Take a week, a month, a fucking year. In the meantime, we'll be gently persuading you. Do you believe the gentle part?"

It wouldn't be gentle. The balding songwriter gathered an ounce of courage. "No. Not this time."

Shinn popped a ripe green Spanish queen olive into his mouth, methodically chewing it and savoring the unique briny flavor. He spit the pit into his open hand, adding it to the six other ones. "How long since your last hit?"

No answer.

"How long? Three years?"

Gideon was silent.

"How long since you wrote a song?" He raised his voice.

"I've brought two new writers in the last six months. Now you can suck their blood. What do you want from me?"

"What do I want?" Shinn laughed. "I'm like a kid in an amusement park. I always want more. Another ride, another sno-cone, more cotton candy." He picked up another olive from the tray and put it in his mouth. The only sound in the room was his methodical chewing. A moment later he spit the pit into his waiting palm. "And I want a little respect. I want you to respect the fact that I've never gone to the police with the evidence. I've never turned you in. It's been three years since the accident and you're still walking around free as a bird. The contract, Gideon."

Respect? This slimy, low-life asshole wanted respect? It was intimidation. Rule through fear. Nothing more. Pike had met Shinn's father only one time, but he knew immediately where this creature had crawled from. The apple didn't fall far from the tree.

"And if I say no this time?"

"What happened the last time, Gideon?"

He was confused. He gave Shinn a puzzled look.

"Rusty? Remember how he looked when they pulled his body from the water?"

Jesus! The crushed skull, the bloated face and limbs, and chunks of skin missing where fish had feasted.

"You said you had nothing to do with that!"

"Don't believe everything I tell you."

Pike closed his eyes. There was too much at stake.

"And what about this interview you're giving? The story I hear is that you want to talk about your business relationships. You want to go public with what happened, put it all out on the table? Tell me, Gideon. Is that really what you want to do? Do you think that's safe for all concerned?" Shinn put his face inches from Pike's, his hot breath blowing onto the songwriter's face. "Are you that stupid? Are you?" He turned in disgust.

Shinn walked to the sink, nodding to his partner, a big man with an open-collar shirt and an ill-fitting sport coat. "Ever hear how olive pits sound when they grind up in a garbage disposal? Listen."

He switched on the appliance and dumped the pits into the drain. The harsh grinding sound filled the small room. Metal against seed, chewing them up.

"Stand up, Gideon. Give me your hand."

"No! You wouldn't."

"No. I wouldn't. I don't have the stomach for it." Shinn smiled, the perfect white teeth against the dark skin. He looked into Gideon's eyes. Turning to the beefy man next to him he said, "Sam. Take his hand."

Sam grabbed Pike's hand and pulled him from his chair.

"No."

"Yes. Can you write if you can't play piano?"

"Jesus! No. Jimmy, please."

"I know what olive pits sound like. I know what chicken bones sound like. Human flesh and bones? I've never heard that sound."

CHAPTER TWO

Sever rolled over and looked at the clock. Who the hell was calling him at 8 A.M.? Too damned early. The Stones had been in Chicago last night, and he and Keith had some catching up to do. Man, there was a lot of catching up. That man should be dead by now. He grabbed the receiver and croaked. "Hello?"

"Mick?"

"Ginny?" His ex. The only reason she would call would be if she was —

"Mick? I've got some trouble."

Bingo.

"Where are you?"

"Miami."

"And?"

"I've lost a client."

Sever rubbed his eyes. Lost a client?

"Do you hear me?"

"Sure. You lost a client. How do you do that?"

"I'm editing his book. Actually, it's notes, scraps of paper, stray thoughts and that kind of thing."

"Ginny. I'm lost."

"The company wants me to shape it all into a best-seller, Mick. You know how that game is played. Anyway, the star of the production has gone missing."

"And you're calling me because?"

"You know him well. You've done interviews, articles, stories on him."

"Eventually you'll tell me who this mysterious vanishing man is."

"Gideon Pike."

Sever couldn't help but grin. "Gin, he's done this before. Every time someone tries to get close, Gideon takes a powder."

"I know. And that's why the publisher's asked me to try to work with him. I had a long talk with your friend, Mr. Pike. He assured me that he was ready to sit down and talk about the music that defined a generation. Three days, and he's gone. And Mick, I went up to see him, and the door was unlocked. His condo was trashed. Drawers pulled out, papers scattered on the floor —"

"Ginny, maybe he was in a hurry. And you've got to know this about him, he's a private person. What can I say?"

He could hear her thinking. He swore he could actually hear her mind working. He knew her too well.

"Mick, he told me it was time. He said he had to come clean, do some confessing, and it wouldn't be pretty. I really thought we were connecting."

Sever remembered the last time *he'd* connected with Ginny. It was always a little painful, knowing what had been his was no longer. It had been awhile. "So what do you want me to do?"

"I really want to pursue this project, and I need someone to help me find him."

"You're kidding. Why?"

"Maybe because this is a chance to really do a story that has some meat to it. Mick, I've been editing other people's stuff for too long. It's time to do something on my own. Here's a chance to really find out what makes him tick, and a chance to explore what makes his music so —" she seemed to struggle for the word, " addictive."

"Ginny —" She was on a roll.

"And maybe because I think he's in trouble. You know how you do just about anything to get to the bottom of the story? Your best writing has been when someone makes you dig for the story. Well,

I'm asking you to help me get to the bottom of mine."

"If anyone can do his story justice, I'm sure it's you."

"Mick, you're as close to him as anyone. I mean, the man wrote a song about you."

"Soul of a Lonely Man." Sever had committed the lyrics to memory.

Never content with the man God has made you
Never at ease you just wander alone —

"Mick?"

"I know."

You can't be true to the friends that have found you
You wander this world, 'cause you don't have a home.

"Actually, I think he had a thing for you."

Sever smiled, picturing the balding man with his thick glasses. Definitely not his type.

"So help me find him."

"What if he really doesn't want to be found?"

"He sounded scared."

"Scared?"

"Yes."

"That's it?"

"Mick, he told me his career may cost him his life. Do you understand that?"

Sever was quiet for a moment. "Pike was always a little melodramatic. I think he probably just took himself a little too seriously. Maybe he felt overworked. Pressured."

"He was definitely under pressure. He said he had confessions to make that could get him in trouble, but he felt he had to make them public."

"Ginny, I haven't seen him in a long time. We *were* close, but something happened. I don't know what. We haven't stayed in touch, so I really don't know what's happened to his life." Pike hadn't responded to Sever's phone calls in three years. At first, he'd just called to stay in touch, then to do an interview. It wasn't like Pike to ignore him. Over the years they'd become closer than just business associates. It was hard to put into words, but Sever felt a strong bond between the two of them, and the lack of communication worried him. He called mutual acquaintances searching for answers. They never came.

"He talked about you. He said you were one of the few people who really understood him. He said you've spent time with him, you know where he goes and what he does."

Sever remembered. He was never concerned about the man's sexual preference. That had never entered into the equation. Other people worried about Pike being gay. His record company, his producers, his agent. They wanted to pair him with female singers and actresses like the studios of the '40s did with Rock Hudson. Sever never worried about it. He and Pike were both impressed with each other's talent and level of success. That was enough.

"Mick, remember that night on South Beach? You told me about it, and Gideon reminded me a couple of days ago."

South Beach. They'd been to Mango's, a hot, hip, happening Latin Club on the strip where the salsa band was pumping out the music, and the bartenders were up on the bar, grinding it out for the crowd. Guys with cowboy hats and no shirts and girls in halter tops and hot pants, lewdly gyrating in unison. And the sultry waitress bringing a tray of tubes with neon-colored exotic beach drinks.

"Want a blow job? I give the best blow job on the beach." She shouted above the noise as she uncorked a tube of Baily's Irish Cream and something, then put the closed end in her mouth and tilted the tube to Sever's mouth, draining the sweet liquid down his throat before he had a chance to say anything. Five bucks. A blow job.

Sever and the slightly pudgy, balding guy with thick, horned-rim glasses moved through the crowd, getting closer to the bar, the guy watching the dancers, his head bouncing to the beat as the crowd pressed closer. No entourage, no bodyguards, just Sever and Pike.

"Hey man, I love your music."

"Hey, you're Gideon Pike. Jesus! Why don't you play us a song?"

Men and women doing double takes, and the Latin rhythm intense and hot, boiling over, pulsating with a driving beat.

"Hey, it's Gideon Pike. Is this cool or what?"

Two more blow jobs.

"Hey, gay boy!"

Sever and Pike ignored them.

"Gay Boy — Talkin' to you!" They screamed in his face with the music full blast. Two gay-bashers, looking for a little rough stuff in a city where anything goes.

Pike spun around and worked his way through the tight crowd. He pushed and shoved the revelers from his path, and Sever followed as best he could. Finally, they reached the sidewalk, swarming with a Saturday night rush.

Sever tried to keep up, his bad knee aching from the long night of walking. Pike plowed ahead, taking long strides for a man with such short legs. He was three, four lengths in front. The two men pushed Sever aside as they raced to catch him.

The bigger man, short hair, maybe ex-military with a gut, grabbed Pike's crotch with a death squeeze. His partner ran up shouting "Queer. You fucking fag!"

Sever lost it. The throbbing pain in his knee, any concern for his own safety with two guys bigger than he was, he lost it. He dove into the fray, tackling the military guy, driving him to the hard concrete as the man's head cracked on the cement. Sever leaped to his feet and drove a fist into the second man's gut, catching him with an uppercut as the man doubled over. Neither of them got up. They didn't move at all. Sever tried to catch his breath, the rush of adrenaline and three blow jobs coursing through his veins.

When he finally pulled himself together, Gideon Pike was gone. He'd done it before, disappearing when trouble reared its head. You had to deal with quirks in personalities. It was all part of a relationship.

"Yeah, he pulls the disappearing act a lot. I remember."

"Well, he pulled it on me, too. Can you spare some time? Come on down and give me a hand. Maybe we can find him, and I can get this project finished."

Gideon Pike. There was a time when Sever would get a call at three or four in the morning, at least once a month and Gideon would be on the other end, confessing, complaining, or bashing and trashing someone. "Off the record, Mick. Off the record." And a lot of it would have been A-plus material for Sever's entertainment columns. He'd listened, once in a while doling out some advice, condolences, sympathy, and always suggesting that Gideon go easy on the excesses. Alcohol, blow, pills — almost anything he could get his hands on. Sever often felt like the big brother. He watched out for the singer. He couldn't come down too hard on the man. Hell, he'd been a borderline addict himself, but Gideon Pike was dangerous. Sever had heard he had cleaned up his act in recent years, but Pike didn't call anymore, and they hadn't seen each other in a long time. It might have been since the night that Sever really did save his life. But that was off the record. He'd promised to never mention that night again.

He worked it over in his head. He was between projects. Recently, nothing had appealed to him. So what the hell, it was a chance to see Ginny. Any excuse to see Ginny was good. Being married to her had been a bitch. Not being with her, even worse.

"Yeah. I'll come down. We'll find him, and we'll tell him he's got to quit taking a powder just when the fun starts."

"Hey, baby. I owe you! It'll be good to see you again."

No. If anybody owed someone, he owed her. He'd never been ready for a commitment like that, and by the time he was ready, he'd totally screwed it up. There was a sound in her voice. Maybe there was a chance to put some things back together — or maybe he just needed a new challenge. Relationships should be easier at this stage in life.

They weren't. He couldn't quite put his finger on it, but Ginny sounded like she was interested in more than just the story. Maybe she had a more concrete idea of where the relationship was going. He couldn't wait to find out.

CHAPTER THREE

The Miami airport was just like he remembered it. Long lines of disgruntled passengers waiting for delayed flights, and babies and toddlers screaming by the gates, giving the people who were boarding planes a taste of what to expect for the next two or four or eight hours in the air. Teenagers were sprawled on the floor, resting their heads on brightly colored backpacks, either sleeping through the mayhem or playing video games. And no one spoke English. Announcements seemed to come in every language except Sever's native tongue.

He was the lonely man in a sea of humanity. It reminded him of another Pike song, "Nobody Knows Your Name."

His bag had a couple of changes of clothes, his dopp kit, his laptop and the latest Michael Connelly novel. Anything else he could buy. She met him at ground transportation, coming up from behind and wrapping her arms around him as tight as she could.

"Mmmm! It is so good to see you."

He spun around. She just looked good. That was all he could think. Sever was a man of words, but she took the words away. Her long blond hair maybe a little shorter than last time, a light Florida tan, and a brush of freckles on her cheeks, her cute little ass packed into her tight jeans, and those big eyes looking up into his; damn. She just looked good.

"I think I missed you." He kissed her and she responded, pressing against him. From teenage romance, to a marriage that had failed miserably, the attraction was still there. Boy, was it there.

"What are we driving?" he asked.

She backed off, a playful smile on her lips. "It's you and me, Mick. What do you think? I splurged. It's a ragtop."

She led him to the parking garage, over to the silver Porsche Boxter. "What do you think?"

"It's your style."

"I thought so too." She laughed, put on a pair of dark sunglasses, and got behind the wheel. They pulled out and headed toward the beach. "I know you. Every time you come down you rent a convertible. I just thought we should do it in style this time." The wind caught her hair, and he saw the heads turn as they passed the cars and trucks on the freeway.

The sun beat down, a welcome change from the dreary gray he'd left behind in Chicago. Palm trees and bright red, green, and yellow crotons dotted the landscape.

Billboards welcomed him to dozens of retirement communities, condominium communities, and single-family housing units starting as low as $330,000. Radio stations beckoned with signs that announced their call letters in larger-than-life type.

WE PLAY TODAY'S FAVORITES AND TOMORROW'S HITS.
THE GATOR PLAYS THE HITS OF YESTERDAY.
YOUR SUN COAST SPOT ON THE DIAL PLAYS BEACH MUSIC 24/7.

Whatever you wanted, whenever you wanted. Miami was like New York, a city that never slept.

"There's a billboard up ahead," she raised her voice to be heard against the wind and the traffic, "with Gideon's picture on it. Something about 'when I'm in Miami, I listen to easy-listening WGLP' or something."

"When he's in town? He *lives* here."

"He does, but if he's in town, I sure can't find him."

"Well, that's what we're going to try and fix."

She pulled off and drove down to Biscayne Bay.

"We're staying up there." She pointed to the Double Tree Hotel. "Gideon has a condo in the adjoining building, the Grand Condominiums. It seemed like a good place to be, close to him and everything, but now —" she drifted off. Ginny turned onto Bay Shore, and pulled up to the front entrance of the hotel, flashing a brilliant smile at the valet who took the keys. Popping the trunk, she retrieved Sever's bag. "Still traveling light, I see." She set the bag down on the drive and reached up, brushing his hair from his forehead. "We're doing separate rooms, Mick." She handed him a security card. "I'm in 347. Come on down when you get comfortable." A kiss on the cheek and she walked away.

Sever hung up the sport coat, shirt, and trousers. He checked out the view from four floors up, looking out at the bay. The lazy blue water sparkled with dots of almost diamond brilliance, and small sailboats gently rocked off the shore. Down below was a marina, with some high-priced yachts, all shined up and waiting for someone to take them into open water. Opening the sliding glass door, he stepped out onto the concrete balcony, smelling the mixture of salt air and gasoline, iodine and seaweed and a hint of fresh fish.

Back inside, he splashed cold water on his face, brushed his teeth, and ran his hand through his dark mussed up hair. He'd check his messages, then visit his ex-wife. Here she was, after all this time, asking him to help her out. Hell, after some of the things he'd put her through, he was surprised she was still speaking to him at all. Their affinity for one another mystified him. It was impossible to define.

Childhood sweethearts, they'd experienced a lot of firsts together. Sex, drugs, rock and roll and then experiments that went beyond routine experiences. It was *his* excesses that finally drove them apart. Women and drugs. The early days had all seemed so idyllic, but the lifestyle got out of hand. Sever reminded himself that it wasn't just one-sided.

Ginny had come up with some major surprises of her own. There was her affair with his own business agent, and several other dalliances that he preferred not to dwell on. He dialed his number in Chicago and punched in the code.

"You have seven unplayed messages. Press P to hear the first message."

He pressed P.

"Mick, the *L.A. Times* wants to know if you'd consider a feature piece on music- sharing on the internet. The angle is how it's really fucking up the recording industry." His agent.

The next four messages were from his attorney and accountant. Questions about where to put this asset and whether he'd thought about this investment and that investment, and Sever decided not to deal with it now.

The sixth message was a quick hang-up.

"Press P to hear the last message."

He pressed P.

"Mick. It's been years. Man, I was hoping you were home. I've been talking to your ex-wife. I owe her publisher a tell-all kind of book. I signed a contract a year ago and took the advance. That was my first mistake. Now they want their book. Maybe you know that already. Probably should have come to you in the first place. Listen, there's no simple way to say this, but hell, I've got to confide in somebody. I'm in a lot of trouble, my friend, and I've made it even worse. I'm not sure I can trust anyone in the inner circle. If I tell my story there's a good chance I won't live to read it."

There was a pause. A female voice shouted from a distance. "No!" She sounded frantic. "Hang that up now. Don't you think someone can trace this call?"

"Mick, I need —"The line went dead.

Sever stared at the receiver, as if intense concentration would help pick up the thread of the caller's voice. The line remained dead. He had no idea how to track the call. Gideon Pike believed he was in serious trouble, and he was begging for help.

He'd stood up for Pike before. And to be fair, Pike had stood up for him. When Sever's career had stalled, Pike had stepped in. He'd given him an exclusive interview before the release of his biggest selling album. The syndication of the story had cemented Sever's reputation. He felt he owed Gideon Pike. But more than that, even though the man had avoided him for several years, he was a friend, and there weren't too many real friends in this business.

Now, he had to find Gideon Pike. Not just to help a friend with his problem and not just to pay back a debt. And it wasn't just to help out his ex-wife. The problem was, Sever felt driven. He could never leave a good story alone.

CHAPTER FOUR

He knocked on the door. Nothing. He knocked a little louder. He could hear the television. No answer. He knocked even louder.

The handle turned and the door opened an inch. "You're early. I thought you'd be a while." She opened the door, standing there wrapped in a white hotel towel, her hair damp from the shower.

"Oh. Then this isn't for my benefit?"

"Yeah. It's for you. I missed you. Even an ex-wife can get horny."

"You look great!"

"So? Want to do something about it?"

He hesitated. "Yeah. However, I need to tell you that I got a message on the machine."

She gave him a curious smile, her bright eyes searching his face.

Sever took a deep breath. "Pike called. He said that you were talking with him, but he was afraid that if he told you the story —"

"Yes? If he told me the story?"

"It was cryptic. He said if he told you the story, he wouldn't live to read it."

"Someone is going to kill him?"

"I got that impression."

"Wow." She sat down on the bed.

"We need to find him."

"Maybe we don't. God, Mick. I don't want to end up having this story published if it puts his life in danger."

"No. We need to get to the bottom of this. He's dead serious."

"Maybe that's not a good word to use."

"What the hell could be so serious?"

"Someone didn't want him to talk to me. The line went dead in the middle of the message."

"Didn't want you to talk about what?"

"Obviously, we never got that far."

"So, maybe it's best if we leave it alone."

Sever looked into those eyes that had seen his inner soul. "You don't believe that. You know that I can't walk away, and neither can you. If Gideon's in trouble we've got to find out what it is." He sat next to her and put his arm around her. She pressed against him and put her wet head on his shoulder. The towel dropped below her soft breasts, tan except for a small white strip. Sever stroked her bare shoulder and they were quiet together. Finally, he kissed her on the lips.

She gave him a peck, then stood up, holding the towel close to her. "You came down to help with the story, right? So whatever happens here, right now, is just a diversion. It can't go any further, Mick. I don't need that grief in my life again."

Sever nodded.

Ginny dropped the towel, sat on his lap and started unbuttoning his shirt. "Let's get you out of these clothes. As I remember, you're pretty buff."

CHAPTER FIVE

She flashed a temporary pass to the doorman, and she and Sever walked to the elevator. Twenty-three stories up. "I went up to meet with him and the door was unlocked. He was gone. And I've tried to call him twenty times since then. You'll see. Oh, and the place was a mess. Drawers were pulled out and dumped on the bed — it was wrecked. Anyway, aside from all that, you'll love the view." They rode in silence.

She knocked, then knocked again. "See?" Ginny twisted the doorknob. Nothing.

"Someone's locked it."

"Can I help you?" Sever watched the man emerge from the condo down the hall.

"We're looking for Gideon Pike."

"So am I." He was slim, dark haired with a hint of gray combed back, and a solid Florida tan. "Hi," he reached out his hand. "I'm Tom Biddle. I'm Gideon's manager."

"Mick Sever. This is Ginny." Sever took his hand and admired the firm shake.

"I know you." He gave Sever a half smile. "You did a story on Gideon for *Spin* maybe three years ago. A really deep piece on, what did you call it, defining a generation."

"Yeah. I met you in the studio when he was recording the album, *Working for a Living*. Didn't we have a drink afterwards?"

"You see, your memory is better than mine. I thought we had three or four, but I could be wrong." He laughed.

Ginny stood off to the side, letting the two males bond. "When you two finish catching up, I'd like to ask if you know where he is."

Biddle smiled at her, his perfectly capped teeth were pure white. "I'm sorry. I didn't mean to ignore such an attractive lady. I was hoping you could tell me where he is."

"I was doing a story with him, and he disappeared."

"He does that from time to time. You're the lady who was going to work on his diary."

"Right." She gave him a radiant smile. "Working title, *The Diary of Gideon Pike*."

He stared at her for a moment. "Excuse me. You are very attractive."

She blushed. She got it all the time, but she blushed just the same. "Thank you."

Biddle glanced at Sever. "You're not — together?"

"We were. Ginny and I are former Mr. and Mrs." There was no claim. He'd had his chance.

"Ah." Biddle walked to the door. "Let's go on in and see if we can get a sense of where Mr. Pike may have gone. I usually do a better job of keeping tabs on him. I live next door." He motioned to the apartment down the hall, pulled out a key, and opened the door.

The small entranceway opened into an expansive living room. Thick white carpet covered the floor and mirrored walls gave the impression that the room was even larger.

A white Young Chang baby grand graced the corner of the room, and an entertainment center with a sixty-two-inch television blended flush with the wall. As impressive as the room was, Sever's view went to the solid glass wall at the rear, with its spectacular view of the water.

"You never get tired of the view from up here." Biddle walked to the sliding glass and opened the door.

Ginny's eyes darted furtively around the room. She looked back at Sever and shrugged her shoulders. No mess. The place looked immaculate.

Biddle motioned to Sever and Ginny, and they walked out onto the balcony. The marble tile reflected the warm September sun. The ball of fire hit the water in a shimmering pattern, flashing off the boats in the marina below.

Sever gazed out at the beaches beyond and the causeways with midday traffic, the three giant cruise ships in the channel, and off in the distance when he squinted, he could make out the pastel art deco hotels. It was truly a magical view.

"Over there is Star Island." Biddle pointed to a landmass in the distance. "Gideon used to own a huge place over there. Rosie O'Donnell, Sly Stallone, Gloria Estefan, all have places on the island. Gideon sold his, and got this condo about three years ago. Not as much up-keep."

Ginny stood basking in the sun, her hands resting lightly on the balcony railing. "Any idea at all where he might be?"

"No. I really don't know. I need to find him as soon as possible. His publishing company has been calling me. They're trying to get him to negotiate his contract, royalties and all that, and he decides to take a powder. He was never one for timing."

They walked back into the unit, Ginny admiring the painting on the wall above the piano. A splash of red ringed with orange and yellow streaks, and what appeared to be an open mouth in the middle with thick white teeth and a pink tongue. "This almost looks like the Rolling Stones logo. What's it called?"

Biddle laughed, an infectious chuckle. " 'Man in Misery.' Gideon always said that he was the man in misery until he finished one of his songs."

"Gideon works out?" Sever glanced into the hall, seeing what appeared to be a workout room at the end. A weight bench and rack of weights stood just inside.

"No. Larry Spinatti works out. He's Gideon's partner."

"Partner?"

"For the moment anyway." Biddle walked down to the room. "He works out up here, but he lives on one of those yachts in the bay. I've checked the boat several times, but Spinatti's not around either."

"What happened to," Sever tried to remember the name, "was it Rusty? His attorney and —"

"And partner. Yeah. Rusty. He and Gideon were quite a pair. Rusty passed away about three years ago."

"Sorry to hear that."

"So was Gideon." Biddle motioned to another room off the hall. "This is his library." They walked in, Sever admiring the two full walls of books. A rolling oak ladder reached the top shelf. Biddle walked to the curved oak desk with a glass top, and studied a small stack of papers. "He didn't call me. Usually he'll at least call and say he's going away for awhile."

"Was he upset about anything?"

"Not that I know of. Did you hear something?"

Sever glanced at the books. "No." *I'm not sure I can trust anyone in the inner circle.* "I just wondered if maybe he had some personal business to take care of."

Biddle gazed at him for a moment. "I think he just did one of his disappearing acts."

Sever turned to the desk. "Anything there give you a clue? Plane ticket receipt? Maybe a phone number for a travel agency?"

Biddle laughed. "You're a reporter. No question about it. No, I don't see anything. But then again, I don't know what I'm looking for."

Ginny stood in the doorway. "He carried a cell phone when I was with him."

"Tried it. Several times. I left messages, but no response."

Sever glanced at a wire-mesh wastebasket under the desk. He reached into the basket and pulled out two sheets of crumpled notepaper. There was nothing else in the receptacle.

"Anything interesting?" Biddle looked over his shoulder.

"No." Sever studied the papers for a moment and tossed them back into the basket.

"Well, I should get going."

Ginny walked back to the sliding door. "Could you point out the yacht. Spinatti's yacht?"

"Sure. It's not Spinatti's yacht." Biddle seemed to spit the two words out. "Gideon owns it. He treats his young friends well." He pointed to the bay. "There, the one with the blue trim."

"Hitting?" Sever tried to read the name on the boat.

"No. Hit King. Hard to read it from up here."

They went down the elevator together. "I'll walk you down there. Maybe Larry is back." They exited the rear of the complex and walked along the rows of boats, admiring the sleek ocean vessels with their teak decks, brass trim, and clever names. Biddle spoke to the dark young girl in a string bikini sunning herself on the deck of a boat called *Flying Machine*. She laughed, and said something to him in Portuguese. He responded in her native tongue.

"Moya hasn't seem him." Biddle smiled. "And she notices all the good looking guys, straight and gay."

They reached the *Hit King,* an attractive double decked yacht with the name stenciled in deep blue. SOUTH BEACH MIAMI was stenciled directly under the name, no mention of the owner. A pelican perched on the railing gave them an evil eye, then concentrated on the water, waiting for his next meal.

"Larry!" They waited. "Larry, are you home?" Biddle shouted again. "Well, what the hell, let's go see." He walked over the small plank to the deck, followed by Ginny and Sever.

Sever stepped onto the deck and felt the tacky surface on the bottom of his deck shoes. He glanced down and did a double take. "Tom, Ginny. Somebody's foot prints." He kneeled down. "It looks like blood in the print."

"No." Biddle bent down and studied the prints coming from the stairway. "It's got to be somebody's spilled drink or —"

"Over here. The sink." Ginny had walked into the small galley. "This is blood. Quite a bit of blood."

They gathered around the sink. "We really shouldn't be touching anything," Sever said. "Let's get off of here."

"I don't think you're going anywhere until you tell me what you're doing here."

Sever spun around and gazed at the pistol. The female police officer in the short-sleeved uniform held it steady, pointed at Sever's chest.

"I don't know who you are, or what happened here, but if this is a crime scene, you could be in a lot of trouble."

CHAPTER SIX

"One thing you can't do in a cigarette boat at this speed," Jimmy Shinn raised his voice to be heard over the engine, the spray, and the wind. The blond next to him smiled, her hair whipped back as the boat cruised at seventy-five miles per hour. "You can't smoke a cigarette."

He stroked her smooth tan leg and admired her flawless features. The meeting with his father hadn't gone well and he wanted to put some distance between the two of them, physically and emotionally.

Once again the older man had reminded him who was ultimately responsible for his position, his wealth, and his success. Respectfully, he listened repeatedly to his father's stories of immigration. Tales of Grandfather, who started with nothing. Slave labor conditions in the garment industry in New York, saving every cent possible until the family could move to Miami.

"Your grandfather organized a crew of ten Korean men, who worked on the docks. Food, textiles, and merchandise of all kinds were taken from the docks, and moved into a private warehouse." It was always taken, never stolen.

The taken goods were fenced through another of his grandfather's operations, and the more profitable the business became, the more ruthless the men became. The profits were used to purchase legitimate businesses. Grocery stores, tailor shops, then import and export businesses. Laundered money. His grandfather had practically invented it. And Jimmy Shinn was well aware that Platinum and all of his other business ventures were a direct result of Grandfather Shinn and his father. His father wouldn't let him forget it. It was drummed into his head every day.

His father also scolded him about his purchase of Platinum. Somehow stealing, intimidation, and murder were not as evil as a strip club. Only Platinum's healthy bottom line kept Richard Shinn from demanding that his son close the club.

And thank God for that. Platinum was Jimmy's open door to women. And this girl was special. Well, more special than the last one. April worked for him at Platinum. The manager had brought her to his attention, telling him the customers were lined up to experience her private lap dances. Now, Jimmy knew why.

"Take off your top, baby. Let me see the twins."

She smiled again, a vacuous look on her pretty face, as she un-hooked the tiny knit bra. Her perfect breasts capped with tiny nipples bounced as the boat hit a wave. All natural.

Jimmy watched her for a moment, her silhouette against the South Beach skyline. Even this beautiful girl and the beautiful day couldn't totally get him out of his funk.

His father wasn't happy at all. He'd been in a rage when Jimmy had told him that Pike was gone, and when Richard Shinn wasn't happy, nobody was happy. Jimmy turned the boat in a wide arc and headed back for the house on Star Island. Maybe she could help him forget his father for an hour or so.

"Baby, did you hear from Bridgette?"

She shook her head.

He frowned, shouting against the wind. "You've got to find out where she is. I need to talk to her."

"Jimmy, if she calls I'll tell you. Why is it so important that you talk to her?"

"It's business, sweetheart. Strictly business. I need to find Brid-gette. If you hear from her, you tell me." He looked deep into her eyes, the hint of a threat in that gaze. His father ruled with threats, and

Jimmy Shinn was a good observer of what worked. " Keep asking around, okay?"

The boat hit a wave and rose out of the water. April squealed, and her breasts bounced. Shinn stared at the open water, trying to find another wave to hit.

CHAPTER SEVEN

The detective carefully walked around the bloody footprints. The uniformed officer with the gun and her partner stood off to the side, stoically watching the proceedings.

"Might be something, might not. Who did you say lives here?"

Biddle sat on a lounge chair, watching the officer as he took in the scene. "For the second time, Detective Haver, his name is Larry Spinatti. Why are you guys out here?"

"For the second time, call me Ray. We got a call that there was some disturbance down here. The officers found blood, and then you on the boat. What does Spinatti do?"

"He models."

"What kind of a model?"

"Swim suits, underwear . . ." Biddle hesitated. "You know, stuff like that."

The detective turned and glared at Sever. "Do I know you?"

"We've never met."

Ginny nudged him, putting her elbow in his ribs. It was the "tell them where they know you from" nudge.

"Well, you might recognize me from television. I write articles and do some stuff for MTV."

"I've seen you on some news shows, right?"

"Could be."

The detective turned his attention back to Biddle. "Would I recognize this Spinatti guy?"

"I doubt it. He models for men's magazines. A lot of gay publications."

Haver studied the footprints. "Could have been cut shaving or doing something on the boat. There's not enough blood to indicate there was foul play."

"What about the sink?" Sever asked. "There was blood all over it."

Haver grinned. "Typical amateur sleuth. A little blood looks like a lot. It's thin, it's messy, and it turns bright red when exposed to oxygen. A little cut on your finger and you can color up a tissue or handkerchief really good. Trust me, there isn't enough blood to be that alarmed. Probably just an accident on the boat. My guess is the guy took off to find a doctor, or went to the store to get some bandages."

"So you're not going to look into this any further?" Biddle stood up and stretched.

"I don't think so. Looks like this guy tracked the blood up here," he bent down, "see how it fades on this teak deck? Whoever tracked it, walked off the boat under his own power. Just not enough to go on. I'll run a check on this Spinatti. Chances are he'll be back here in the next couple of days." He nodded to the two officers. "You guys can take off. Thanks for the call."

"Ray," Sever watched the uniforms walk up the pier, "who called with the disturbance complaint?"

"The old guy on the next boat. He called the station house. Seemed to think that some strange things have been happening here in the last several days."

"Strange things?"

"Late parties, strange people. But then he's in his seventies. Lots of things that go on down here may appear strange to a guy like that. By the way, what were you doing here?"

Ginny had been standing by the water, gazing at the boats in the bay. She turned to the detective. "Spinatti was a friend of Gideon

Pike's. I'm doing an interview with Gideon, and he's disappeared. We were out looking for him, and the *Hit King* seemed like a perfect place to start.

"Everyone is disappearing on you." Haver fumbled in his shirt pocket and finally pulled out a business card. "Call me if you hear anything else."

Ginny took the card.

"And you're staying at the Double Tree?" Haver wrote down the hotel on his pad of paper. "Have a good time in Miami." He turned around and walked off the boat.

Biddle stepped on the plank. "I've got to go, too." He ran his hand through his thick hair and gave Ginny a broad smile. "Tell you what. I'm busy tomorrow morning, but we could all get together for lunch. Maybe compare notes?"

"Sure." A slight smile played on her lips. "Why not take down my cell phone number?" Ginny gave him the number, and Biddle stepped off the boat, turning to give her a look when he was halfway down the pier.

"What?" She caught Sever staring at her.

"You tell me what."

"Well, he is good looking. It's not like you don't look at every single girl that walks down the street."

Sever walked into the galley. He hadn't seen her in months. He didn't want jealousy rearing its ugly head. "Ginny, did Gideon ever mention a girl named Bridgette when you were talking to him?"

"Bridgette? It doesn't sound familiar. Why?"

"I'm not sure. When I picked up those papers in the wastebasket, there was a crumpled up note that said 'Call Bridgette.' "

"I never heard him mention her. Was there a phone number?"

"No. Just two words. It's probably nothing."

"He's got a sister."

"Yeah. I remember him mentioning her. Maybe that's who it is. We should probably check that out. She may know where he hides out."

"It's probably nothing."

"We're not getting anywhere. You may not find him, Gin." He picked up a match book on the countertop. Black with silver lettering. Platinum. A Gentleman's club. He flipped it to Ginny.

"Gentleman's club? Female strippers? Doesn't sound like a place Pike or Spinatti would frequent."

"You're wrong. Pike loved music and he loved dancing. It's exactly the kind of place he would frequent. Shall we?"

"Oh, jeez Sever. A matchbook, and now you have an excuse to visit a strip club? Very flimsy excuse."

"Do you have a better idea?"

"No. I wish I did. And don't stand there with your tongue out. If I go with you there will be no lap dances!"

CHAPTER EIGHT

They had dinner at Nicki Beach on Ocean Boulevard. The trendy restaurant with its faux beach was packed with young people, girls in tight tank tops, skirts slit up to the waist, and skin tight jeans. Sever felt old. Older than the hills. Then the waitress, a young lady with a giggle that punctuated each sentence, recognized him and he didn't feel quite so old.

"You're the guy who writes about rock stars. I read one of your books." She giggled, and took their order.

"You really want to go to this strip club?"

"Ginny, Pike liked dance clubs. When we'd go out, that's where he wanted to go."

"But a female strip club?"

"I've been to a couple with him. He's a big hit with the girls."

"Sticking fifties in their G-strings?"

"He appreciates attractive people. What can I say? Look, we'll ask some questions, and we won't stay long. I promise. Hey, you asked for my help."

Sever saw Mark McGrath, Sugar Ray's lead singer turned television host, holding court on one of the beach chairs in the powdery white sand just two seats away. He was surrounded by beautiful girls, each one vying for his attention. Sever walked over and McGrath immediately stood up, breaking free from the adoring fans. He shook Sever's hand.

"Hey, man. Good to see you. I haven't had a chance to thank you for the piece you did on the band. You actually made us sound human." He smiled that boyish smile that drove girls wild.

"I like your sound. I hope you guys are around a long time." He motioned to Ginny, who walked over and shook the singer's hand.

"This is the Ginny, the former Mrs. Sever."

McGrath nodded. "Never should have let this one get away."

Too many people making the same observation. It became increasingly harder to remember the bad times. There were some. Fights that almost became brawls. And Sever kept thinking that maybe the years would give them both maturity to handle the problems and give the relationship another chance. Hell, he wasn't any more mature than he had been. He knew it, and worst of all, Ginny knew it.

They went back to their table and worked on the broiled grouper with grilled vegetables on the side. When it was gone, they each ordered another ice-cold Corona with fresh lime.

"Mick, you never said a word to Tom about Gideon's message."

"I told you, he said he *didn't trust anyone*. And he specifically mentioned the inner circle. I assume Biddle is inner circle."

"Yeah. It's just that somebody needs to know how serious this might be."

Sever tilted the cold beer to his lips and drained a third of the bottle. "And what about someone trashing his condo? And yet it's all nice and tidy when we go in today. Could be a maid, or it could be that the person who tossed it went back to straighten up the mess."

They were both quiet for a moment. The hum of voices, the Latin music drifting on the open air, the smell of grilled meat and fresh spices was almost hypnotic.

"We'll figure this out," Sever said. "We'll find him. In the meantime, I've got to pretend that I never heard that message."

"I can't pretend that I didn't hear him tell me he was scared." Ginny was adamant. He told me it was time to finally come clean. And then he said that there was only one thing hanging over his head that could stop him from telling his story. You had to hear him, Mick. He was frightened. And I have no idea why."

*   *   *

The garish neon sign out front flashed a bright red. *Live Girls 24 hours a day.*

"Is there a place nearby that features dead ones?" Ginny frowned, and followed him into the block building. "I hope that parking lot attendant can drive a stick."

Sever paid the $30.00 cover, and the bouncer at the door gave Ginny the once over.

They chose a table a couple seats away from the stage.

"Do you remember the first time I took you to a strip club?" Sever covered her hand with his.

"I think I invited you. You weren't going to take me, so I took you. I needed to see what all the commotion was about."

"And?"

"Juvenile."

"And the male strip club you and your friends Linda and Vicki went to up in Lake Geneva, Wisconsin?"

She smiled. "That wasn't juvenile. That was — educational."

"Yeah. You know, I think the problem with us was . . . "

"Oh, hell, there were a million problems with us. The biggest one was that —"

"We were too much alike."

"Yeah. There was that."

"Do you ever think what it would be like if —"

She bristled, the frown lines in her forehead deepening. "Don't even go there, Sever."

The little blond waitress stood in front of them in a G-string and bra, looking very attractive and very bored.

"There's a two drink minimum, drinks are five bucks a piece. If you buy a dancer a drink, it'll cost you ten bucks, and there's a minimum twenty percent tip on the bill." She stood there, daring them to place an order.

They ordered two Coronas and Sever watched the dancer, a slim brunette in a tiger-skin bikini. After the second song, she took it off and worked the brass pole, climbing her way to the top, then slithering down like a smooth-skinned, flesh-colored snake.

"There's something very Freudian about that act." Ginny studied the girl.

"Educational. See?" Sever smiled at the waitress as she returned with their beers. "Excuse me, do you know a guy named Larry Spinatti? May be a regular?"

She shook her head, took his twenty dollar bill, and started to leave.

"Ma'am."

She turned and frowned.

"What about a guy named Gideon Pike? Does he stop in from time to time?" Sever reached into his pocket and pulled out another twenty. He laid it Jackson side up on the table. The blond cautiously walked back.

"Why do you want to know?"

"He's a friend, and I'm looking for him."

"Yeah. He comes in sometimes."

"Do you know him?"

She looked at the twenty, then shook her head. "No. I could lie to you, but I don't know him. April does."

"April?"

"Yeah. She dances the slow stuff. She dances to his music. He gets a kick out of it."

Ginny looked up at the young girl. "Is she here?"

"Not tonight."

"When does she work?"

The girl glanced back at the bar, then reached over and took the twenty. "When she feels like it. Or, when her boyfriend lets her."

"Boyfriend?" Sever kept pushing.

"I've said enough. She might be here tomorrow. Why don't you stop back then, but God, don't tell her I told you, okay?"

The girl walked away, stuffing the tip into the waistband of the G-string.

Ginny watched Sever as his eyes followed the waitress. "Any excuse to come back?"

"Hey, somebody knows him. And he frequents the place. It's a start."

CHAPTER NINE

Sever was up early, observing the traffic as it started to build on the causeway over to South Beach. He took the elevator down to the lobby and left by the rear entrance, watching the wharf slowly waking up. He could smell the raw gasoline as boats were fueled, and nodded to a couple of young men who were swabbing the deck of the *Billionaire Bob*. There probably was a Billionaire Bob. It would take that kind of money to own and maintain a boat like that. The Brazilian girl, Moya, from yesterday was nowhere to be seen.

He wandered down to the *Hit King*, almost bumping into a little guy with a stocking cap and wide sunglasses. He wondered if the seventy-something neighbor might be keeping a lookout. The yacht rolled gently in the water, but there was no sign of anyone on board. Sever walked up the plank and gazed at the deck. No footprints, no blood.

"They were working on it late last night."

Sever spun around and saw the older man, a cup of steaming coffee in his hand. He stood on the deck of the neighboring boat, dressed in cargo shorts, a blue knit shirt, and deck shoes. His deep tan was set off by his full head of white hair. The mystery man who called the cops.

"Mops, buckets, two of 'em about 2 A.M. this morning."

"Do you know them?"

"Nah. I got in about 1:30, and I was —" he smiled, "busy. I

happened to come up on deck as they were finishing up. I don't think they saw me."

Sever nodded. "Mick Sever."

"Brady White. You a friend of the guy who lives there?"

"I've never met him, Mr. White."

"Please, call me Brady. So what's your interest?"

"He's disappeared, and so has the guy who owns the boat."

Brady sipped his coffee. He gazed at the blue sky for a moment. "Gonna be a hot one. Tell me, Mr. Sever, do you know who owns the *Hit King*?"

"Gideon Pike."

"Nah. Used to. He still uses it. Let's his friend stay there, but he doesn't own it."

"Who owns it?"

"Hit King."

"Hit King?"

"The publishing company."

"Yeah?"

"Yeah. I try to keep up with who owns what down here. Over there," he pointed to a yacht with gold trim "Boyce Johnson Corporation. The company that makes toilet valves." He chuckled. "Toilet valves. And the one on the other side, Brad Kominsk. Played center field for the Indians. Jay Waggoner, the CEO from I-Rad who skimmed about $600,000,000? He owns the *Elizabeth W* over there.

"But Hit King is Pike's publishing company."

White smiled and took another sip of his coffee. "Not quite."

An attractive brunette stuck her head above the stairs on White's boat. "Brady, do you have coffee?"

"Right here, baby."

She walked on deck, a short robe pulled around her. Brady pulled her close and kissed her on the cheek.

"This is Cindy. Cindy, Mick."

The old man was doing well for himself. Cindy was about thirty-eight to forty and was in great shape. She smiled at Sever, and took her cup of coffee from a table.

"Well, Mick, Cindy and I are going to breakfast in a minute, so I'll leave you to your search. If you need anything, look me up."

"Brady, if Larry shows up, or Pike, I'm at the DoubleTree, right there." He pointed up at the towering hotel. "Could you call?"

White nodded, put his arm around Cindy and steered her to the galley. Sever headed up the dock. He could do with some breakfast himself. Maybe Ginny would be up, and they could drive down to the beach and visit the News Café.

CHAPTER TEN

The News Café was packed. The outdoor venue was popular on a warm morning like this, and locals, business people, and tourists all joined in the mix that was uniquely South Beach. Newspapers from around the world were spread next to omelets, plates of fresh fruit, waffles, and syrup-drenched French toast. Men in bold solid color ties and women in gray, black, and blue suits sat next to shirtless men and girls in string bikini's while the 7:30 A.M. traffic was wall-to-wall just fifteen feet away

"So somebody cleaned the entire boat?"

"Brady says they cleaned it all."

"Brady." She laughed. "You go for a ten-minute walk and come back with a new best friend. You're amazing, Mick."

"Ginny, tell me about the notes. The ones he gave you to start the process."

"It was all about publishing. And not much about *his* publishing."

"Whose?"

"Paul McCartney, Michael Jackson, Diane Warren —"

"I don't follow."

"Neither do I. He told me it was important to understand the music publishing business. He had notes on Paul McCartney's publishing company. You probably know more about this than I do, but —"

"No. Go on."

"Paul McCartney doesn't own the Beatles' songs. He got out-maneuvered and outbid by Michael Jackson, but he still owns a bunch of songs."

Sever remembered. The Beatles had sold their songs to a publishing company to avoid tax consequences. When the publishing house decided to sell the songs, Jackson beat McCartney to the punch.

"But, Sir Paul owns all of his songs since the Beatles. All of Buddy Holly's songs, all of Meredeth Wilson's songs like everything from *The Music Man* — and he owns all the songs from *A Chorus Line, Hello Dolly,* and *Guys and Dolls*. Mick, he even owns Carl Perkins' 'Blue Suede Shoes'."

"I didn't realize it was that extensive."

"That's just the beginning. And he gets like fifty percent of the royalties for every song, every time it's played or recorded, or the sheet music is sold. Plus, big bucks when they use these songs in commercials. He bought these songs as investments. And now, Paul is worth about one billion dollars."

"It's a great story. But what does it have to do with Pike's story?"

"He said understanding how lucrative the publishing business was had a lot to do with his current situation. It was very important to him. He wanted me to do some research on the Beatles' songs, and he wanted me to look into Diane Warren's publishing company. He said it would be good background when he got around to explaining his predicament."

Sever watched the flow of people on the sidewalk as he sipped the orange juice and took a bite of his bagel. Ginny had a ham and cheese omelet, toast, bacon, and coffee. He had no idea where she put it all.

"Mick, do you know who she is?"

"Who?"

"Diane Warren."

"Sure. She wrote 'If I Could Turn Back Time' for Cher, 'Rhythm of the Night' for LeBarge, songs for Celine Dion —"

"Like maybe 1,500 tunes. She makes almost twenty million dollars a year, Mick. I think we're in the wrong end of the writing business."

"So that's as far as you got? Nothing about Gideon Pike?"

"That's it."

"It's funny, but Brady mentioned publishing this morning."

"That doesn't sound like something that just pops up in conversation."

"He says that the *Hit King* yacht isn't owned by Pike. It's owned by Hit King Publishing."

"Nitpicking. Gideon owns Hit King Publishing."

"Brady says, very cryptically, 'not exactly'."

"And you asked what he meant?"

"At the time it didn't seem important."

They both sat silent, Ginny sipping her coffee. The heat and humidity of the Miami morning was already heavy and Sever could feel small dots of perspiration dotting his forehead and arms.

Ginny pushed her plate aside, leaving half a strip of bacon. "So if he doesn't own *Hit King,* does it have something to do with his disappearance?"

"Probably nothing." Tom Biddle walked up, smiling at them, "Good morning. Boy, you guys get an early jump on things. I thought I was an early riser."

"I thought you were busy this morning. You said you weren't free until this afternoon." Ginny nodded at the empty chair at their table. Biddle pulled it out and sat down.

"This is where I'm usually busy. Having breakfast and getting my thoughts together. What are you two talking about? Publishing and Gideon's disappearance?"

"You're down here a lot?" Sever asked. He tried to smile, but it wasn't in him.

"Oh, I'm down here two or three mornings a week. It's the best food and the best people watching on the boulevard."

"Does Gideon own Hit King Publishing?"

He seemed to look into Ginny's eyes. "No. He sold it."

"Anything strange about the sale?"

"No. Straight business transaction."

"Who owns it?"

Biddle flagged a waiter down and ordered a cup of coffee. "Guy named Jimmy Shinn."

"What about him?"

"What do you want to know? He's a local businessman, he's got a lot of irons in the fire, owns a big house over on Star Island."

Sever pushed his chair back. "Maybe if we called this Shinn, he could shed some light on —"

"He's never at Hit King, Mick. He's as hard to pin down as Pike. My philosophy is this. Gideon's like Little Bo Peep's Sheep. Leave him alone, and he'll come home, wagging his tail behind him. Look, I need to find him too, but knowing Mr. Pike, he'll take his sweet time about coming back."

"One more question. You said Rusty had passed away."

"That's right."

"Who's his attorney now?"

"Guy named Lou Frey. He's really good. No personal relation with Gideon, but he's a damned good lawyer."

"Have you checked with him?"

"I called his office yesterday. The last time he spoke with Pike was a week ago."

"When was the last time you saw him?"

Biddle glanced at his watch, studying the date. "Said hi to him in the hall about three days ago." He nodded to Ginny. "Yeah, about the same time you lost track of him."

"Well," Sever reached for his wallet to pay the bill, "it sounds like we're covering all the bases. This Star Island, you said Gideon owned a place over there at one time?"

"He did."

"And Shinn lives on the island?"

"Yep."

"I'd like to see it."

"It's just over there. You can get on by driving, although you've got to be visiting someone who lives there. They have a gatehouse and guard at the entrance."

"Well, let's rent a boat." He looked at Ginny. "We can ride around it."

Biddle chuckled. "There are certainly a lot of ways to see Miami."

"I assume we could rent a boat at the marina by the hotel."

"Do you need a guide?"

"No. Thanks. We'll be fine. But tell me what to look for."

Biddle sipped his coffee, letting his eyes connect with Ginny. "It's a stone-gray mansion, and you'll see a huge flower bed right down by the water. It's about halfway around the island. You two be careful. I'll be around when you get back and maybe we can still have that lunch?"

Ginny smiled. "Sure. We'll compare notes."

Sever paused. "Any chance you could call this attorney, Lou Frey, and set up an appointment a little later?"

"I'll call him from my cell phone right now. If he's got some time, I'm sure he'll be glad to see you."

"By the way, Gideon has a sister. Do you know where she lives?"

"No. I don't even know her name. He doesn't talk about her. I get the impression they aren't close." Biddle shrugged his shoulders.

Sever and Ginny walked back to the car and headed to the hotel.

"You're right. He is good looking."

"Oh, Mick. Are you jealous?" She toyed with him.

"If I was jealous, I'd have to be jealous of every guy who's ever met you."

"You glib-tongued devil!" She leaned over and kissed him.

You couldn't be 'friends' with the opposite sex. He believed that. It didn't work. It didn't work, because one or the other was always trying to make a move. It was always this intricate dance. In this case, he was the one dancing.

CHAPTER ELEVEN

"Got a 17-foot runabout, 150 horsepower Johnson outboard on it. That should get you up and down the coast and out to the island. $170 for half a day." The tanned young man with the ponytail and long-billed cap was matter of fact. You wanted it or you didn't.

"Sure," Sever pulled his American Express card out.

"You drive a boat before?" He wore the bill of his hat low over his face, and kept leaning back to look at Sever as he signed for liability.

"Yeah. No problem. We'll probably be back in a couple of hours."

They walked down to the docks and the man introduced them to a seaweed-green boat. The faded, torn, yellowed upholstery had seen better days. They climbed in and the man with the hat pushed them out as Sever started the engine.

"Biddle's calling the attorney, Lou Frey. Maybe we can see him this afternoon."

She nodded. "Do you think he's got any ideas?"

"If a guy is going to disappear deliberately, I think there's a chance he'd call his attorney and accountant. Just my guess."

Sever eased away from the dock, familiarizing himself with the simple dash. Cutting back on the choke, he slowly increased the speed and took a deep breath of the salt air. The sailboat up at Navy Pier in Chicago was nice, but being on the ocean was a whole other experience. He coasted past the gleaming yachts, looking up at the *Hit King* as they went by. Brady was on his deck, cell phone in hand and he waved, seemingly surprised to see Sever. They headed toward the island, and Ginny took off her cover-up and lay back in the seat, letting the morning sun do its magic on her skin. God, she looked good. Was she ever going to age?

He pulled closer to the island, easing back on the throttle. The homes were huge. Ginny sat up and pulled a brochure from the pocket of her cover-up.

"Want to know what we're looking at?"

Sever glanced at her. "You're always prepared."

"Over there," she pointed to the shore, "I *think* that's the latest celebrity house. Sylvester Stalone. They're still working on the pool in his front yard."

They coasted by, Sever running the engine on idle.

"Somewhere, maybe there," she pointed, "is Rosie O'Donnell's house. They filmed the Al Pacino movie, *Scarface*, there. And Edith Piaf's house is somewhere over there. The pool at that house was used in the movie *Cocoon*."

"And Julio Iglesias, Tommy Mottola,"

"You and Tommy go back, don't you?"

"When he and Mariah Carey split up, I wrote a story. He hasn't talked to me since."

Two sailboats were moored offshore and Sever gave them wide berth. A small boat with a skier behind buzzed fifty feet out from the island. Sever kept an even speed, rounding the tip of Star Island as he watched the shoreline for a stone-gray mansion with a flower bed by the water.

"Ginny, we've been over this before, but I keep wondering if Pike is just being paranoid. We could invest a whole lot of time in this project, and it may turn out he just doesn't want to be found."

"He called you, Mick. Reaching out."

"And so did you."

"I wanted the story. Now I'm worried. I want to find out if he's okay."

"I do too."

A speedboat appeared at the bend, the full throttle of the engine roaring over the still water. Sever admired the boat and its plume of water spouting from the rear. He gazed at the shoreline, watching the emerald green lawns.

The red speedboat seemed to steer erratically, finally making a beeline for the shore.

Ginny watched the boat with interest. "If he makes a sharper turn, he'll be heading right for us."

He did. Aiming for a direct hit.

"Jesus," Sever shouted. "Ginny, get ready to jump. Seriously!" He pushed the throttle forward, aiming toward the shore, the Johnson engine slow to respond. Too slow.

"Mick, this is some kind of a joke!" She screamed over the roar of the engine.

The red boat now bore down on them, Sever giving his boat full throttle, weaving and dodging. The speedboat never wavered at twice the speed, heading straight for the runabout.

"Can't you do something? He's going to hit us!" She grabbed his shoulder, holding on for dear life.

Now it was one hundred feet, now eighty. Sever could smell the burning fuel, wondering if the driver meant to kill them, spilling their bodies into the bay. He changed direction, pointing the small boat out to the open water. It did no good. The red menace stayed on course.

"We're going back to shore." Sever could tell they didn't have a prayer. "Once we get near the marina —"

The boat was almost on them. Sever could see the driver, a large man in a black tee shirt and shorts. Although he was still too far to make out details, Sever could swear that his eyes were glinting like pieces of flint. The red boat cut across the bow, then spun in a tight circle and headed for the rear of the runabout.

"Jesus, Mick!"

The driver was close enough now. Sever could see the wide smile on his face, the thick arms and legs on the man and the brown skin. The speedboat engine roared like a chain saw motor, ready to cut them in half. The boat clipped the runabout, and Sever's hands were knocked free of the wheel. He grasped for it, and this time the man's craft slammed into them full speed. Sever and Ginny both were knocked to the bottom.

The runabout veered crazily, then spun in a circle and the speed-boat circled for one more assault. Sever grabbed the wheel again as the speedboat plowed into him dead center.

The boat jerked violently. He tried to gain control, struggling to keep the small craft upright and then he saw the jagged hole in the fiberglass.

"Mick! Oh, God, Mick."

The boat seemed to split apart, the frame ripping in two, and in a crazy, erratic motion, the two halves leaned to the left and slowly sank into the sea as Sever grabbed a life jacket and tossed one to Ginny. *God, please don't let anything happen to her.* He had two fleeting thoughts as he hit the cold salty water. A good captain always goes down with the ship, and he hoped American Express would cover the insurance.

CHAPTER TWELVE

The young couple on the deck boat were renting too.

"Man, that wasn't just an accident," the sunburned man shook his head emphatically. "Tanya thought at first it was some guy just playing games, but that sure as hell wasn't a game."

"He was trying to kill you." The girl spoke rapidly, a regular chatterbox. "He was trying to kill you, no doubt. I mean he just kept smiling and aiming right for your little boat, and, my God, I thought he was going to kill you. Really. Kill you."

Sever and Ginny sat on the rear seat as the boat headed back to the marina. He got the message. The guy was ready to kill them. "Did you see where the boat went after he hit us?"

"Back toward South Beach. The first thing I thought about was chasing him, but in this thing?" The guy gave him a glance, then concentrated on his destination.

Ginny toweled her hair. "Thanks for picking us up."

The tiny brunette in the shiny blue bikini laughed. "Jeez, you made our morning. They were trying to kill you! Really. Think of the story we'll be able to tell when we get back to Connecticut."

She met him in the lobby, freshened up, but a little shaky.

"You okay?"

"I lost breakfast."

"Maybe you want to stay here for awhile. I can make the next call by myself."

She glared at him. "Somebody tried to kill us. I'd like to find out why!"

They walked out, and Sever pointed to a cab in the front lot. Neither of them felt like driving after the morning experience.

Lou Frey's office was up on Biscayne Boulevard. The cab driver pointed to the bleachers lined up by the side of the street. "They're going to run the Miami Grand Prix again. Couple of days from now this street will be packed. It'll be crazy, but it's good to see the business."

He dropped them off in front of the ornate building. "Somewhere in there." Sever paid the fare, left ten for a tip, and they entered through the revolving doors.

Frey's secretary, in a long black skirt and high-necked white blouse, seemed stern and officious, announcing them on the intercom, and having them wait on a leather sofa.

"Exactly what are we going to ask him?"

Sever leafed through a deep-sea fishing magazine. "It's a fishing expedition."

"Like the strip club?"

"Well, I think that was more fun that this will be."

"Anything will be better than the trip this morning."

"Ginny, what are you thinking?"

"Somebody doesn't want us looking into the disappearance of Gideon Pike."

"It could have been something else entirely."

"What?"

"Mr. Frey will see you now. Walk this way, please." Sever thought about trying to imitate the secretary's walk, but he figured he'd need a stick up his ass.

Lou Frey sat behind his desk and didn't bother to get up when they were escorted in.

"I don't have a lot of time. What can I do for you?"

They sat down in the straight-backed chairs in front of the desk.

"I'm working on a book with Gideon Pike, and without any explanation he disappeared."

"I'm his attorney, Ms. Sever. I'm not a bodyguard or his guardian."

Sever bristled. "We're simply asking if you have any idea why he would have abandoned the project, and where he might be now."

"I have no idea. Is that all?"

Sever let his eyes wander to the paintings on the wall.

"David Bowie painted that, Mr. Sever. And over there, John Mellencamp. The two behind you are by Tony Bennett, and the block print of Elvis over there was done by Ron Wood of the Stones."

Sever stood back up and walked over to the pieces, admiring each one. He'd met all four of the artists. Finally he turned to Frey. "Can you tell me what happened to Rusty McCain?"

"Ah, Mr. Gideon's former attorney. Rusty went for a swim and drowned."

"How?"

"No one is sure. By the time his body washed up, two weeks had gone by. It was badly decomposed but it appeared he'd hit his head."

"Foul play?"

"It was ruled as accidental drowning. Mr. Sever, I really do have important work to do."

"You took over after Rusty died?"

"I did."

"You and Gideon —"

"Rusty had a more personal relationship with Gideon."

"Do you deal with his publishing company at all?"

"That's privileged information."

"And you have no idea where he might be?"

"None."

"Mr. Frey, is there anything you can tell us?"

"I see no reason to tell you anything."

Sever looked at Ginny. She was frowning and biting her lip. "Mr. Frey, did you know Gideon Pike before Rusty's death? Did you know about him, who he was?"

"Certainly. Who doesn't? I did some work for him. Rusty was —" he paused, a pained look on his face, "there is no reason to tell you this but I will. Rusty was going to retire, and I was already doing a good deal of work for Gideon. Now, if there is nothing else, I really am quite busy." He stood up and ushered them to the door.

"The painting behind your desk," Sever stopped, walking back over to the colorful red, yellow, and white piece, "Who did this?"

"Gideon Pike. It's similar to the one he painted that hangs in his condo."

"Pike painted that?"

"He did. He's quite a talented man, Mr. Sever. If you're his friend, I'm surprised you didn't know that."

"One more question. When Tom Biddle called you to ask for an appointment with us, did he mention that we were renting a boat to see Star Island?"

Frey gave him a cold, hard look. "He may have mentioned something about it."

Sever nodded, and he and Ginny walked into the hallway. The door banged shut behind them.

They took the elevator to the lobby.

Sever stopped and closed his eyes for just a moment. "I met Rusty. He was maybe thirty-eight years old. Tops."

Ginny met his gaze as they walked onto the sidewalk. "Doesn't sound like retirement age."

"That's what I was thinking. Exactly what I was thinking."

CHAPTER THIRTEEN

Sever remembered the interview with Pike four years ago, after a crazy weekend in New York. It was the first time he'd heard about the book idea — the diary. There'd been the concert at Madison Square Garden with Paul McCartney, a decadent private dinner at "21" with about twenty friends and hangers-on, then a night on the town that neither of them remembered too well. The conversation took place the next morning, over strong coffee, aspirin, and a pitcher of Bloody Marys. The story had started off with Pike threatening to write his memoirs. And Sever had written the story just the way the conversation had played out. Several months later the *New York Times* ran Sever's full interview when Pike received a Grammy for lifetime achievement:

> "I'm going to write a book. I'm going to tell the world what's it's really like to be a road dog." Gideon Pike has been a 'road dog' for part of four decades, traveling and telling his stories night after night. His music and his performances have become a hallmark, a benchmark for other song writers and performers to measure themselves by. Now he wants to become an author? He's already proven there's no stopping his determination.
>
> "I keep a log," he told me, after we'd spent a rather wild night of drinking and carousing around

Manhattan. "I write something every night, without fail."

I asked him if our evening out would appear in the log and the book to follow.

"Yeah, it probably will. You know how weird the entertainment life is. I don't think anyone has ever really written about it from this perspective. At least not the perspective I'm talking about. It will read like a diary."

I did remind him that I'd written several books about the wilder side of fame and rock and roll entertainers.

"Oh, I'll cover the wild side, but as far as the fame, I've never really stopped to enjoy it. I think I've been too busy trying to perfect my craft and put out a good product."

Outsiders didn't understand. How could entertainment be hard work? Big bucks, constant adulation — this wasn't work. It was Dire Straits who had the lyrics, "Money for nothing and your chicks for free." But it *was* work. Worrying every minute that you weren't on top of the charts. Desperate to top your last success, and looking over your shoulder every waking moment to make sure no one was catching up with you.

Entertainment journalism was the same. You were always watching the other guy, trying to stay one step ahead.

In the article, Sever had explored the similarities between writing books versus songs.

"If I don't feel the passion, then the song and the words mean nothing. Every song is a story, Mick, just like you write. And if a song doesn't have passion and," he paused, "a ringing truth, it's got nothing."

At that time Sever had felt closer to Pike than he'd ever felt before. He understood the singer, and Pike understood him. Writers, the ones who took their craft seriously, were a rare breed. People with a strong sense of honesty and passion. Ginny was a writer, and he knew that was one of the reasons *they* bonded. Most of the time. Pike wrote music, some of the lyrics, and performed his art, and Sever had felt a kinship with him that was stronger than with almost any other performer he knew. He couldn't fathom what had happened to that relationship. But while Pike didn't write *all* the lyrics that he sang, he understood the passion of words. And simple words, thoughtful phrases, complex verse, brought people together.

Rusty, Pike's attorney and partner, had met them that day, after the debauchery, the revelry, and the hungover conversation, then he and Pike had left for the West Coast.

Sever'd seen Pike a couple of times since then, and had endured a bizarre evening with the songwriter that scared the hell out of him, but that conversation that became the article — that coming together of two wordsmiths, was a defining moment in their friendship. They understood the power of the written and delivered word. Mightier than the sword.

And Sever never forgot that Gideon Pike's friendship and openness was largely responsible for his career. Pike had given him that interview when Sever's career seemed stalled. Several times when things got slow for Sever, Pike had picked up the pace with a great story, a song, or a memorable experience. Sometimes Sever wondered if that *was* the basis of their friendship. Always good for a story. But because of it, or in spite of it, he and Sever saw their fame and fortune surge. No. It was deeper. He truly missed the guy. He missed the conversations, the intense feelings, and the general camaraderie.

Despite the friendship, Sever was never truly aware of the pressure the singer/songwriter felt until a fateful night a little over three years ago. A wild party, drugs, and a situation Sever had promised to keep secret for his entire life. Pike had gone off the deep end. It was as if he'd decided to become invisible. Again, it was off the record. Sever kept it to himself. There but for the grace of God —

CHAPTER FOURTEEN

Biddle answered his condo door, dressed in linen slacks and a soft, tan polo shirt. "I heard you had some excitement out by the island."

"You heard that? Excitement? It was a little more than just excitement!"

"Down at the marina. I just heard that —"

"We never did get to see the house. Somebody decided we didn't need to be out there on that boat. Any reason you can think of why someone would take a run at us?" Sever asked.

"Not one reason, Mick. I've lived here for five years, and I've never heard of anything happening like that."

"Well, that's reassuring." Sarcasm seeped into his voice. "You don't have a clue? Because I've got to tell you, man, this *excitement* scared the shit out of us."

"Man, your guess is as good as mine. I don't have a clue. Listen, do you still want to do a late lunch? My treat. I hate to think you'll remember Miami for that freakish boat incident."

"Maybe. But, Tom," Ginny motioned to Pike's condo, "we were wondering if you'd mind letting us in one more time."

Biddle gave her a questioning look.

"Without going through Gideon's things or invading his privacy," she hesitated. "We're not going to tear the place apart or anything, but I guess I thought there might be something there, maybe on his desk or a night stand, that we overlooked. Do you mind?" She gave him a pleading look, her eyes two pools of blue.

"Sure." He grinned. "No harm in that. He always has me look in on the place when he's gone. Just so you respect his privacy. No going through his drawers or anything like that."

"Agreed."

"Good. So, we're on the same page. Come on." He walked down to Pike's door, pulled out the key, and unlocked it.

Sever took notice of the painting by the piano. The signature was bold white on a red background. He hadn't noticed the name before. "You didn't tell us Gideon painted this."

"Yeah. Quite talented, our Mr. Pike."

"Lou Frey has a similar painting in his office."

"When you asked me to call him and set up a meeting for you, I should have warned you. Frey is such a warm, sociable guy." Biddle laughed.

Ginny walked to the painting and touched the thick texture. "It's so vibrant. The colors almost light up the room. It really is good."

"Gideon paints portraits, too, when he has the time."

"Anything else in here that he did?"

"I don't think so. He's done Dick Clark, James Taylor, George Michael, Eminem —"

Ginny smiled. "Eminem? You're kidding."

"No. Gideon is really good. He ends up giving them away to the people he paints. He even did a picture of me. It's hanging in my hallway." He gave Ginny an inviting look. " I'll show it to you sometime."

Sever walked into the library while Biddle and Ginny went through papers stacked by the kitchen sink. He was tempted to open drawers, look through files, but Biddle certainly wouldn't approve. He looked down at the wastepaper basket. The crumpled papers were gone. Gone. Maybe the maid? He looked again, kneeling down to see if they were under the desk somewhere. No papers.

He rose up and saw the small metal object on the desk. He hesitated. He might be able to use it later. He covered it with his hand and —

"Anything of interest?" Biddle stuck his head in the door.

"Nothing that says 'this is where I'm hiding out.'"

"Well, then I think it's time to go. How about lunch?"

Sever looked at Ginny. She shook her head.

"No." Sever held his hand up. "I don't think this would be a good time. After the morning we had, I think we may want to take a break. Maybe we'll hook up later."

"I hope so." Biddle locked the door and walked down to his apartment nodding his goodbye.

"You'll have to go visit him sometime and see the portrait." Sever anticipated her reaction. They knew each other much too well.

"Do you think I'd be safe?"

"You weren't safe with me today."

"Good point. For just a minute, just a brief moment, I really thought we might be killed."

"Yeah. Me too."

"And do you want to know what else I thought?"

"Sure."

"If I had to go, I was glad I was going with you."

He wasn't sure if that was a good thought, or a bad thought.

CHAPTER FIFTEEN

They went down the elevator to the lower level, and walked through the hotel entrance to the lobby.

"So, you want to come up for a drink?"

Sever nodded. "After everything that happened I could use one. Or two."

In her room she opened a mini-bar bottle of Dewar's Scotch. Pouring equal amounts in each glass, she added a splash of water. "Here's to the Green Demon. May she rest at the bottom of the sea." They clinked glasses.

"You named the boat?"

"We could have gone down with her. I figure she should have a name."

Sever straddled the desk chair. He gazed at her, sitting on the bed where they'd made love not long ago. "I saw in your interview notes there was something about Gideon's lyricist, Ed Komack. I've never met him, but I always had the impression they were pretty tight?"

"Apparently as tight as a partnership like that ever is. Gideon hadn't said much about him. I've got his phone number. Do you want to call him?"

"I'll do it." Sever reached into his pocket. "You know that key that Biddle used to open Gideon's door?"

"Yeah."

"There was one just like it in the library."

"Was?"

"It isn't there now."

"Where is it?"

Sever pulled out the key and laid it on the desk.

"Mr. Sever. That's against the law."

"Mrs. Sever. I've broken the law before. Somebody tried to kill us today, and I think we need to search that apartment a little more thoroughly to see if we can find out why."

CHAPTER SIXTEEN

Ginny had given him the number for the lyricist. It had been in the notes that Pike had given to her to sift through. Edward Komack was to have a major part in the book. He and Pike had come up through the ranks together, lyrics and music. Lennon and McCartney, Gilbert and Sullivan, and just like all musical partners they'd had a rift. Rumors said theirs was about the money. Pike didn't feel that Komack should get an equal split, Komack thought the music was only a vehicle, that the message was more valuable. So the Rogers and Hammerstein of the '70s, '80s, and '90s had split. Pike wrote his own lyrics or collaborated with other writers. Komack worked on independent projects, and wrote lyrics for up-and-coming rock stars. But the industry agreed, neither was as strong individually as the sum of the whole. In the last six months, they had reconciled and were talking about making their first collaborative album in over a year.

He made the call from his own room. Sever had never been comfortable doing an interview with other people around, and Ginny wanted to take a short nap, resting up for the Platinum Club and whatever else the evening would bring. He hoped her plans involved him.

As the phone in New York rang, Sever glanced farther down on the page. Komack was writing the lyrics for a musical based on Hugh Hefner's life. He smiled. The Playboy mansion in L.A. had always been one of his favorite spots. And before that, the Chicago mansion.

Could be a hell of a play. The phone rang a third time and someone picked up.

"Yeah?"

"Edward Komack?"

"Who wants to know?" A soft voice, with an edge.

"Mick Sever."

"What do you want?"

"I'm trying to find Gideon Pike."

The voice was distracted, as if Komack was on the computer or watching television, and wasn't interested in the conversation. "Unh huh."

"Do you know where he might be?"

"Nah."

"Edward, he's been missing for several days. A friend of mine was doing a book and —"

"Oh, yeah. The diary thing. He was determined to do that. Wanted to set the record straight on some things."

"You haven't seen him?"

"Two weeks ago. He was up here. I ran some songs by him and he was supposed to be working on melodies."

"Nothing since then?"

"He does this. Goes away when he's stressed out."

"But *where* does he go?"

"Little hideaways."

"Edward. Do you know where these hideaways are?"

Silence on the other end. Sever could hear what sounded like someone punching the keys on a computer keyboard.

"Edward?"

"Yeah. I'm here."

"Is there a reason to be worried?"

"Do I sound worried?"

"Let me put this another way. Was there a reason he was worried? Was something stressing him out?"

I'm not sure I can trust anyone in the inner circle.

There was silence on the other end.

"Edward?"

"People think that entertainers have it easy. Fame, fortune, but it's a business. And just like with any business, there's stress. Okay?"

"Do you know where these hideaways are?"

"Nah, I don't know where they are. Half the time he's hiding out, he's hiding out from me."

CHAPTER SEVENTEEN

April Morn crawled across the main stage at the Platinum Club, wiggling her naked rear end and making sure her perfect breasts swayed hypnotically beneath her. She reached the lip of the stage, and gazed seductively into the eyes of the kid with his hat on backwards. He held out his one-dollar bill and she ignored it, pulling his head toward her, nestling it between her two fleshy orbs. The kid's buddies started whooping it up. The dancer backed away, nipped the bill with her teeth, stood up, and gathered her panties and bra. She shoved the generous number of tips into a small bag, and waltzed off the stage to a mild applause.

"Ladies and gentlemen — hell, there ain't but two or three ladies in the crowd, let's have a hand for April Morn."

"You want to talk to her? Or do you want her to nuzzle you with her mammary glands?" Ginny seemed half-serious. A hint of jealousy perhaps?

"I want to talk to her. Unless *you* want to offer some money and take her back to the private area."

Ginny frowned. "Go ahead. Have a good time, but bring back some good information."

"You don't approve?"

"I think this is a wild-goose chase."

Sever smiled at her. "I've got some of my best stories on wild-goose chases."

"Oh. So now this is *your* story?"

April seemed to be in a bidding war with the young guy and three other men flanking her as she pulled on her underwear. Sever walked up and dangled a $100 dollar bill between his fingers.

She flashed him a golden smile. "Hey sailor, you want to go to the champagne court?"

The kid with the backward hat gave him a menacing look, then walked back to the stage with his two friends, shouting catcalls at the new girl now on stage.

She took his hand and led him to the back room. Two other partially dressed girls were dancing in front of older men, but in the dim light it was hard to make out anything else. April sat him down at a vinyl booth.

"Bottle of champagne, sir?" A burly bouncer type appeared in a tuxedo shirt with a bottle of cheap champagne. "Fifty bucks."

Sever forked over another bill, and the man walked away.

April started to take off her top.

"Hey, there's no need." Sever looked into her eyes. "I've got some questions. For $150 I should get some answers, okay?"

She stopped and backed away. "What kind of questions?"

"Simple questions. You dance to some of Gideon Pike's songs."

"Yeah?"

"Do you know him?" The room smelled of cheap perfume and cigars.

She was quiet. Wondering whether to walk away, or wait for more money.

"Do you know him?"

"Sure. I know him."

"Is he a regular?"

"What's a regular?"

"Does he come in on a regular basis? Once a week, once a month?"

"I —" she paused, looking over her shoulder. "I haven't seen him in a couple of weeks. Is that all?"

"Do you know where he might be?"

"Look, Jimmy wouldn't want me talking about this."

"Jimmy?"

She looked around the room. "Jimmy."

"Talking about what? I just asked if Gideon —"

"Gideon and Bridgette."

His eyes widened. "Bridgette? Who's Bridgette?" The name on the scrap paper in Pike's apartment. Sever closed his eyes for a brief second. Cha-ching. There was a connection.

"Shit." She wrapped her arms tightly around her upper body. "I think you need to leave."

"April, I think I need to get my money's worth. Who was — who is Bridgette? His sister?"

She gave him a puzzled look, the furrows deep in her bow.

"Not his sister? A friend?"

"Christ, will you just leave? Please."

"April, I'm trying to find Gideon Pike. That's all. Can Bridgette help me? Can you?"

April chewed on her bottom lip. "I asked you nicely to leave."

"You can walk away anytime."

"No. I can't. I can't walk away at all." She looked toward the doorway back into the club. "Bob! Bob! The guy's getting fresh!"

The burly guy in the tuxedo shirt barreled into the room and was at the booth in five long strides.

"What's the matter, bud, can't keep your hands to yourself?"

The bruiser grabbed Sever by his shirt collar and picked him up.

"No reason to get physical. I was asking the lady some questions." Sever pushed at him. In a flash the big man had Sever's arm twisted behind his back.

"Move it, bud. Out back." He shoved him, Sever feeling the pressure in his shoulder and elbow, past a surprised dancer and her partner, to the back of the darkened room and out an emergency exit.

The blast of heat from the blacktopped parking lot hit him, just before Bob did, three times in the stomach, fast and hard. Sever toppled over on the paved surface and threw up everything in his stomach. Almost everything. He vomited again and got rid of the rest.

CHAPTER EIGHTEEN

Jimmy Shinn studied the figures. Serious money. The last box set of Pike's oldies, or classics, as the industry leaders called them, was doing nicely, even if he did have to hold the record company's feet to the fire. It wasn't like *they* didn't cook the books on a regular basis. All record companies did, but he made damned sure he got every penny he had coming. When *he* was taking a cut, they bristled. But what they didn't know, they couldn't worry about. And what they didn't know was that he was overproducing the CDs by printing an extra 200,000, then selling them to independent reps. The reps sold them to dealers. He paid no royalties, no commissions, and nobody was the wiser. A cash business with no paper trail. He walked away with almost a million in under-the-table money. Meanwhile, the box set was selling on the legitimate market and had rocketed to #2 on the charts. Another four or five million in just the first four weeks.

That pain in the ass Komack didn't have to know about the unreported figures. Pike wouldn't find out about them. Producers, arrangers — they were stiffed too. If he cut out the writer, producer, musicians, and arranger — hell, Jimmy Shinn could rake it in. This business was like having a license to print money. Even when the computer-sharing companies like Napster had been trying to horn in on the business, even with Apple and the iPod, there was a pile of cash to be made. This was the greatest shakedown in history. His father should have been proud of him. But there was never enough for the old man. Some devil that centered himself in the patriarch's soul drove the man to accumulate more and more. And Jimmy knew that same devil owned a piece of him.

The cell phone buzzed on his hip and he removed it from the holster.

"Mr. Shinn?"

"Yeah."

"A guy named Mick Sever was in Platinum asking about Gideon Pike."

"Asking what?" Sever. First Ginny Sever, trying to pry a tell-all story from Pike, now her famous ex. He thought maybe it would all go away. No such luck.

"Asking if Mr. Pike came in here."

"Who was he asking?"

"Sir, he was asking April."

Shit. She was dumb enough to talk to him.

"Mr. Shinn. We took him out back and asked him not to come back."

Shinn held the phone at arm's length and studied the emerald green accounting chart on the screen. "Telling him — warning him won't be enough. Do you understand me?" Bob was a loyal employee, but he needed to be tougher. If someone got in the way, eliminate him.

"Mr. Shinn, no disrespect, but you don't pay me enough to do anything else."

Shinn was quiet. He'd killed men for saying less. He could feel his heart pounding in the cavity of his chest. He could actually hear the rush of blood and adrenaline coursing through his veins. "Bob, you need to take care of problems like this. If it means you need more money, then we'll work it out." He hung up the phone.

The old man was going to be pissed. It was Jimmy Shinn's business, but he always worried about the old man. Old man, shit, was that any way to refer to the patriarch? Old-world loyalties, family values, it started to lose something here in the glitz and glamour of the Miami high-life. Filial piety, a respect for the parent. The father-son relationship was deemed the most important part of a Korean family. Like a full-time job. Shit, it seemed like a full-time job just keeping the old man off his back. Yeah, yeah. He owed his fucking existence to his father, his lifestyle to his grandfather and the whole lineage of Shinns. Where did it end? He had a serious problem right now, and he didn't need to second-guess his father's feelings.

He was responsible for what was now happening. None of his revered ancestors were going to take the blame. He was just trying to get control of a situation. And he didn't have a kid to pass on the blame. Too bad. He could have made his offspring's life a living hell. He'd had a mentor to teach him the ropes.

He punched in nine digits and hit send, sitting at his white lacquer-polished desk, running his pen under the numbers. Nobody ever claimed that there wasn't a little risk in running your own business. Or running your father's business. He just didn't want his father giving him any more shit. His father knew why Pike was being black-mailed, and he was worse than Jimmy when it came to bleeding someone to death. The senior Shinn would hold on with a death grip until he couldn't get any more out of someone, then he'd cut them loose.

The voice on the answering end, "What?"

"What? What? You fucking say hello and show some respect!" Shinn felt like reaching through the phone line and strangling the guy. It was time to take out his anger on someone.

"Says the number is blocked. I thought maybe you were trying to sell me long-distance service."

"I'm not selling shit. How about I come over and pop you?"

"I'm sorry, Jimmy. What can I do for you?"

"Sever's getting to be a real pain in the ass. I'm getting tired of him, and so is my father."

"Your father?"

Shinn shook his head. They didn't care about his father. They cared about Jimmy. He controlled himself. "Bob let him off with a warning. I want you to do something about it. A little more permanently."

"Give me a couple of days? Let me think it through."

"When you think, it scares me." Shinn opened the drawer in front of him and pulled out a Cuban Cohiba. He clipped the end and put the cigar to his lips, letting his tongue touch the rough end and taste the savory tobacco.

"Two days. That's all I need."

"To get rid of Sever, or to find Pike?"

"I may have a lead on Pike. I'll figure out what to do with Sever."

It sounded like a lie. The guy had no idea where Pike was. Shinn gritted his teeth. "No complications."

"I know."

"If you find Bridgette and the kid, you'll find Pike."

"Jimmy, that's what we're working on."

"You know where they are?"

"Not exactly, but I've been thinking about the Sever situation. He's looking for Pike as hard as we are and—"

"And I don't need that son of a bitch Sever finding him first. I own that mother-fucker. Pike is mine."

"And he's about ready to bolt, and tell his story."

Shinn was quiet.

"So, why not watch Sever and his ex. If they can flush Pike out, we'll grab him."

Shinn pursed his lips, letting the idea roll over in his head. Sever and his ex looking for Pike. Shinn's troops looking for Pike. As long as someone kept an eye on Sever. He pulled out an engraved gold Zippo lighter. To JIMMY, WHO LIGHTS MY FIRE. Some bimbo he met in Rio. He couldn't even remember what she looked like.

"Fuck it. Keep a damned close eye on him." He closed the flip phone and lit the cigar, turning it slowly for an even burn. That first mouthful of rich smoke was often times the most satisfying. This time, it wasn't.

CHAPTER NINETEEN

"Are you sure you're up for this?"

Sever frowned. "I'm up for finding out why I'm being used as a tackling dummy. We're lucky the son of a bitch agreed to see us, and I'm not going to waste the opportunity."

"Agreed?" Ginny pursed her lips. "You threatened his secretary."

"Yeah, there was that, too."

Like a matronly female prison warden she walked into the room in almost a march cadence. "Mr. Frey will see you now." Her words were clipped.

Ginny stood up and offered her hand to Sever. He took it and eased out of the chair. Together, they walked back into the lawyer's office.

"I told you I had no knowledge of Gideon's whereabouts. I will however admit that his disappearance has me somewhat concerned." Frey wore a pair of reading glasses and clenched a pen between his fingers, as if interrupted from writing something on the tablet in front of him. He made no offer for them to sit down.

Ginny took the lead. "So you are concerned that your client has disappeared?"

"He's done it before. But this time there is business to attend to. Business that needs Gideon's attention. Mrs. Sever, I'd like to introduce you to my assistant, Charles Strict." Frey picked up his phone, punched in three numbers, and asked the person on the other end to come into his office.

"This is Charles Strict. Charles, Mr. and Mrs. Sever."

The young man was no older than twenty-five, with razor-cut blond hair. He smiled at them, a boyish grin spreading on his face. "Hey, good to meet you. Mr. Frey told me that you're looking for Gideon Pike. He's kind of assigned me the same task."

Frey jotted something down on a pad, peered up over his reading glasses, and nodded toward Strict. "Now that you know Charles, you can contact him when you need something. I can't guarantee he'll give you any information, but at least you've made the connection. Now, if there's nothing else, I have work to do."

"Mr. Frey. Let me change the subject."

Ginny shot Sever a look.

"What kind of legal advice can you give me about a case of battery?"

"Battery?"

"I was at a club —"

"What club?"

"The Platinum Club."

"Mr. Sever, I charge $250 an hour."

Sever pulled out his wallet and peeled off a fifty and two one-hundred dollar bills. He laid them on the desk.

"Proceed."

I talked to one of the dancers. She knew Pike. I asked her the same basic questions I've asked you, and she reported me to a bouncer."

"And he beat you?"

"Yeah. Sucker punched me. Do I have a case?"

"Do you have proof?"

"I have bruises and it's hard to keep food down."

"Mr. Sever. You've paid me $250 for advice, so listen carefully. Here's your advice."

Sever watched the attorney as he slid the two bills across the desk and deposited them in a drawer.

"Stay away from the Platinum Club."

Strict motioned to them, and the three left the office.

"He's really a nice guy if you give him some time." Strict softened his smile.

"I haven't got that much time," Sever said.

CHAPTER TWENTY

Sever looked at his watch. Even though he knew it was ten minutes fast, it helped him be on time. 2:10 A.M. Ginny put the key into the slot and turned it. The door opened.

"The guard in the lobby saw you. Is he just going to ignore our visit?"

"I told you, Gideon gave me a temporary pass card. As long as I have it, they don't care."

"Not a great security system."

She walked in. "Sever, we're here. That's what's important." She turned to him, and in the faint glow of the evening light filtering through the glass patio doors he saw the serious look on her face. "We can walk away now. This isn't our battle. I'm afraid maybe it's gotten too serious."

"Have either of us ever walked away from a good story? Or from helping each other?"

"Maybe it's time."

"Nah. If Pike's in trouble, I want to help. There aren't too many people I feel that way about. Ginny, I saved his life one night. I've got to complete this."

She studied him for a moment. "The night in Miami?"

Sever kept his lips tight. He'd promised never to talk about it. He flipped on the flashlight, guiding the beam over the entrance. A digital clock on the microwave glowed luminescent green. 2:01 A.M.

Ginny switched on her flashlight and the two beams searched the living room.

"It's an interesting painting. He does have some serious talent." Sever let the beam play over the artwork above the piano. Dark red paint fading to shades of lighter red and then pink. A free-form brush stroke with flashes of white, all thickly layered in a three-dimensional texture. There was something sexual about the piece.

"I'll check the master bedroom. Why don't you do the library?" Ginny headed down the hall.

Sever walked into the first room off the hallway. The rolling ladder stood against the shelves. He checked the basket again. No crumpled paper. The paper had been there the first time. Pulling open the top drawer in the desk, he shuffled through the stack of papers. Receipts, invoices, and financial papers. Nothing in the pile seemed unusual. Methodically he went through each drawer. There were copies of reviews, profiles, and stories from *Time* magazine, *Newsweek*, *Rolling Stone* and *Reader's Digest* dating back almost twenty years. In another drawer he found tablets of notes that seemed to be ideas for songs. Nothing out of the ordinary.

I pray for you each night. (keep the religion out of it, but the emotion in.)

"The Way I Feel." About a guy who is in love, but the other person is unaware.

> *Did you ever love someone so*
> *Love someone who didn't know*
> *Try to live a lie so it won't show*
> *I know the way you feel —*

The stray beam caught him unaware. He spun around and looked into the light.

"Mick. Somebody's been here since we were here. In the kitchen. Two drawers are open. They weren't open when we were in here with Tom."

"You're sure?"

"I'm sure."

"Biddle says he checks up on the place from time to time." He could see her outline in the bright light.

"Yeah. Maybe. It looks like someone was cooking. There's a pan on the stove and I know it wasn't there the last time we were here."

"Anything in the bedroom?"

"No." She frowned. "I feel like a pervert. Here I am looking through his underwear drawer, and there's a box of letters from some guy named Jason. Oh, then I even stumbled across a box of Trojans. But I really think someone was here."

She walked in and trained the light on the bookshelves. "Have you been through all the desk drawers?"

"Almost." He opened the bottom drawer.

She pulled a book off the shelf. "Look at this. A leather-bound *Huckleberry Finn*." She flipped through the opening pages. "First edition. How much do you think this is worth? Oh, and he's got a bunch of Hemmingways. God, Mick, look at this. A signed Raymond Chandler first. I don't know first editions that well, but it looks like he's got a great collection."

Ginny climbed the ladder and holding the light with one hand, reached up to the top shelf where two books sat off to the side. "Here's a couple with no titles at all." She pulled them from the shelf, and climbed back down.

"There's nothing here." Sever closed the drawer. "We can check out the closet in the hall."

"Mick, like your fishing expeditions, we have no idea what we're looking for." She opened the first book.

"We'll know it when we see it."

"Oh, my God."

"What?"

"It's a diary. A real daily diary." She laid it on the desk and opened the second book. "In two installments." Sever trained his light on the book as Ginny thumbed through it. "Look. It stops about eight days ago. It's that current."

"It's the log he talked about. We need to take these two volumes back to the hotel."

"What? We can't do that. What are you thinking?"

"Oh?" Sever gave her a quizzical look. "We can steal a man's key, break into his apartment, and yet we can't borrow his books?"

He caught Ginny's smile in the dim light. "I'm not arguing the legality of what we're doing, Mick. If we take the books, someone may know we were here."

"What if this diary tells us where he is?"

"Or tells us why we're targets for people with boats and fists?"

"That too." Sever shined the light on her face. "Are you comfortable with this?"

"No, but I do want to find out where he is, and why we're getting hassled for looking."

"Okay."

"So, we both want to get to the bottom of this. For Gideon's sake — and, maybe for ours."

There was nothing left to say.

Sever noticed the green numbers on the illuminated clock on the desk. They'd been there twenty minutes. He had no idea whether someone would be coming back, or if maybe security had been alerted when they walked by the desk, but he was starting to get nervous. It was time to get out. "Let's check out the closet before we go."

Sever walked into the hall and opened the sliding doors. A collection of jackets, snap-brim caps and several umbrellas hung from the metal rod. Playing the light over the floor he saw the rolled canvases.

"Hold the light while I unroll these."

The first canvas was the face of a young woman. She smiled from the painting with full, sensuous lips. Her eyes stared directly into Sever's. It must be the way the flashlight caught the colors, green eyes, with pale blue eye shadow. He looked into the eyes, wishing he knew more about her. Rolling it back up, he opened the second painting. Spreading it out on the floor, they gazed into the face of a young boy, maybe five or six years old.

"Family? Might be his sister." Sever admired the skin tone and the blush in the boy's cheeks.

"I know he's got a sister and a nephew."

"Good looking kid. And his sister —" he pointed to the rolled painting, "That is a beautiful woman."

"He's painted those eyes so that they're —"

"Hypnotic?" He rolled up the portrait of the child, and opened the third canvas. A man's head appeared, dark haunting eyes with coal-black hair. Again, the skin tone was lifelike. This time, the skin was a darker color and the eyes had a slightly Asian appearance. There was no smile. The expression was a tight frown. Sever could almost sense the negative energy.

"Roll it up, Mick. That one scares the hell out of me."

Sever rolled it up and pushed the canvases back into the closet.

What looked like a rolled up blanket on the top shelf caught his eye. He carefully pulled it down. The blanket was bound loosely with a piece of twine. Sever laid it on the ground and carefully untied it, opening the wool fabric. Ginny took an end and helped him spread it on the floor. The patchwork square prints were light pastel colors — mint green, pale yellow, tangerine orange. The center of the blanket was lightly smudged a charcoal gray and the cloth gave off a heavy smell. Sever ran his finger over a smudge.

"Oil."

"Oil?"

He shrugged his shoulders. "Oil. Like a lubricating oil." He rolled the blanket back up and loosely tied it with the twine. He lifted it up to the shelf, and passed his light over the interior of the closet one more time.

"Nothing else?"

"No. Let's go." It was at that moment they heard the key turn in the lock.

CHAPTER TWENTY-ONE

Switching off the two flashlights, they froze. The key turned again, and again. Someone was jiggling the door handle, then pounding on the door. The door stayed closed. Sever quietly stepped into the entranceway.

"Mick," she whispered. "What the hell are you doing?"

He walked to the door and looked through the peephole. A leggy blond in a sparkling green mini-dress and high heels balanced unsteadily in the middle of the hall.

"Tom?" She appeared to be drunk, shouting the name again. "Tom! You bastard."

Sever watched with fascination as she stared down at the key in her hand. Then, she stumbled down the hall toward Biddle's condo. He lost sight of her.

"What the hell is going on out there?" Ginny's coarse whisper broke his concentration.

"Some girl was looking for Biddle. She's got a key, but the wrong apartment."

"Are you sure?"

"I'm sure. If Biddle's there, he could be in for a rough night." He turned the light on his watch. "Or early morning."

CHAPTER TWENTY-TWO

He couldn't sleep. Something about the apartment was unsettling. The diaries, the paintings, or the fact that someone had been there. There was a simple explanation for that. A maid, a lover, Biddle, maybe his attorney, Frey. But something was playing in a corner of his mind and he couldn't shake it.

He thought about reading the diaries, but he'd left them in Ginny's room and he didn't want to wake her. Sever opened his laptop and turned it on, staring at the familiar glow of the screen and waiting for the Windows chimes. This wasn't his story, but he thought better when he wrote. Writing helped him organize his thoughts and right now he needed organization.

He typed in a title. *Where in the world is Gideon Pike.*

1) Hiding out?

 Where? And why?

2) Dead?

He surprised himself. He hadn't really thought about that possibility. Biddle, Pike's manager, seemed mildly concerned about Gideon's disappearance, but only because there was a contract to sign. Frey, his attorney, said it happened all the time and it didn't overly concern him. Komack, his lyricist, said Pike often hid out and sometimes hid from him. No one seemed concerned about Gideon Pike. Or maybe they all appeared just a little too casual. And he couldn't tell anyone except Ginny about the message. *I'm not sure I can trust anyone in the inner circle.* Of course that raised another question. Who exactly was in the inner circle?

Sever listed the names. The lawyer, Lou Frey, Tom Biddle, maybe his lyricist Ed Komack. He included April from Platinum and Spinatti from the *Hit King.* Then he reviewed the incident with the rental boat, and the confrontation at Platinum. He was still sore from that one.

There was another avenue. Ginny had mentioned the sister, the painting of the young lady with the deep green eyes. Did she live close by? Were she and Pike close? He knew almost nothing about the man's personal life. It just never came up in conversation.

And finally, what if Pike was dead? Ever since he'd joined Ginny in the hunt for Gideon Pike, someone had been after him. Someone had tried to kill them with a boat. Someone had kicked the shit out of him at Platinum. It seemed to be related, and if someone was determined to stop him from looking into Pike's disappearance, maybe they were afraid that he and Ginny would find a corpse.

Sever didn't even want to go there.

At 5:30 A.M. he shut the computer down and closed his eyes.

He awoke an hour later, something still nagging him, like a hazy picture that wouldn't focus.

He pulled on a pair of jeans, a tee shirt, and his deck shoes and took the elevator down to the lobby. He exited from the rear and walked the dock, listening to the early seagulls cry.

Two pelicans swooped down ten feet from him and made a morning catch. The fresh, tangy scent of the saltwater made him feel alive, and the ever-present pain in his knee was barely noticeable.

He saw the squad car pulled up next to the dock. The lights were flashing, and a second car drove up, red and blue lights throwing eerie patterns on the boats. The two officers got out and started quickly down the concrete walkway. Sever followed. The source of the commotion, about five boats down, was the *Hit King.* Maybe the old man, Brady White, called in another disturbance. He quickened his pace. He noticed the Brazilian beauty in a short wrap, standing on her deck, straining to see down the row.

"Any idea what's going on down there?"

She turned slowly, studying him for a moment. "Mr. Sever."

"You know who I am?"

"A friend of Mr. Biddle. You're the man who was married to the attractive blond lady."

"You're very observant."

"I study people. It's a hobby." She smiled. "I don't know what happened on the *Hit King*, but I would guess there is some sort of a domestic disturbance. Is that what you would call it? When there is an argument or fight that is family related?"

Sever nodded. "Did you see anything? Hear anything?"

"No." She sounded disappointed.

A slender brunette in a tee shirt and thong walked onto the deck from down below. "Moya, what is it?" She gave Sever a brief glance and stood beside the Brazilian, taking her hand.

Moya turned to the tanned girl and squeezed her hand. "I don't know, but Mr. Sever was heading in that direction. He'll report back to us."

Sever considered the possibilities, nodded, and walked down the dock.

Arriving at Brady's boat, he stopped. The rest of the dock was roped off.

"Kind of a mess over there."

Sever looked up. Brady was standing on his deck in tan shorts and a polo shirt, a martini glass half full in his hand. "You see what's on that boat, you might want a stiff one too." He held out the glass as if making a toast.

"What happened?"

"Come on board. You can see better from here."

Sever climbed up the plank as Brady pointed to the boat next door.

"The blood is back. Plenty of it."

"Who?"

"I think it's the model. Spinatti."

"Jesus. Somebody killed him?"

White took a sip of the colorless liquid. "Sure you don't want a drink?"

"It's a little early."

"All I know is that somebody shot him in the head. Bullet to the brain." He swallowed the last of the martini.

They watched the police move about the boat, and Sever saw from the corner of his eye the man moving down the dock. Detective Haver. He tried to remember the first name from the business card he'd given them. Ray. Ray Haver. His head was lowered and he walked with long strides. He glanced up at White and Sever.

"You called this in?"

The old man nodded.

"You're a neighbor, I suppose you see things."

Brady White nodded again.

"Don't go anywhere," Haver said. "I've got a lot of things to talk to you about." He took a long look at Sever. "Do you always show up when there's a problem down here?"

"I study people. It's my profession."

"You're in the Double Tree, right? If you decide to check out, call me first. I'm very interested in anyone who shows up before and after a death that might be murder."

"It's purely coincidental."

"It's very seldom that someone tells me they were actually involved in the crime." Haver reached into his shirt pocket and pulled out a business card. "Did I give you one of these? Makes no difference, have two. You call me if you suddenly remember anything." He turned and walked onto the *Hit King*.

"Brady, I believe I will have one of those concoctions. Sever nodded at the martini glass.

"And I believe I'll have another," the old man stepped to a small bar and poured.

"What did you see?"

"I was asleep. I didn't get in until 1:30, and there was no sign of anyone. About 2 A.M. I hear some carrying-on somewhere close by. It's hard to tell when you're on the water. Sounds play tricks on you, but I assume it was over there."

"What kind of sounds?"

"People stumbling around. Bangin' into things. It's not unusual. People here tend to stay out late, and come home with a buzz on. But this sounded close, so I assume Spinatti was just getting in. And that's early for boaters."

"And the gunshot?"

"I went back to sleep. Never heard another thing. Then I got up early this morning. Kerri had an early flight, and there was all that blood."

"Kerri? The girl from the other day?"

"Uh, no. Different girl."

"There you are." Ginny called up from the dock, watching their conversation. "An officer tried to stop me from coming down here. What happened?" She walked up the plank.

"Ginny, this is Brady. Brady, Ginny."

Brady held out his tanned, wrinkled hand. He gazed at her with clear, blue eyes framed by his bushy white eyebrows. "You're a beautiful lady."

She smiled.

"Brady says that Larry Spinatti was shot last night."

"You're kidding."

"No. Detective Haver is over there now."

"Jesus, Mick. Pike's gone, we almost get run over by some angry boater, you get beat up at a strip club, Gideon's former attorney washes up drowned, and now his partner is killed." She sat down in a canvas sling chair, and watched the action on the *Hit King*.

"Brady, who would have wanted him dead?"

"Probably the same people who bloodied him up the other night."

"You still think —"

"I don't know, pretty lady. He was involved in the entertainment business, and from what I've seen and read, that's not a pretty place to be. You'd know better than I would."

"But to murder someone?"

"Well, he had several boyfriends about the time he and Pike got friendly. They'd be on the boat at all hours. Maybe somebody got jealous."

"Maybe —" She sounded skeptical. "You know, all I wanted was a story."

Sever watched the team next door carefully dusting a white powder on the railing, as three men carried a stretcher out from the galley. "You got one, Ginny. You've got one hell of a story."

CHAPTER TWENTY-THREE

"So you're still a little tired?" They sat in the small bar off the hotel lobby. Ginny snacked on pepper poppers and nursed a margarita.

"I'm still a little tired. Did you get a chance to look at the diaries?"

"I did. I read a lot, but most of it is just rambling. A diary of his thoughts, and once in awhile he talks about his activities. Some of it consists of lists."

Sever sipped his Scotch. "Of what?"

"I don't know. A list of names and titles. I thought it might be songwriters and songs."

"People who have songs published by Hit King?"

"There's a lot to read. The entries are numbered and I read like five or six, then skipped to the end. He just rambles, and unless you know the players it doesn't necessarily make any sense. Actually, it's very disappointing. You can look at it later. Maybe you'll figure it out."

"In the last entries is there anything that gives a clue as to where he went?"

"Mick. Don't you think I'd check for that? There's nothing. He writes about working with Ed again. Little things like, he hopes Ed understands. I'm not sure about what. And he mentions Boots and Kick.

"What?"

"He signs off each page with Boots and Kick. I'd need a translator to understand most of it."

"Boots and kick?"

"They're capitalized. Boots and Kick, my good luck charms."

"I'll take a look."

"It's very cryptic."

"Anything else?"

"He talks about an accident, but unless you know the situation, the writing makes no sense. And he obviously hasn't written anything in those books since he disappeared."

"What accident?"

"Mick, I told you, I don't understand. About every three or four pages he says 'if it wasn't for the accident.' Or, 'The damned accident.' Read it. You'll see for yourself."

"I would bet he's still keeping a log. He's jotting down thoughts as we speak. He wrote almost every day. Anyway, I'll read them. Maybe something will jog my memory."

"You're right. He's probably writing about why he bolted, and we don't have those journals. You know, it still bothers me that someone had been in there."

"Ginny, it could have been the cleaning lady."

"Drawers were open. Things seemed out of place. A cleaning lady doesn't leave things worse than she found them." She picked up another popper and took a bite.

"Biddle."

"He checks up, not messes up."

"Alright, Spinatti, when he was doing his exercises."

"He won't be doing those anymore."

They were both quiet for a moment.

"We don't know everyone that Pike knows. Maybe his sister was looking for him."

"I have a funny feeling, Mick. Like it was someone who broke in."

"Oh, that would be wrong." He gave her a sidelong glance.

"Well, we did it for the right reason."

"So you think if you can figure out who's been visiting Pike's apartment, you'll be able to find Pike?"

"It's a fishing expedition, Sever. Remember?"

"I was hoping the diary would give us a clue." He heard the music and glanced at the television above the bar. A sleek Korean automobile went cruising up a winding road, the camera closing in on a gorgeous brunette behind the wheel.

It may be the time, it may be the place
It may be the smile that she wears on her face,
It may be the reason, it may be the season
She may be the love of your life.

Ginny glanced up at the screen and smiled. "Gideon. There he is. I didn't think about looking at the TV."

"Gideon Pike is everywhere." Sever watched the commercial as Gideon's music faded.

"Except where he should be."

"Do you remember that song?" Sever looked back at her.

"Before it was a car commercial? Sure. 1985. "The Love of Your Life." It was up for a Grammy, and I think Lionel Richie won that year for 'Three Times a Lady'. Gideon should have won it."

"Yeah. But Gideon won his share over the years." Sever looked back at the screen, but the commercial had disappeared.

"He gets paid every time that commercial plays?"

"He does," Sever paused, "or his publishing company does."

"And the publishing company pays him?"

"That's the way it works."

"But Mick, he doesn't own Hit King."

"No. He *did*. He was a shrewd business man. He started it, ran it, but Biddle said somebody named Shinn owns the company now."

"Gideon did own it."

"I'm sure he did. He had some young songwriters at one time who published their music with him."

"It was so important to him. The way the publishing business worked."

"Did he ever tell you what the catalog of songs was worth?"

She took another sip of the margarita, swirling it in her mouth. "He talked about everybody else. He mentioned Barry Gibb, from the Bee Gees and how he changed publishers and went to Warner/Chappel because they told him they could sell a lot more of his songs to the advertising industry. He talked about Michael Jackson, and how Sony loaned him two hundred fifty million dollars — pawn-shop-value — for the Beatles catalog —" she paused. "Do you believe that? They loaned Michael Jackson *two hundred fifty million* to get a piece of the Beatles songs. And then there was Diane Warren and some others — but nothing really about *Gideon's* songs. You've got to remember, Mick, I only spent about three days with him before he split. I thought maybe you'd know something about this."

"We never talked about the legal aspects of his songs. We talked about writing and performing. Nothing about his publishing."

Sever saw him come in. Biddle nodded to them, and ordered a beer at the bar. The bartender drew a draft, and Biddle walked over.

"Hey. I understand you were down by the *Hit King* this morning. It's unbelievable about Spinatti."

"Pull up a chair." Ginny motioned to one at the next table. "Is there anything new?"

"They didn't tell me anything. The old man on the next boat said he thought there were several people there last night. That detective was still on the boat when I left."

"Any motives that you know of?" Sever sipped on his Scotch, the smokey, amber liquid rolling on his tongue. Tropical drinks were fine, but a good, smokey Scotch was something he savored.

"Don't know. There was speculation about a financial deal that may have been a little shaky, or maybe a love affair that went wrong? You just never know."

"Tom," Ginny finished the green margarita and took a bite of the sour-lime garnish. Sever could never understand how she could do that. She didn't even make a face. "Have you heard anything about Gideon?"

"No. I am getting worried. It's important that he be here day after tomorrow to sign the publishing contracts. Legal stuff for the song rights and everything." Biddle took a deep breath. "You know, I shouldn't be talking to you about this. It's Gideon's business, but I figure you want to find him as much as I do, so we're all in this together. I talked to Lou Frey today and he's getting a little anxious too. Oh, and by the way —" Biddle took a long swallow of beer as if pausing for dramatic effect. "Spinatti's body showed signs of bruising and it appeared that he had some cuts on his chest and arms. They had started to scab over, so the police think he was injured a couple of days ago."

"The blood on the deck the other day? It just gets stranger and stranger." Ginny looked over at Sever.

"You know," Sever pushed his chair back and looked at both of them. "It sounds more and more like Pike's life may be in danger."

"It could be this has nothing at all to do with Gideon —" Biddle left it hanging in midair.

"Or," Ginny watched Mick for a reaction, "he's already dead. And that thought has crossed my mind."

"Come on. You guys are creeping me out." Biddle gave them a time-out sign. "Gideon is fine. He just needed a little time. You'll see. He'll be back day after tomorrow."

Ginny frowned, her eyes scrunched up. "How is he going to feel when he finds out his partner was killed?"

They were silent; the television providing the only sound in the nearly empty bar.

And police today are looking for singer songwriter Gideon Pike as a person of interest in the shooting death of Miami model Larry Spinatti. Spinatti, found shot to death on the singer's yacht early this morning, was said to have had an on-going affair with Pike, and this afternoon there is reason to believe Gideon Pike may have been involved in the murder. Shawn?

Sever stared, his mouth hanging open, not believing the screen as a tanned, thirty-year-old pretty-boy did his best as a reporter.

That's right, Wendy. Just down this concrete dock is Gideon Pike's boat, the *Hit King*. Neighbors here tell us that Spinatti had been staying on the boat for the last six months. Occasionally the music legend would visit the yacht. Pike's condominium is located just above the marina at the Grand Condominium complex.

The camera pulled back, showing pretty-boy standing on the dock. Then the picture dissolved and the tall Grand complex came into view.

Although no one seems to have seen any activity last night on the boat, police say they have reason to believe that Pike may have visited the boat late last night. We'll stay on top of the story, Wendy, and let you know if there are any late-breaking developments.

"Jesus!" Biddle sat there shaking his head. "Where the hell did that come from? Nobody called *me*. I'm only his fucking manager! He's supposed to have been on the fucking boat and we can't find him? Jesus!"

"It could be a set-up." Sever struggled for an answer. The Gideon Pike he knew was not someone who would be a suspect in a murder.

"Who would set him up? And why?"

Ginny drummed her fingers on the table in a burst of nervous energy. "Tom, you keep saying there's no problem. You keep saying that he'll be back. Yet every time Mick and I ask questions, things get violent. Now Gideon is being dragged into a murder investigation. Maybe it's time we admit that his disappearance doesn't seem to be the normal, run-of-the-mill getaway that he's famous for. Maybe this time it's serious."

"It just got a lot more serious." He was quiet for a moment, staring off into space. Finally he pushed his chair back and stood up. "Damned right!" Biddle walked out of the bar, his half-empty beer on the table.

CHAPTER TWENTY-FOUR

"Here. The estimated value of his songs." Ginny reached over from the bed and handed the diary to Sever.

"Shinn has the catalog valued at — Jesus — two hundred forty million?" He leaned back in the desk chair and contemplated the stunning figure.

"Read on. He and his lyricist apparently have a little problem with the publishing company."

Sever picked up the volume and read aloud. "Writing credits still go to Eddie and me, if Hit King ever pays. Eddie says we should let it take its course. Of course, Eddie always says 'let it take its course.' I don't think Eddie knows what the hell happened. If it ever 'took its course' I'd probably be crucified."

Sever stopped reading. "Writing credits. A publisher and the writer split the royalties."

"They split the royalties?"

"They call it 200%. 100% to the writer, 100% to the publisher."

"Strange."

Sever nodded. "Not like book publishing."

"So, when Pike owned the publishing company, he took *all* the money." Ginny was picking it up.

"That would be my guess. Now, Shinn gets half."

But the publishing company ends up collecting the money and writing a check to the writers."

Ginny nodded. "Your agent collects all your money and pays you. Same thing."

Sever smiled. "My agent only takes 15%."

"You've still made some money for her. Those monthly jaunts she takes all over the world to watch the birds?"

"Pike's saying that Hit King isn't paying."

"So he and Ed aren't getting paid and Hit King is keeping all the money?"

Sever looked at her. "That's got to be a fortune."

"Song publishing is a huge business."

"And," Sever looked back at the diary, "He says he might be crucified. Our boy is in big trouble over something."

"He doesn't think Eddy knows. Knows what?"

Sever leafed through the pages. "Here's something else. He talks about his sister and her son. Pike sends her a check to keep him in private school."

Ginny lay curled on her bed, reading the second volume. Sever let his eyes wander over to her, her tanned legs set off by white shorts. Barefoot, she curled and uncurled her toes as she studied the diary. He forced himself to look away. There was always that confusion when he was around her.

"Here, Mick. He mentions him by name. Kyle."

"Kyle?"

"I don't know. I think that's his nephew. He just rambles." She read aloud. "'Kyle looks more and more like his mother. Thank God. The father is not good looking, and not very bright.'"

"His sister is divorced?"

"Yeah. Apparently Gideon didn't care for the guy. Ugly and dumb."

"The father is ugly and dumb. And what if we'd had kids?"

"You don't even want to go there. Beautiful and smart, but boy would they be screwed up. Mick, if there is a God, thank him that we never had kids."

Sever gave it a passing thought. "We were too caught up in ourselves to ever give attention to a kid."

"We probably still are."

"Does it strike you as strange that after all the problems we've had, we keep coming together?"

She ignored him.

"Ginny, I'm serious. What's the bond?"

"We're friends."

"No. That's not all of it. I don't believe that men and women can be good friends. There's always sexual energy that gets in the way."

"So, what? We're still "dancing" as you call it? We still believe that somewhere in the distant future we'll be together?"

"Yeah. I believe that we're still dancing."

"Mick, I love you. But we're friends. Very special friends. We're not getting back together. Not now, and not at any time in the future. I'm sorry."

Sever stared at the pages in the diary, registering nothing on the page.

"Mick?"

"Well, I think we'd have to read these page by page to get any useful information. You'd be hard pressed to write a book about him based on these limited thoughts."

"Hey," he could feel her eyes on him. "You know we're not getting back together. Why even suggest it?"

Sever was silent. It had been what? Two years into their marriage? He'd been on the road with Zeppelin, just before drummer John Bonham died after a drinking binge. Mick was in London, staying at some five-star hotel and overnighting with a gorgeous nineteen-year-old blond when Ginny had walked through the door. Surprise. From that point on, he was pretty sure the relationship wasn't going to last.

"Mick, right now I just want to know where Gideon is, and if he's alive. And I think the information about the publishing of his songs could be very useful —"

"Except we have no idea how, or if, it ties in to his disappearance."

"My thoughts exactly. Mick? What's Boots? Kick?"

"Huh?"

"I told you. He signs off on some of the pages with *Boots. Kick. My good luck charms.*"

"Boots kick. Maybe they're the footwear he prefers."

"Boots as a good luck charm?" She shrugged her shoulders.

Sever pointed his finger at her. "The condo —"

"Who was there?"

"Yeah. I've got a thought."

She sat up, her halter top straining at her breasts. "Go on."

"There's only one way to see if anyone goes in or out of that condo."

"Stand in the hallway and watch?"

"No. Too obvious. And we can't hang out in the lobby all night. Security might not appreciate it."

"Then?"

"The dock. If we go down to the *Hit King*, we can look right up at his condo. The curtains are gauze. The blinds in the library were cracked open. We could spend a couple of hours tonight, and see if there are any signs of light. If we see a flashlight or someone turns on a light, we can use your pass to get up there and see who it is."

"Where is this going, Mick?"

"Fishing expedition, Ginny."

"And if someone is going in and out at night?"

"It might be Gideon."

"God, I hope it is. Then again," she gazed out the glass doors of the balcony, "I hope it's not. He could be in a world of trouble."

CHAPTER TWENTY-FIVE

Brady White poured liberally from the Dewar's bottle. He added a splash of water and handed the glass to Sever. "And for the lady?"

"Mick says you make a mean martini."

"I do, pretty lady. Gin or vodka? No, wait. You're a vodka girl. I can tell."

She laughed. "How?"

"You're blond and beautiful. I've mixed drinks for hundreds of women, and if she drinks a martini, the attractive blond girl always drinks vodka." His eyes sparkled as he gave her a grin.

"Thanks for letting us use your boat."

"Get yourself into some serious trouble if you try to use my neighbor's boat. All that yellow tape over there? Crime scene, do not trespass under penalty of law."

The boat gently rolled as a wave runner ran close to shore, someone getting in their last minutes of fun before dark. A slight breeze sent the hot, humid layer of Miami atmosphere into motion, but a moving hot and humid atmosphere was still hot and humid.

The drinks were cold, and felt good going down.

Brady stretched out on his lounge chair and motioned for Sever and Ginny to sit as well. "I've got a pair of binoculars here," he handed a leather case to Sever, "These are from my fishing business days."

Sever admired the leather case. He opened it and took out the binoculars. "You were in the fishing business?"

"I was."

"Commercial fishing?" Ginny sipped at the vodka.

"Charter boats."

"Where?"

"Right here. Ran a charter fishing company. Eight boats."

"Must have been successful," Sever said. "Eight boats."

Brady nodded. "Foreign tourists, northerners, they were all a big part of it. Started off with one boat, then I helped a buddy get his boat. Then another, and another. Pretty soon we had a fleet of 'em. I owned the company."

Sever watched the old man intently, a new level of admiration for the white-haired guy.

"Wow." Ginny's eyes were wide. "So what happened?"

"I sold the business. Years ago. Made some damned good money."

"And then what did you do?" Sever took a swallow of Scotch.

He smiled, and gestured at the hotels on Biscayne Bay. "Oh, a little of this, and," he pointed out to South Beach, "a little of that."

"Invested in property? Pretty shrewd."

Brady nodded again. "The values don't seem to go down. Can't sing, Mick. Can't write, and I can't build toilet valves like the guys who own that boat over there, but I do pretty well."

"I guess you do."

"Mick, I was thinking, if Gideon is the one who's going into the condo, he might look for the diaries." Ginny set down her glass and stood up. "I really should get those diaries back into that library."

Brady's eyes danced back and forth between Sever and Ginny.

"We, uh, borrowed a couple of books from Pike's library." Sever nodded toward the condo. "Diaries. We thought they might shed some light on where he was."

"Mick, I'm going up."

"Now?"

"Now. If Gideon comes back, that may be the first place he looks. I should have done this before."

"Ginny. You can't just waltz in there and put them back."

"I waltzed in and took them out."

"Someone may have missed them already. Let me go up there."

"No. If Biddle saw you, you'd have no excuse, and he knows I have the pass card."

"So what's your excuse?"

She thought for a moment. "I want to see his portrait that Gideon painted."

"This isn't a good idea, babe."

"Mick, I don't want Gideon coming back and seeing those diaries gone. Breaking and entering won't exactly help our professional relationship. If he'd wanted me to have them, he would have given them to me."

"Ginny. This isn't a good idea."

"In and out, Mick. There's no one there right now. No big deal. This won't take long. I'm going. Give me the key. I'll be back in fifteen minutes."

He handed her the stolen key, and she walked off the wooden plank at a brisk pace.

"She'll be all right, Mick," Brady said. "You know as well as I do that once a woman's mind is made up, there's absolutely no changing it."

They watched her walk up the gray concrete to the hotel. The evening lights from the Double Tree and the Marriot next door had yet to come on and they lost her in the dusk.

CHAPTER TWENTY-SIX

Somewhere close by Sever heard the tinkling of glass on glass and soft laughter. The heavy bass of a sound system seemed to ebb and fade in the distance as a boat moved slowly through the bay. The sound of water lapping at Brady's yacht was more pronounced than during the day. Somehow, the gathering darkness seemed to amplify the sounds.

The old man sat still, occasionally sipping his martini. Stars were hard to see with the lights of the Sealine Marina burning the darkness away, and shadows moved as boats rocked on the rolling water. The creaking of the *Hit King* moved across the water and entered into the cacophony of night sounds.

Sever glanced at his watch, squinting to see the numbers. She'd been gone fifteen minutes. Three or four minutes to get to her room, pick up the diaries, then go back to the lobby. All right. Maybe six minutes. Maybe she went to the bathroom. Ten minutes tops.

"Another drink?"

"No. Thanks. I want to be ready."

"For what?"

"I don't know."

Then she goes to the lobby, swipes her card at the desk, and goes back up the condominium side. Twenty-three stories. The elevator takes a minute, she goes up — another minute, walks down the hall, goes into the condo, and puts the books back. Another five or six minutes. Then five minutes to come back out. Twenty-two minutes. He realized he'd been holding his breath, and he let it out.

"Yeah. Make it a short one, Brady."

Brady moved to the bar and poured the Scotch into Mick's glass. "She's a catch."

"Fisherman's talk?"

"She's a catch, Mick. They don't come along too often."

"What's your story? You seem to do fine with the ladies. And you seem to enjoy variety."

Brady gave him a faint smile. "Lots of lonely women in the world."

"Were you married?"

"Was. Two kids."

"Just didn't work out?"

"Worked out fine. She died giving birth to our second child."

"Jeez. I'm sorry. I didn't mean to —"

"I know about the good ones. Never found one as good again. So, yeah, I do okay for an old guy. But I really do believe that when you find that special lady, you got to hang on. 'Course, I just met you. I don't pretend to know your situation. Just seemed to me —"

Sever took the drink. He could feel the alcohol course through his veins.

He felt primed for whatever happened tonight, but he wasn't sure that was a good thing. A slight buzz might slow him down.

"I think maybe it's because I'm no threat. Older, wiser, not a serious candidate for romance. So if they want a little fling, a little danger in their lives, Brady White may be the answer. Hell, Mick, sometimes I get referrals."

Sever watched him in the darkness. "Referrals?"

"I go out with a flight attendant, and she tells her friend. I get a call a week later and there's another notch on the bedpost. I don't pretend to understand it. I just know that there are a lot of lonely women out there. And," he paused and took a drink. His eyes drifted out to the bay, "and a lot of lonely men."

Sever put the binoculars to his eyes and trained them on Pike's room. The windows were dark. He thought he'd see something from her flashlight, but everything seemed black. He might have missed it. He trained the lenses on her hotel room. Eight floors up, seven rooms over. Nothing.

He went back to Pike's windows. Then to Ginny's. He could go back and forth in less than a second. Pike, Ginny. Pike, Ginny.

"No sign of her."

"There will be."

Pike, Ginny. Pike — a light.

"There she is."

He handed the glasses to Brady.

"I see it. Single beam, bouncing around. Shouldn't take her very long."

"No."

Brady gave him back the binoculars.

Darkness, then the bobbing beam, back again. It seemed to shut down, then flash, then shut down again. A flash, then total darkness and a repeat of the pattern.

"She's got to be telling us she's in and the books are in place." Sever threw back a swallow of Scotch. Relief. Ginny was on her way back.

"May take several nights to find this guy," Brady said.

"Brady, we have no idea who was up there. This is all speculation" He kept the lenses trained on Pike's apartment. "It's just taken a more serious turn now that the cops are suggesting Pike may be a suspect in Spinatti's murder."

A bouncing beam in Pike's condo stole his attention. She was still there. The beam went dark, then picked up in the next window. Pike's bedroom or the library. Hell, he couldn't remember.

"She's still there."

"It's taken longer than we thought."

"Yeah. I'd just feel a whole lot better if she would —" He stopped.

"What?"

"Shit." A chill ran through him, stopping at his heart.

"Mick, what is it?"

"There's a second beam."

"A second?"

One beam in the main room, where the piano and the painting were. One beam in the second room, the library?

Sever stood up. "Come on. Give me a signal." The beams continued to play in two separate rooms.

"Mick, maybe she's on her way back. Might be two other people, just like you and Ginny the other night. It may not have anything to do with her."

"It may not. Should I take that chance?"

Brady was quiet.

"Should I, Brady?"

"No."

Sever handed him the binoculars and set his Scotch on the bar. "Keep this. I'll be back."

He walked off the wooden plank and onto the concrete dock. His knee was throbbing, but he jogged to the end of the dock. He wanted to make much better time than Ginny had made.

CHAPTER TWENTY-SEVEN

April was on her knees. Shinn admired her smooth taught buttocks as she leaned between the knees of the NASCAR driver. Johnny something. Shinn loved fast cars, but guys racing around a track for hours at a time bored the shit out of him.

Celeste worked on the other driver. This being their first time, Shinn told the drivers the hummer was on the house. Hell, the girls worked for him. Football players, baseball players, actors and now this. He'd seen them all.

The private back room was built with a mattress type floor, springy to the step. Plush, red velvet benches surrounded the oval-shaped room, and almost every customer's wish was granted. This wasn't the room the regular $150-a-pop customer saw. This was only for the elite. April and Celeste were hand picked to take care of this caliber of customer.

Johnny something looked up at Shinn, sitting silently by the door. "Oh shit. This little girl knows what she's doing, Jimmy. Damn! Oh, shit."

It wasn't that Shinn enjoyed watching so much, although he did receive some sort of perverse pleasure watching his current squeeze giving the celebrity a blow job, but he wanted the men to know that they owed this unique treat to him. As long as he remained in the room, they had to know that Jimmy Shinn was responsible for getting their ashes hauled. And as long as these lovely ladies were swallowing their cocks, the two drivers were perfectly willing to accept the fact that Shinn was watching the proceedings.

His cell phone vibrated. He opened it.

"This is not a good time."

Richard Shinn's voice was loud. "It makes no difference to me what time it is. I asked for a report, and I have yet to receive it."

Jimmy Shinn stood up and walked out the door. He stood in the hallway between the club and the private room, and closed his eyes. "Father," it sounded so stilted. Always had. But it's what the old gentleman demanded. Maybe it was time to break with family traditions. He'd realized there was a difference in the types of respect you paid people. *Demanded* respect, or *earned* respect. Theirs was demanded. He was sure of that. There had never been a close moment in the father-son relationship. Never a Little League game moment, or a talk about the birds and the bees. There had never been a discussion of joining the family business. It was expected. The bond was expected, part of the heritage. No questions, please. Just live by the code. Honor thy father. Damn demanded respect.

One time, and one time only, he'd talked to his mother about the relationship. He'd been about fifteen, and the stilted, formal family life had finally driven him to her. He gathered up every last ounce of courage that he had, and spoke to her as if he'd written a prepared script.

"Mother. I respect you. I respect my father. But I have friends who . . ." he fought for the words, knowing what he had to say and scared to say it. "They go on vacations with their parents." He waited for a response. When there was none, he continued. "People I know have discussions with their families. They go to sporting events and celebrate holidays together."

She bowed her head and walked from the room, never uttering a sound. He stood there, dumbfounded. He'd prepared the talk for a month, and she dismissed it in a second. Jimmy Shinn never made the effort again. Domination, threats, and a total respect for authority — that was family life as little Jimmy Shinn had known it. As an adult, nothing had changed.

"Father, I have no report." Cell phone conversations were easily intercepted. Nothing he said could be clear and concise. Everything had to be vague. "The party you're seeking is still missing."

"Missing? With your resources? Do I have to hire an outside firm? We have him in a very compromising position, and I will not allow you to lose him now. Do you understand?"

He was quiet, seething inside.

"Do you?" Richard Shinn had raised his voice.

"I understand."

"Find him, or I'll hire someone who will."

"No. No. Don't do that. I'm very close."

"Son. I assume the situation by the docks this morning was a signal to our friend."

Shinn grimly smiled. "Yes, Father. That's why I'm asking you to please give me just a little more time. I feel very strongly that we have the situation well in hand."

"And if you don't?"

"If I don't, there is plan Kyle."

"Make one of your plans work. And soon."

The old man hung up, the click loud in Shinn's ear. Threats. Richard Shinn didn't make idle threats. Not to his friends, not to his enemies, and not to his son. And Jimmy didn't know if he was truly frightened by the older man and his demands, or if his subservience was habit. Anyway, this was not a Little League moment. Jimmy Shinn quietly opened the door and walked back into the room.

"Shit, oh shit. SHIT." Johnny something was bucking his hips, choking April. With a last loud "SHIT," he drew back and collapsed against the wall. April wiped her hand over her mouth and stood up, heading for the restroom. The other driver must have expired minutes before, and was sipping on a Jack and Coke.

"Gentlemen, I assume you're both satisfied? I would ask that you tip both of the girls, and join the rest of the customers. I'm sure they'll be excited to see two famous NASCAR drivers."

They stood, tucking in their shirts and zipping up. Shinn followed them into the club.

No matter what his father wanted, there was still a business to run.

He sat at the end of the bar, watching the drivers shaking hands with several customers around the center stage. Sipping on a Coke, he thought about the matter of Sever and his ex-wife. Like two loose cannons, they were all over the place. Something had to be done.

The local investigation of Spinatti's murder would go through its slow, methodical process and Shinn had no doubt what the outcome would be. But Sever wasn't part of that process, and this investigation didn't need a wild card. Jimmy Shinn didn't like elements that were out of his control, and Sever was out of control. Two more days. He'd give them two more days. If the two Severs didn't come up with Pike, they were useless, just like Larry Spinatti.

Where the hell was Pike? Jesus, he knew how important it was that they find the songwriter. This added pressure from his father was driving him crazy. And for the first time he truly admitted to himself that maybe he didn't fear his father any more. Maybe fear had just become a habit. Maybe he was pursuing Pike for himself, not for the old man.

He paged Sam on his phone. "We need a meeting. Call our friends, and meet me in half an hour. We need a plan."

Shinn left from the rear exit and climbed into his olive-green Lexus convertible. He settled into the leather seat, and started the engine. A little drive would help settle him down. Then he'd come back and meet with Sam and the group. He found himself looking forward to that meeting. He and Sam always found a unique way of solving problems.

CHAPTER TWENTY-EIGHT

Sever reached the brown tile steps that led up to the lobby, barely noticing the waterfall cascading beside him. He took the steps two at a time, his knee throbbing but holding strong. Through the glass doors and down to the security desk. No entry card. Two uniformed guards stood behind the desk, one reading a Spanish newspaper, the other half asleep. Sever stopped and caught his breath. He owed her. He'd made her life miserable, and more to the point, he was still dancing. She was still the love of his life. Hell, yes, there was still a future.

Three black-and-white monitors sat on the curved, marble-topped reception desk. On one monitor, Sever could see the entire elevator area, six elevators in all. The entrance to the elevator area was through the card-activated doors behind the desk. The sleepy guard looked up at him, as if to ask if he could be of assistance. Sever ignored him and walked to a newspaper rack. He pretended to scan the headlines of the *Miami Herald* as the guard settled back in his chair. Ginny was up there and so was someone else. He had to make something happen soon.

Sever picked up a paper and turned so that he could see the elevators. No one was going in; no one was going out. He needed some activity. They might ask him for identification if he followed someone on their way in, but if he could time it so he was at the card-activated doors when someone else was coming out, it might seem like a coincidence. Someone had to be going out for the evening. There were forty-three floors of condos. Somebody, please, somebody. Hurry.

An elderly lady in a pink and yellow sweatshirt and sweatpants walked by, swiped her card, and the glass doors opened. Sever was tempted, but he noticed the guard glance up again. Then he saw motion on the screen. The first elevator on the left opened and some guy stepped out. The older woman seemed to be saying something to him, and Sever reached into his pocket and pulled out two quarters. He dropped the quarters on the desk, held up the newspaper, waving it at the guard so he'd know what the quarters were for, and slowly walked toward the doors, timing it perfectly. As the man walked out of the doors, Sever slipped in.

He held his breath then slowly exhaled. No one raced in, looking for him. He pushed the button on the control panel and number four opened immediately. Sever stepped in, pushed twenty-three, and wiped perspiration from his upper lip. Maybe the humidity, maybe the stress. The elevator rose, slower than he remembered. Painfully slow. Finally the soft belltone sounded and the door opened. He stepped out, trying to remember if he walked left or right. Left. He could see the condo, all the way at the end of the hall.

The doors were on the left, an atrium on the right. A straight drop off to floor six, protected only by a railing. Sever glanced down. Open seventeen stories, all the way down to the pool area. The protective railing was strung with small lights, and when he looked down, or up into the immense opening, there were rows and rows of the decorative bulbs. It started to make him dizzy. He took long strides, moving as quickly as possible. No pass card, and no key. If he couldn't get in, he'd try Biddle. It may take some explaining afterwards, but right now he needed to get into that condo. If anything happened to her —

He double-checked the number on the door. 2333. Cautiously he put his ear to the door. No sounds at all. He tested the knob, slowly turning it. The door was unlocked.

He eased it open and stepped inside the pitch-black entrance-way. No pass card, no key, and he'd made it this far. Now he needed a weapon. The only thing he had was the newspaper, still clutched tightly in his hand. He wasn't sure how much damage he could do with the *Miami Herald*.

CHAPTER TWENTY-NINE

The door silently closed behind him. The room felt as if the life had been sucked from it. Hot, humid and no sound at all. He listened intently. No air-conditioning. The kitchen was to his immediate right, but there wasn't even the quiet hum of a refrigerator. Sever stood still, letting the surroundings soak in. Maybe thirty seconds passed, and he heard nothing. His eyes adjusted and he could see the distant lights of South Beach through the gauze curtains. He laid the newspaper on the counter and moved straight through to the living room. The sliding glass doors were open, and a slight breeze moved the thin material.

Deliberate, soft steps. If someone was here, they may be aware he'd come in, but Sever hoped that they wouldn't know exactly where he was. He actually hoped no one was there. Maybe Ginny was on her way back to Brady's boat. Maybe the whole thing was a false alarm.

Stepping out on the balcony he saw Sealine Marina below. He glanced over at Brady's boat and waved. He couldn't see if the old man was on deck or not. Several small tables and lounge chairs were scattered about the tiled balcony but there was no sign of anyone. In the distance the headlights of cars crossing the causeway over to South Beach caught his eye. He stepped back in and walked quietly back to the hallway. His shirt stuck to his body. The humidity, no air-conditioning, plus the sweat from his run up the pier. No sounds.

None. He hadn't been aware of this oppressive silence the last time he'd been here. Something was different.

The room on the right was the library. This is where he'd seen the flashlight from the deck of Brady's boat. Slowly, he walked down the corridor, five, six steps. He turned into the room, holding his breath. Blinds covered the window, barely cracked open to let just a hint of evening bay light in. He wanted to turn on the overhead lights, look up at the top bookshelf, and confirm the two diaries in their original setting.

That's what he wanted to do. Caution being the better part of valor, he didn't. Not enough light to see. But, there was the ladder. He paused. Thirty seconds. There was no sound at all. Sever stepped on the first rung of the ladder, then the second, third, fourth and fifth. He tried to remember exactly where she'd pulled them. Ginny would have been sure to put the two volumes in the exact same spot.

He made a guess. The light was too dim to see the books. He ran his hand over bindings. There was no space between any of the books. This was a good thing. The missing diaries would have opened a — shit!

A space. A wide space opened up. Just about where he thought the books should have been. Ginny hadn't put the books back. Why?

Sever stepped back down the ladder. He massaged his knee, trying to wish the pain away. She didn't put the books back. So where was she? Back on Brady's boat? In Biddle's condominium?

One bedroom, the workout room, and two baths left to explore. With no light, it was going to be a bitch. Sever crept out of the library, pausing in the hallway. Still not a sound. Then it hit him. There was no LED light from the microwave oven in the kitchen. No illuminated clocks in the living room, kitchen, or library. He was sure he'd seen one or two the last time he was here.

The power was out. A circuit breaker had flipped off. It was as if someone wanted the condo to be dark. Softly, quietly, he stepped down the hall, feeling along the wall for the first opening. This was the guest bedroom, where Spinatti kept his exercise equipment.

There was no open window, no light creeping in. Sever stared for several moments, waiting for his eyes to adjust. They didn't.

Running his hand along the wall he stopped at a machine. Maybe a Weider exercise station. Beyond that his knee bumped something. He reached down and felt the slanted bench. Weights would probably be nearby. He could feel the edge of a rug up against his shoe. Sever slid his shoe forward. It wasn't a rug. Whatever it was didn't move. Maybe a footstool, or a piece of soft-side luggage. He nudged it and heard the noise. It wasn't the object on the floor, it was behind him, ever so faint. A gentle whoosh. The shattering crash on his head felt like the world exploded. Bright lights flashed inside his skull and sharp shots of pain raced to every part of his body. It only lasted for a second, and he felt himself crumpling to the floor.

CHAPTER THIRTY

He wished he were invisible. Not the kind of invisibility where no one could see you, but the kind where no one noticed you. Where you could walk through a crowd and no one would look. Head down, an anonymous face in the crowd.

But people knew. People looked, and pointed, and some came up and told him how much they enjoyed his stories. And others came up and told him how much they hated them. He was paid to have an opinion, paid very well, and sometimes people didn't agree. He'd had death threats from rappers, angry letters and threats from agents, managers, and record companies, and just plain threats from a jealous husband or two. A lot of people just didn't like his opinion.

A couple of years ago, he'd been on Ocean Boulevard. Traffic was crawling, then stopping altogether in the see-and-be-seen craziness of South Beach. And the girl he was with, maybe Bobbi, said "Let's walk. It's faster." So they parked the rental car and walked the busy sidewalk, jostled by the crowd, watching the Porsches, the Bentleys, and Rolls Royces. He'd seen the silver convertible, a make and model he didn't recognize. The sleek machine was crawling with the rest of the traffic, moving inches intermittently.

Sever walked right into the middle of the narrow street to get a closer look. An Astin Martin Vantage. Glancing up, he caught the eye of the driver, Ben Affleck. Seated next to him, hair pulled back was his then fiancée, Jennifer Lopez. She gave him a glance, then a second glance that became a glare. Sever nodded and stepped back onto the sidewalk She hadn't appreciated his opinion. He'd slammed every record she'd made. He'd written scathing reviews in *Rolling Stone*, *Spin,* and half a dozen other publications. It was his opinion she should have stayed with acting. He was paid for his opinion. He didn't like her records.

He looked over his shoulder and saw her eyes following him, a deep frown on her face.

"God, Mick. Was that Jennifer Lopez?"

"Yeah."

"Do you know her? She looked like —"

"No, forget it, Bobbi."

Sometimes he wished he were invisible. Totally invisible. If he'd been invisible in the hotel that night, the night Ginny had walked in on him, he might still be married. Or maybe the nineteen-year-old blond should have been invisible.

Sever watched the brilliant flashes of yellow and orange behind his eyelids, and realized he was somewhere else. This wasn't South Beach. He was unbearably hot. He wiped at his face and felt the sweat. And whatever he'd had to drink had left him with one hell of a hangover. His head throbbed and his hands shook. He tried to open his eyes again, but they seemed to stay shut. Everything had suddenly gone black. Then he saw the light. Not the flashing lights, but a single beam of light, and he wondered if this was the light that you see when you have a near-death experience. The light that leads you to the next stage. Jim Morrison had written the song, "Break On Through to the Other Side." Was this the other side?

He was dizzy, his head swimming, and he felt like he might throw up. The light was bright in his eyes, causing his head to throb even more violently. Even with the pain, he knew he wasn't really ready for death. If there was an afterlife, if there was a heaven, he had a ways to go to make up for life on earth.

The white, bright beam stayed on him, and he closed his eyes. He drifted off where the pain wasn't as bad, where the light wasn't so bright. He didn't always like to be recognized in life, and he certainly wasn't ready to be recognized in death. There was work to do. It was important. Ginny was in trouble. His childhood sweetheart, the first girl he'd smoked dope with, the only girl he'd ever loved. There had to be something he could do. He'd fucked up her life and he owed her. Ginny. And he still had to find Gideon Pike. He remembered.

He could still sense the light, fading gradually. He wished he were invisible.

CHAPTER THIRTY-ONE

The light was back. The pain in his head had subsided somewhat, little sparks shooting off occasionally, but not the incessant throbbing that had made him nauseous. He wasn't going to die after all.

"Mick?"

Ginny? It had to be her voice. Hell, she'd been there so many times. Almost every time. When he jumped from the stage in Toronto in a drug-induced stupor and broke his leg, when he woke up with head-banging, gut-retching hangovers, or been higher than a kite. She was there when he got the shit kicked out of him in the parking lot at Platinum, the strip club. It occurred to him that this visit to Miami was turning into a very painful experience. He turned his head ever so slowly, afraid to anger the pain god.

"Are you all right?"

He was lying on a bed, a pillow propped up under his head. "I wouldn't want to tackle a ten-mile hike right now."

"Thank God. I was afraid maybe there was some permanent damage."

"You hit me?" It made no sense. He blinked, trying to see her face. He couldn't see beyond the light. "Get the light out of my eyes."

She lowered the beam. "No. Of course not."

She'd probably had good reason to. His philandering, carousing, and party-down rock-star lifestyle should have earned him several slaps to the face. But she never did. When Sever refused to grow up, Ginny just walked away.

"Who hit me?"

The responding voice was soft, somewhat timid. Sever'd heard it before. He couldn't quite put his finger on it but —

"Me. I hit you. I'm very sorry, but things have gotten a little intense and I was trying to protect myself."

Sever tried to sit up but fell back. Ginny took his hand. "Take it easy, Mick. He can explain everything."

"Somebody tried to kill me. Can he explain that?"

"I thought you might be one of *them*."

Sever couldn't see the face in the dark. "Would somebody turn on the goddamn lights?"

"We can't find the circuit breaker." Ginny sighed. "We've looked, but so far it's eluded us."

"Who tried to take my head off?"

Again, the voice. "I did. I'm really sorry. I don't go around cracking people's skulls as a rule."

"Who the hell are you?"

"Ed Komack."

Ed Komack. The voice on the phone in New York. The guy who wrote the lyrics. Eddy, who along with Gideon, wasn't being paid by Hit King Publishing.

"We've met," Sever found strength in his delivery.

"On the phone. You called me in New York. Look, I'm afraid things are a little out of control."

"You think?" Sarcasm dripped from Sever's voice.

"I thought maybe I'd killed you."

"I wasn't sure myself. What the hell did you hit me with?"

The shadowy figure held up a large bottle. "Champagne. Come on, man, you were breaking and entering."

Sever was quiet for a moment. Of course the man was right.

"Do you know where Gideon is?"

Komack paused. "Not for sure."

"Maybe?"

"He called me. I knew where he was then. Things have changed."

"Look," Sever pushed himself into a sitting position. The reflection of the flashlight highlighted the man's face. Closely cropped hair, a high forehead, bushy eyebrows, and glasses. He'd seen his picture before. Maybe in *Rolling Stone*, or *People*. And he remembered an A&E special on Pike and Komack. *Behind the Music*. "Look, I'm losing my patience."

"Mick," Ginny in her damned condescending voice. "He's explained a lot of this to me. You need to hear it. Just be patient. Ed?"

Komack sat down on the bed. "I was in New York when you called. I'm working on a musical and —"

"I know. Let's get back to why we're all here in this room."

"You told me that Gideon had disappeared. I told you he does that from time to time."

"Go on."

"He called me. Right after you did."

"He's all right?"

"It depends on what you mean by 'all right.' "

"Ed, what did he want?"

"Why should I tell you?"

"Because I assume we're all after the same thing. Finding Gideon Pike. Maybe you don't get it, but I've put my life on the line for this guy several times in the last forty-eight hours. I genuinely like the man, and I'm concerned for his safety."

Komack's voice grew quiet. "He was afraid for his life. And afraid for mine."

Sever remembered a time when Pike *hadn't* cared about his life. And Sever had been there then. It only seemed fitting he was here now, when the man apparently wanted to live. Should he tell Komack he'd received the same message? *Don't trust the inner circle*, and Ed Komack was certainly part of that circle. "Afraid for his life?" Sever could feel the little jolts of pain in his head every time he raised his voice.

"Mr. Sever, you know Gideon. He's somewhat prone to exaggeration. He feels he's been threatened. I thought that might be a little exaggerated. But it's a long story going back years ago. It has to do with Jimmy Shinn, our publisher. He," Komack cleared his throat, "he controls the catalog of songs that we wrote."

"I know that."

"Jimmy and the people at Hit King Publishing are in control of our publishing rights, but before they took over, Gideon and I had negotiated an agreement with White Sand Records — that's our recording company — all of the *recording* rights to all of our songs would revert to us the first of next year."

"That means?" Sever winced. Brain cells were exploding at an alarming rate.

"I hesitate to tell you all of this. It really doesn't seem to be any of your business."

Sever worked the sympathy angle. "Look, you almost put my lights out permanently. Humor me."

The soft-spoken man nodded. "Gideon and I would own one hundred percent of the recording rights. Not the publishing rights, but the recording rights. They're different. We could release all of our hits, box sets, compilation albums — whatever we wanted — on our own label. Except for the publishing rights and distribution rights, all the profits from CD sales would be ours. The rights could be worth hundreds of millions."

Sever closed his eyes. Hundreds of millions. "Why would White Sand Records give up all those rights?"

"Because at that time we agreed to sign a new, four-record deal with them. That deal worked out for both of us. They made a killing on those four albums over the last eight years, and, they'll still have distribution rights to our new label."

Ginny jumped in. "So, you see, even though White Sand Records wouldn't have the recording rights, they still get a cut of the profits because they use their sales force and distribution force to help release all of the Pike/Komack songs."

"What's this label?"

"PK records. Pike, Komack. Pretty simple."

"So Gideon feels his life is in danger, but you think he may be exaggerating?"

"I don't know how to say this." Komack balled up his fists. Ginny kept the beam on the floor, letting the reflection bathe the room in a ghostly light. "I can't be too specific, because there's a lot involved here."

"Damn it. Just say it."

"Jimmy Shinn feels we should cut him in on the recording deal. When Gideon refused, he says Shinn threatened him."

"Threatened him with what?"

"Look. There's something between those two that I —" he closed his eyes and was silent for a moment, "I can't talk about it, all right?"

Sever paused. It was time to break it down interview style. "This guy owns the publishing rights."

"Yes."

"He makes millions every year on songs you and Gideon wrote."

"He does."

"Why did you give up the publishing company? How did Jimmy Shinn get it?"

Komack took a deep breath and let out a sigh. "There was some bad legal advice," he hesitated as if weighing his next statement, "and maybe more threats."

"Bad legal advice. Lou Frey?"

"I'd rather not say."

"Rusty? Gideon's first attorney?"

"I can't talk about it. But it happened. Now, Hit King wants the recording rights."

"And what about the threats?"

Komack shook his head. "You don't need to know anything else."

"If someone is threatening Gideon, he's got a secret. Something he doesn't want anyone to know." He hesitated, feeling the throbbing return to his head. "Ed, do you know anything about an accident?"

The cryptic diary message. Something about *if it wasn't for the accident*.

"Jesus! Can't you just leave it alone? We're talking about a man's life here. It's his life, not yours. Go away, will you? You're going to fuck everything up if you keep prying."

"Is it life or death? How serious is this? Was there an accident?" Sever wanted to push on, beyond the throbbing pain. He'd saved Pike's life before. He was never to talk about it, or write about it, but he couldn't let Pike's life end now.

"Of course it's serious. Very serious. Any time you talk about hundreds of millions, you're talking serious. But as I said, Pike tends to exaggerate things. This threat on his life is probably one of those times."

Sever gingerly touched his head and winced. "Why would you two even think about cutting Shinn in?" There was no answer. "Because he threatened to kill you and Gideon?"

"I didn't say —"

"God damn it. You said Gideon thought his life and your life were in danger."

"That's what *Gideon* thinks. Gideon. Look. Gideon owns a controlling interest in our partnership."

"And?"

"He and Shinn have a thing between them. That's all I can say." Irritation crept into Komack's voice. Sever knew he couldn't push him much farther.

"If he's threatened, is Gideon going to give in and let Shinn have a piece of the recording rights?"

Komack shook his head. "If I could find him, I'd give you an answer."

"You really don't know what this *thing* is? You're telling me that you don't have any control or interest in this relationship."

"Yes. No. I'm telling you it's none of your damned business, and you're way out of line in asking."

"And you have no idea where he is?" There was always a time to back off an interview question.

"Look, Sever. If I did, we wouldn't be having this conversation.

I'd be talking to him and getting the answers to all of these questions."

"You came back from New York because?"

"Because," the soft voice got softer. "Because of something else. Not Jimmy Shinn or the business. I came back because I think Gideon is in serious trouble. The police are suggesting he may have murdered Larry Spinatti, and I think that may be true."

CHAPTER THIRTY-TWO

Sever rested while Ginny and Komack searched for the circuit breaker. They found it in a utility closet off the master bedroom. Komack went around to all the rooms, shutting the blinds and pulling the heavy curtains across the sliding glass doors.

"No reason to advertise that we're here. Someone may be watching."

Ginny flipped a switch in the living room and the track lighting came on, covering the soft-white room in an amber hue.

"I'm still waiting to hear why you think he killed Spinatti." Sever sat down on the piano bench, looking over his shoulder at Gideon's painting, the obscene, red mouth leering at him. Aspirin and a glass of soda water had helped the headache.

"You know, it seems to me you've got one hell of a lot of nerve. You and your lady friend." Komack's voice went up. He'd seemed to recover from his apologetic nature regarding Sever's bash on the head, and with the lights on he seemed to muster some bravado. "This is my business partner's condo. I've got a key that *he* gave me. The question still is, why are you here?"

Sever glanced at Ginny. She walked over and sat down next to him. "I told you, Ed. I was working with Gideon on the book and he —"

"Yeah. But that doesn't give you the right to break into his condo."

"Well, we did. And, like I told you before Mick came up, we found the diaries. We simply thought they might give us a clue to where he is. We want to find him just like you. Let's quit with the cat-and-mouse game."

"You want him so you can get your story. I want to find him because he's in trouble. Big difference."

Sever gave Komack a long look. "It seems to me that you want him because he's the brains behind your partnership. You want to protect this business."

Komack stared back. "Please. I'm not the one who has an extravagant lifestyle."

"Gideon's always lived with some excess." Sever remembered interviewing the superstar at a four-thousand-square-foot penthouse overlooking Central Park in New York. The view had been spectacular. Gideon believed in living large.

"Oh, Mr. Sever. Houses scattered around the world, including the one on Star Island. The yacht. The art collection. The Lear jet."

"I remember. He seems to have downsized." Sever waved his hand at the surroundings.

"You don't understand any of this. Why not just drop it and leave."

"Because we want to find him." Sever glanced at Ginny.

"Well, Mrs. Sever, did you find any clues in the diaries? The ones you were so anxious to put back?"

"We didn't have time to go through them entirely, and I'm not sure we would have understood everything anyway." Ginny brushed her hair back with her hands, tucking it behind her ears. "So we're guilty of breaking and entering. We're guilty of stealing. We're guilty of trying to find Gideon."

Komack sat on a bar stool at the kitchen counter. "He asked me to check on one thing when he called. He said he needed something from the hall closet. Have you two been in the hall closet?" His eyes stared intently from under the bushy eyebrows.

Sever looked toward the hallway. There wasn't anything he could think of that they hadn't seen. "We glanced through it."

"Did you take anything?"

"Not from the closet. Just the diaries from the bookshelves."

"Look," there was a very serious tone of voice, "I need you to be honest with me. What did you find in the closet?"

"Nothing." It was time to forget the inside circle warning. Sever sincerely believed that Ed Komack was worried about his partner.

"You searched through it. What was there?"

"Clothes," Ginny said. "Jackets, hats —"

"An umbrella," Sever added.

"Paintings." Ginny squinted, as if picturing the three portraits. "Three paintings. Is that what you want to know? The portraits? We looked at them, we didn't take them."

Komack seemed to stiffen for a moment. "No." He stood up. "I'm sorry about tonight. I'm sorry I hit you. Both of you. But you've got to understand that first of all, you," he pointed at Ginny, "come sneaking in, and I had no idea who you were."

"You could have asked before you hit me and taped my hands."

"Somebody turned the breakers off. Any idea why?" Sever rubbed the back of his head.

He walked to the door, looking back at them. "No idea at all. It was dark when I got here." Komack stared at Sever. "You know, I got into writing songs because of the creative side. It was a chance to express myself, and make a lot of money. But it turns out it's all about business. A dirty, nasty business. There's a sinful amount of money to be made and everyone wants a piece of it." He gazed at the floor. "Not just a piece. Too many people aren't satisfied until they have the whole enchilada. That's the nature of the business." He looked up and opened the door. "I think it's time that you two leave. Now."

Sever stood up, getting his balance. He was still a little light-headed. He and Ginny walked to the door. "We're staying at the Doubletree next door."

"Mr. Sever. I'd just as soon you forgot what I told you. I can take care of this, okay?"

"Ed, if you need help,"

"Help? Help me by leaving." He motioned to them to leave.

They walked to the elevators, neither of them speaking. Ginny carried what looked like a purse in her hand. When they reached the lobby, Sever broke the silence.

"You're okay?"

"My head's a little sore. But he didn't hit me hard like he hit you. Jesus, Mick, you really are lucky you're alive."

"Hey, I'll be all right. Why don't you go up to your room. I've got a drink waiting on Brady's boat."

"I should argue with you. You really got clobbered."

"I'm fine. Seriously."

Ginny looked into his eyes, trying to see into his soul. "Okay. You're on your own, Sever." She started toward the hotel side of the lobby. "Oh, Mick. She held up the canvas bag in her hand and smiled. "I never did make it to the library. There still may be something in here worth reading. We'll just have to hang on to the diaries for awhile longer."

CHAPTER THIRTY-THREE

When the last album with White Sand had been released, Sever had written a short piece for *Newsweek* without talking to the singer. Pike had cut him off. Refused his phone calls and wouldn't call him back. It was as if Pike had decided Sever was persona non grata.

> Gideon Pike still has style. He and partner, Ed Komack, have stayed true to their rock and ballad style on their new release *A World Gone Mad,* but they've broken new ground, and for the number of years they've been in the business and their substantial body of work, that's not an easy feat.

He'd gone on to praise the stylish album, and question a rumor that Pike may never record again. Pike never responded to the article. Sever had hoped it would be a way to renew the friendship. It was unlike Pike to ignore a story in the press. Several months, then a year. He'd tried again, but there was no reply. He'd called Pike's William Morris agent, some girl named Cathy Naab, but the answer was that Gideon Pike was busy. On the road. Traveling. Performing in Australia or somewhere in Europe. Now, Sever wondered if Komack's cryptic comments had something to do with the distance Pike had put in their relationship. Was there a secret that Pike wanted to keep from

Sever? Komack kept warning him off. And he kept wondering about the reference in the diary to an accident. Maybe Komack was right. He should walk away from it all. But he couldn't. The story was too good, Ginny was by his side, and friends in the business like Gideon Pike were hard to come by. Even friends who distanced themselves from you. And maybe, just maybe, his estranged friend was dead. Jesus, the idea kept rearing its ugly head. He didn't want to think about it.

He walked up the plank to the deck of the boat, still feeling a slight headache.

"Brady?"

He couldn't remember ever seeing a name on the vessel. He stepped off and searched the side, a dim light mounted above the marina helping him find his way. Murky shadows like dark clouds swirled over the water and the boat as it rocked gently on the surface.

Old Man and the Sea. Sever could barely make it out.

Fitting. Brady was a Hemmingway character himself. He may have been the Old Man. Sever'd met *the* old man in Cohimar, Cuba, years ago. Gregario Fuentes. Fuentes had been Hemmingway's chef, boat captain, and his best friend. He was 102 at the time, and full of life. Brady would probably make it to 100 and still be going strong.

"Brady?"

No answer.

Sever walked back on the deck. His glass of Scotch sat on the bar, undisturbed. He picked it up and walked to the railing, pouring the caramel-colored liquid into the water. The way his head felt right now he didn't need anything else messing with it.

Walking back up the concrete dock he saw the blue and red rotating lights. Cops. Again. Quiet this time, but obviously on a mission. That son-of-a-bitch Ed Komack *had* called the cops. He quickened his pace, hoping to be off the dock before they arrived.

The lights swung in front of the hotel and condo complex and disappeared from view. Sever pushed his bad leg, feeling the ache every step of the way. He had to get to Ginny. If it was Komack who'd called the police, they'd be looking for Sever and Ginny. Reaching the back steps with the waterfall he had a sense of deja vu. Up the steps to the lobby. There was no sign of the cops.

He walked to the condo desk with the two guards and the three monitors.

"Something going on?"

The two uniformed security guards had been engaged in an animated conversation. The taller of the two gave him a hard look. "Didn't you just come out a couple of minutes ago?"

"Yeah. I was visiting a friend."

"What floor?"

Sever saw no reason to lie. They were unarmed security guards. The cops were nowhere in sight. And besides, there were at least twenty condos per floor. "Twenty-three."

"That's where something is going on."

"Any idea what?" If they said it was a case of breaking and entering, he was going to bolt. Get to Ginny's room, and take off.

"No. They wouldn't tell us anything else."

"Mr. Sever." Detective Ray Haver waved from the entrance to the lobby. "We keep running into each other." He held out his arm as he approached as if to shake hands.

Homicide. He wouldn't be here for a simple break in or burglary. Sever took his hand.

"Ray, right? It's a little late for investigations." Sever looked at his watch. "Or a little early. What's going on?"

"Ballistics report. Two officers are up there checking things out."

Sever felt himself go limp. He took a deep breath, and longed for the Scotch he'd tossed overboard. "What things?"

"You're a reporter, right? After you told me you did some television, I looked you up. You get some pretty good coverage. A couple of books, a movie —"

"Yeah. But what about ballistics?"

"Are you working on a story?"

"No." Ginny was working on a story.

Haver nodded his head. "It appears that whoever shot Spinatti did it from a distance."

Sever waited for the rest. Haver pulled out his badge and flashed it to the two security officers. "I'm going up to twenty-three."

"A distance? What kind of a distance?"

"From this building. There's a straight shot from Gideon Pike's condo to the *Hit King*. We're checking the place out. We heard he might be up there tonight. You know Pike, right?"

From the condo? Jesus Christ, half an hour ago —

"Mr. Sever?"

"Call me Mick. Yeah, I know him. I've interviewed him before."

"Ever been to his condo?"

Sever hesitated. "I was there a couple of days ago. His manager let me in. We were trying to see if there were any signs of where he might have gone."

Haver started toward the door to the elevators. He turned. "So this manager has a key to Pike's place?"

"He does. He watches the condo when Pike's not there." He probably should have shut the hell up.

Haver reached in his pocket and pulled out a small tablet, flipping through it until he found the right page. "Tom Biddle?"

"That's him."

"And you've been in the condo?"

"I told you —" If they checked for fingerprints, they would know he and Ginny had been there.

"Ever been in Biddle's condo?"

"No."

"Did you ever see a rifle in Pike's place?"

Sever thought for a moment. "No. We were only there for a short time."

"Do you know if Pike owned a rifle?"

"I have no idea."

Haver stuffed the tablet back in his pants pocket. "Okay. Thanks for your time. If you think of anything, let me know." He nodded again and walked through the doors.

Sever watched him on the monitor as he stepped into an open elevator and disappeared from sight.

"Jesus!" The shorter guard was staring at Sever. "They think Mr. Pike shot the guy on the boat? I thought that was just a rumor."

"I don't know if I'd go spreading that around. It sounds like they are just doing some checking."

"The guy is the greatest! Gave us a tip at Christmas, five hundred bucks apiece. Hell, management never gave us a bonus that big since we worked here. There's got to be a mistake."

"Did you ever see him with a rifle?"

They looked at each other and broke out laughing. "I've never seen any of our tenants with a rifle. It would be a little out of place. People don't just walk in with exposed weapons." The taller guard stepped out from the desk. "The cop said you're a celebrity?"

"I wouldn't go that far. I'm a writer."

"Well, if you write this story, make sure we're in it."

Sever smiled and walked toward the hotel portion of the lobby. "It's not my story."

He took an elevator up to Ginny's floor, and knocked on her door. After a minute he heard her unlatch the chain.

"Mmmm." She wore a long, thin white teeshirt and it appeared there was nothing underneath. "If you're here for what I think you are, I've got a headache. Seriously."

"So do I." He told her about the cops.

"Whoa! And they think Pike shot Spinatti from the condo with a rifle? You know him, Mick. What is he, a sharpshooter?"

"I can't see it. It just doesn't fit."

"You haven't seen him in almost three years. From everything we've heard he's been under a lot of stress."

"Yeah. There's that."

So what do you think Komack is going to say to them?"

"Komack may not have been there." Sever pulled out the desk chair and straddled it.

"He was there when we left. Mick, I hope he left before they showed up. He could incriminate us."

They were both quiet for a minute.

"I don't think Komack was there when they showed up. The cops would be calling on us by now!"

"It's unthinkable. Pike, shooting someone from his balcony."

"Ginny, Komack wanted to know what we found in the closet."

"And you told him."

"Not everything. I forgot one thing."

"What? I thought you mentioned everything."

"The blanket."

"The blanket?"

"It was rolled up, oil smudged on the inside?"

"Oh yeah. The blanket." She was on the bed, her legs curled underneath her.

"Nothing was in it."

"Right."

"Something had been in it."

She looked puzzled, then recognition dawned in her face. "Oh, my God. He kept a rifle wrapped up in the blanket?"

"That's my guess."

"Mick, there was nothing in that blanket the night we were there."

CHAPTER THIRTY-FOUR

The meeting broke up at 1 A.M. The participating parties had gone home, or wherever you go in Miami at 1 A.M. A lot of clubs didn't start cooking until then, and Jimmy assumed they'd be checking them out. He thoughtfully chewed on an olive and spit the pit into his hand.

He wanted to hold his father off for two or three more days. The old guy was pushing, demanding, calling him two and three times a day to force some direction or to make sure he was staying on task. Yelling at Jimmy for not finding Pike, and threatening him for not getting control of Sever. The man was controlling, never letting go. The old man's death might be the only release of his stranglehold on the business. He was constantly scolding him for not showing enough respect. Old school Korean. Damn it, you respected your father no matter what an asshole he might be. And *his* father didn't seem to understand that things hadn't been easy.

The business was changing. Every day something new came down the pipeline. The original Napster was out of business, but college kids were exchanging free tunes through university Internet hookups. CD sales had slowed down, but now there were new Web downloads charging for music. MP3 format and iPod, and they all looked like promising commercial outlets for recording companies. And new artists like Norah Jones, 50 Cent, and Usher were taking the world by storm and making millions of dollars overnight.

The most comforting fact was that standards from the '70s and early '80s were almost more popular now than they were during their heyday. Pike's concerts were sold out as soon as they were announced. The recording rights in three years would be worth more than even Shinn could imagine, and he'd worked far too hard to let those go.

But this wasn't considered *work*. According to his father. His *father*. No, this wasn't work. Work was slaving away on the loading docks. Stealing machinery parts, crates of produce, and sewing machines under the watchful eyes of security cops. Work was what his grandfather and father had done. According to his father, all Jimmy ever did was play.

And he could use a play date or two. He thought about flying the Lear to Vegas where they comped him at the Venetian. Or maybe taking April to Aruba for a couple of days, but he wasn't sure about April. What had she said to Sever? And he was restless, thinking about moving on. The new girl, Misty Rain or whatever the fuck her name was, had let him know she was available and willing. Did it matter if he got girls because of his money? Because he was in *the business*? Not really. Hell, he was good looking. Dark skin, dark hair, dark eyes. Some girl told him that his eyes smoldered. He liked that. He was smart, with personality. Even if he hadn't owned a strip club or didn't have a piece of Gideon Pike — he could still take his pick.

He popped another olive into his mouth. He should have forced the issue. Should have had Sam stuff Gideon's hand down the disposal. But the concerts would have been cancelled — permanently. Hit King made money every time Pike played a concert — every time he played one of his songs, every time a fan walked out of a concert and bought a CD. There was still a lot of money to be made from Pike. But now, he wasn't so sure. Gideon Pike had become a big risk, and if Pike was killed, there would only be Komack to deal with. Maybe that was the best way to approach the situation — work with the weak link, Komack.

Shinn stretched and stood up from the antique desk. He glanced at his solid-gold Rolex again and picked up the keys to the Lexus.

Twenty-four/seven, hot and cold women at Platinum. It was time to see what kind of action he could stir up. Misty Rain sounded promising. And Gideon Pike would show up sooner or later. Probably sooner. God knows there were enough people looking for Pike. The cops, the Severs, and Shinn's own group.

Right now it was time to pull in some favors, bought and paid for.

He walked to the sink and threw the olive pits down the disposal, flipping the switch, and listening to the grinding.

He might need the cops to help pull Pike back from his hiding place, and cops could be had for next to nothing. Everything in life was relative. If you made sixty thousand dollars a year, ten thousand was a king's ransom. If you made millions every year, you wanted millions more. And if you had a father who was never satisfied, well, he'd have to deal with that. Deep in his heart he knew he'd never be in this position if it weren't for the old man. He could have been the son of a grocery store owner, mopping up spilled milk and other crap off the cheap tile floor every night, or ringing up somebody's six pack. He owed his father for the opulent lifestyle he led.

But now, now it was his turn. He'd forced the sale of Hit King, and in the process proven that he could run the business, make millions, and still have a life. He was certain his father had no life outside of the business. His father. Damn his father. His father was the blessing, and at the same time the curse. It was time to show some backbone. It was time to stand up to the man, and tell him to quit micromanaging the business affairs. Because if the old man didn't back down — Jimmy Shinn was afraid he would be forced to back him down. And that went against everything his culture stood for.

In the garage, the sleek, olive-green machine waited for him, hardtop down. He climbed in, feeling the soft, tan leather surround him. Turning the key, he listened to the quiet power beneath the hood. Shinn drove around the island to the exit, nodding to the lone gatekeeper, a stooped old man who looked like he'd had his white, wispy hair cut by a weed whacker. The man nodded back. Some poor son of a bitch who retired from a job up north and couldn't afford the lifestyle down here without another job. The gatekeeper had been there for years. Jesus, what a loser.

Shinn turned right on the causeway, away from South Beach and back toward the city. He just tapped the pedal and the Lexus leaped around the BMW in the right lane, came in tight on the bumper of the Audi in the left lane, and he laid on the horn as the Audi quickly moved to the right. He gave it more gas.

He remembered a night about three years ago, drunk, weaving through cars — what he thought was one of the *worst* nights of his life. One of his dancers, dead in the Platinum parking lot. Jimmy Shinn remembered. And because he remembered — because of his memory of that night, it had turned out to be one of the *best* things that ever happened to him. And he intended to keep it that way.

This early morning's traffic was light, and in Jimmy Shinn's life there were no speeding tickets. Favors, bought and paid for. He drove through downtown Miami, along the Miami River for a short distance, then jumped on 95 and hit 110 miles per hour before he finally calmed down. He could deal with his father. The time had come.

At 1 A.M. the club was slow, guys still hoping to get lucky at the singles bars. After 2 A.M. when they realized that their charm, wit, and looks had failed them, that's when they showed up. That's when they'd pay twenty bucks for a lap dance, or fifty bucks for a private party. That's when they sprang for a fifty-dollar bottle of cheap sparkling swill, and twenty bucks for a fruit-flavored water for the lady, hoping to get a little action, bought and paid for. And wasn't it safer that way? A professional wasn't going to tell your wife, or start calling you at work. A professional was going to shove her tits in your face, stroke you until you came, and say goodnight. Seemed like a safe bet. Safer than the pickup bars, no matter how fancy.

April was working the main stage, lewdly grinding her shaved pussy inches from some college kid's face, and she gave Shinn a nod as he walked in. The barmaid had Jimmy's Grey Goose and grapefruit before he reached the bar. Shinn flashed her a smile, and sat down.

This was good. They kept time to his beat. They catered to his whims. The bass punched through the sound system, drowning out all else as his thoughts drifted back to the poor bastard at the gate. How could people live like that? Losers like that had no concept of another lifestyle. Or maybe he did. Maybe the old, white-haired guy knew and hated Shinn for it, every time he peeled out in his ninety thousand dollar car.

April stepped off the stage to scattered applause. She accepted the dollars thrust at her, pulled one old man's head to her chest and kissed his cheek, then made a beeline for the bar. Struggling to get her tiny bra snapped, she approached Shinn.

"Hi, baby."

"You're sweaty. Go dry off."

She frowned. "Aren't you glad to see me?"

His eyes gazed beyond her, looking for Misty Rain.

"Jimmy?"

"Yeah, sure. I've got some stuff on my mind."

"So do I."

Oh, shit. Here it comes. She wants a more permanent relationship. She wants to get out of the club, and be a model or a kept woman. Shinn stood up, drink in hand. "I've got to get back to the office. Maybe we can talk later."

"I talked to Bridgette."

He stopped. "Where is she?"

"She wouldn't tell me."

"I told you —" God. His threatening tone sounded like his father.

"I know. I know." She whispered above the loud music and din of voices. "You said if she ever tries to contact me, find out where she lives. I tried, Jimmy. Jeeze, I tried."

He threw back a swallow of the drink, barely tasting the tart beverage. "What did she say?"

"She said she was all right, and she hoped nobody was worried about her."

"And?"

"Well, I didn't tell her that you were looking for her. That would have freaked her out."

"Is she going to call again? Did you set up a time?"

"I didn't think about it. It all happened so fast and I was so surprised."

"Jesus. What the fuck good are you?" He slammed the glass on the bar. "Useless as tits on a boar hog."

Tears rolled from the corners of her eyes. "I thought you'd be happy that she called."

"You don't know shit, do you?" He signaled for another drink, and pointed to the office. "Is Misty working tonight?"

She sniffed, wiping her face with the back of her hand. "She's on a break. She should be back any minute."

Shinn gave her a cold stare, his piercing eyes dark and focused. "Tell her to bring the drink to my office."

April looked at the floor. "So I won't see you any more tonight?"

"I don't think so. And if Bridgette calls again, you'd goddamned better find out where she is."

CHAPTER THIRTY-FIVE

Biddle's phone rang four times and the machine picked up. "Hello. I'm not able to come to the phone, so you know the routine." Sever hung up.

"Not there? At 2:30 in the morning?" Ginny raised her eyebrows. "The man has a late-night lifestyle."

"Nobody's home. Brady wasn't on the boat, Biddle's not around, must be a party and they forgot to invite us." Sever stretched out on the bed. His head throbbed and even laying back on the pillow hurt the bruised skin. Kornack had really laid him out. "Do you have aspirin?"

Ginny went into the bathroom and came out with three tablets and a glass of water. He swallowed them and closed his eyes. Little green flashes of fireworks went off behind his eyelids.

"I remember bringing you back from some hangovers like this." She watched him, seeming to study the effect the pills were having. "As bad as you'd get, there was something comforting about the fact that you'd come home for your remedy."

Sever was silent.

"But when you stopped coming home —"

"Hey. If memory serves, you had your share of tying one on. And toward the end, I remember nights when you never showed up at all."

She shrugged her shoulders. "Maybe we're too much alike."

"You think?"

She walked over and kissed him on the cheek. "I wish I knew what it was. We should despise each other, and instead —" She let it hang.

"You're there for me when I need you. And I'd like to think I'm here for you. I just have trouble thinking there's nothing more."

Ginny was silent. The absence of sound filled the room.

Sever closed his eyes, and forced himself to think of the problem at hand. Gideon and Komack had both said Pike thought his life was threatened, and now he was missing. And how did that lead to the shooting death of Larry Spinatti? Did Spinatti work for Jimmy Shinn? Maybe Spinatti was the muscle and Shinn was using Spinatti to pressure Pike. It was all too confusing. He'd have to learn a little more about Jimmy Shinn. The guy had a high profile, so he should be easy to research. And what about Pike? Alive or dead?

He felt himself drifting away. In the distance he could hear a voice, maybe Ginny, saying "Mick?" "Mick?" but he was too far gone to respond.

Ginny was in the shower when he woke. He could hear the water, even picture it caressing her body as she washed. Sever winced when he turned his head, the tender skin alive with nerves. The constant throbbing had stopped. She'd taken off his pants, and pulled the sheet over him. It appeared she'd slept on the other side and he smelled her pillow, picking up a hint of the Key West jasmine perfume she liked. He glanced at the clock on the end table. 7:30 A.M. About four hours of sleep. She'd turned off the water, probably toweling her blond hair. Then, she'd wrap the towel around her, leaving the damp hair trailing down her back and around her shoulders.

The bathroom door opened and she stepped out, wrapped in the thick, white cotton towel.

"Hey. I got a little worried about you. How's the head?"

"Better. What are you doing up so early?"

"I thought I'd try Biddle again, and maybe you could go down and talk to Brady."

"You and Biddle?"

"He lives right next door to Gideon. For God's sake, he may have some new information. And in the meantime you can see what happened to our white-haired friend on the boat. Aren't you a little surprised he didn't call and check up on us last night?"

"Now that you mention it."

"You need to go get cleaned up. Scoot." She threw his pants to him.

"We'll get together for lunch?"

"Sure."

Sever pulled on his trousers, slipped on his deck shoes, and grinned. "Now you're being modest?"

She stood there, the towel tightly wrapped around her compact frame. "Go."

"Hey, don't tell him we were inside Pike's last night. Just that we know the cops were up there."

"Komack might have told him already."

"Let's assume he hasn't."

"Okay. Now please, go."

He went.

Brady was throwing a bucket of water overboard. "Hey, Mick. You must have come back and finished the Scotch? Or a pelican got it."

Sever walked onto the deck. "You were gone when I got back."

"Yeah. Took a late-night walk. Went up to the security desk and asked those two boys if they'd seen you, and they assured me you'd been down, so I wasn't worried. What happened?"

"A friend of Pike's was up there. He thought I was breaking into the condo so he hit me with a champagne bottle."

"Champagne?" He frowned. "Full or empty?"

"Full."

"Ouch."

"Brady, look up at Pike's condo."

Brady glanced up at the building, bathed in bright orange in the early morning eastern sun. "What am I looking for?"

"The cops think someone shot Spinatti from up there with a high-powered rifle."

"Mmm. Good scope, accurate shooter, could be. It's not that far and Spinatti probably wasn't a moving target."

They sat down in deck chairs and watched the orange-tinged clouds on the horizon. A lazy seagull circled overhead, mournfully calling for his breakfast.

Sever looked back at the Grand. "What do you think? One shot?"

"Like I said. You get a good rifle and good shooter."

"I think Pike had a rifle. But it's not there now."

"So if he shot the boyfriend, he'd want to dump the weapon. Maybe right here, in the bay. It'd be like finding a needle in a haystack."

"Did you ever hear Pike and Spinatti quarrel when Pike would visit the boat?"

Brady was quiet for a minute, watching the warm sun burn off the early morning mist. "I heard things."

"What?"

"Things."

Sever had interviewed hundreds of people. Hundreds? Probably several thousand. There was a rhythm to an interview, just like a song. Each one was slightly different. You let the interview find it's own tempo. He bit his bottom lip, and let the silence build.

"Lover's quarrel."

Sever waited. Another minute passed.

"Everybody has differences. Those two did. Some nights they'd sit out on the deck and just talk. Other nights they yelled."

Brady closed his eyes and sat motionless for another two or three minutes. "Pike accused Spinatti of only being in the relationship for the money."

"The money? Pike's money?"

"See, that's what I thought. But the two of them were talking loud, so I couldn't miss what was said. Pike accused him of being paid off. He kept saying something about Spinatti being on the payroll.

This *they* he kept mentioning. 'They must have you on the payroll. They must think you can influence me. They must be paying you off.' He insinuated that Spinatti was only in the relationship because *they* were paying him to pressure Pike."

"Pressure him to do what?"

"Never got to that. He and Spinatti apparently knew. And I was trying my damnedest to ignore the conversation."

"So someone was paying Spinatti to stay in this relationship with Gideon."

"It's what Pike seemed to think."

"When was the last time you heard them argue?"

"Ah, maybe a week ago. Just before he disappeared."

"No idea who *they* are?"

"What do you think?"

It was Sever's turn to be silent. He wasn't sure what to think. If the boyfriend Spinatti was working against Pike, maybe Pike had a reason to shoot him. He tried to picture Gideon Pike with a rifle, shooting his lover. People snapped over the smallest of matters.

He surveyed the boat. "No overnight women? You seem to have guests on a regular basis." It was time to change the subject.

"No. Nobody last night."

"Did you ever see any women on the *Hit King*?"

"Once or twice. I shouldn't say this. Nobody's business, but I think Larry Spinatti went both ways. He did have an occasional woman on board."

"Did you know any of them?"

"Nah. Just an observation. Pike brought a woman down here several times. A real looker."

"Pike?"

"Pike."

"He's got a sister that lives in the area." Sever looked out over the water. "Can you see Pike shooting Spinatti? I never knew him to be a sharpshooter."

Brady stood up and stretched. "Got no more to say on the matter, Mick. I don't speculate on things like that."

"Love affairs are tough, Brady."

"I still see a spark in your eye for Ginny. There's some chemistry there."

Sever ignored the comment. "How about you, Brady. Is there anybody you'd spend some time with? Serious time?"

"Ah, Mick. You know, if I found a lover who I trusted, I'd stay with her. There are times when I really miss that trust. Someone you have a bond with. I could go with that person and hide forever. Just the two of us. We could become —"

"Invisible?"

"Sure. Maybe."

"Brady, you see what goes on down here. I think you probably know more than you admit. Did Pike spend a lot of time down here? Could he hide down here? Would someone put him up?"

The white-haired man gave him a weak smile. "The man can't hide down here, Mick. First of all, everybody is looking for him. This is the first place they look. Second of all, *this* lover is dead."

"*This* lover? Are there others?"

Sever watched the old man. The gentle rocking of the boat and the warming morning air seemed to lull him and Brady's eyes closed again.

"Brady, did Pike have another relationship?"

I could go with that person and hide forever? Is that where Pike was hiding? With a lover? Or with a loved one. Someone who loved him?

"Brady. I think I may have an idea where Gideon is. Brady?"

The old man was breathing deeply and Sever watched the rise and fall of his chest. Finally he stood up and walked back down the plank to the concrete dock. He hated interviews that raised more questions than they answered. He would have liked another twenty minutes with White, but with the late hours the old man kept, hell, he had to sleep sometime.

CHAPTER THIRTY-SIX

He called her room from the lobby, but Ginny wasn't in. Hopefully *her* interview hadn't nodded off in the middle of a conversation. Sever didn't have the keys to the Porsche, so he grabbed a taxi in front of the Doubletree and took a ride to South Beach.

The News Café was busy with its international clientele reading newspapers from around the world. He read the ambitious menu with interest, but settled for black coffee, a bagel with some Philadelphia cream cheese and the *Miami Herald*. The News was a great place to watch the world go by.

After breakfast he walked it off. Ocean Boulevard was already busy, the cars streaming along the oceanfront street and the sidewalk packed with tourists and the workers who catered to the tourists. The pastel-colored hotels, restaurants, and clubs shone brightly in the early morning sun. Pinks and blues and shades of tangerine, they wore their colors proudly. The Beacon, Colony, Boulevard, Satellite, Pelican, Mecaluna, and Waldorf Towers. They all exuded their personal art deco charms.

Sever passed Mangos and he remembered the night he'd punched the lights out of the two guys who were giving Pike a rough time. Where the hell was Pike?

His thoughts drifted back to Ginny. She was probably closer to the answer than he was. Tom Biddle was Pike's next door neighbor and his manager. He had to know something. Maybe there was a piece of information he'd forgotten about, or possibly something would jog his memory. Something Pike once said or did.

Sever walked, jostled occasionally by the stream of pedestrian traffic. He half expected to see Gideon walking the opposite way. Or maybe driving a yellow Mazzarati on Ocean Boulevard. As he walked by Lardios, he heard the music. Stopping for a moment, he listened to the lyrics. For some reason, Pike could hit the right sentiment at the exact right time.

> How much depth and understanding?
> Who knows what it means?
> Is it just a scratch of surface?
> Or the truth that we have seen?
> In the morning the window dressing
> Is clean and fresh and new.
> Pretend that last night never happened
> In the misty morning dew.
> Hold me close and tell me lies
> That I'll accept as truth
> That we'll stay close for all our lives
> The lies that I like most.

"Window Dressing." A huge hit about five years ago. Sever held his place for several seconds. The lies struck home. He and Ginny didn't see each other enough anymore to tell the truth. *We'll stay close for all our lives, the lies that I like most.*

He stopped at the next café and opened the newspaper. Sipping a strong Cuban coffee, he read the second section.

> Police last night raided the residence of pop singer and entertainer Gideon Pike at the Grand Condominium complex. A police spokesperson said that ballistics reports from the shooting death of male model Larry Spinatti showed that the rifle bullet ap-

peared to come from a high-rise in the Grand complex.

At the time of the raid, police say no one was present in the residence. Pike's whereabouts are unknown at this time.

Ed Komack apparently had left. But where the hell was Pike? At the bottom of the bay? What if he'd been on the boat, and a gunshot knocked him in the water?

He found a pay phone in the lobby. Ginny answered on the second ring.

"So how did the interview go?"

She was quiet.

"Ginny?"

"Good. Really good. He's a very neat guy, Mick."

"What does that mean?"

"Well," she paused again as if composing her thoughts. "You're a former husband."

"Guilty."

"You're a current lover."

"A couple of nights ago." He thought about the unexpected pleasure.

"I'm not sure I can tell you how I feel."

"Tell me."

"I like him. A lot. We have a lot in common."

"Like what?"

She was quiet for a moment. "Maybe it's that we both deal with ego-driven artists."

"Are you including me in that category?"

"Not *just* you, but yes. And he's dealing with Pike and his little quirks, and, well, it made for some very interesting conversation. I understand where he's coming from."

Sever swallowed his reply.

"Anyway, Tom's going to meet us at Lardios at 12:30 for lunch. He can fill you in."

Sever sucked it up. "Give me a heads up."

"Well, Gideon may not be the choirboy you and I thought he was."

"Oh?"

"Apparently he got himself into a financial jam."

"It happens."

"I'm talking about the rumored Michael Jackson financial kind of jam. Millions of dollars."

"So what does that have to do with his disappearance? And what about Shinn's threats?" He was irritated with this little game. Either give him the information or not. Oh hell, it wasn't the little game. It was her interest in Pike's manager. He let out a breath.

"Let's talk about it at lunch."

"Fine."

"Mick, what did you find out this morning?"

"Spinatti and Pike argued."

"When? About what?"

"A week ago. Brady seems to think Spinatti was being paid off to pressure Pike."

"For what?" She sounded frustrated. It was her story, and he was tempted to hold back. The truth was, he wasn't comfortable sharing everything.

"He doesn't know. I'm thinking it might have been about the contract for recording rights. Ed Komack told us that Shinn wanted a share of those rights."

"Well, there's no more pressure there now. Spinatti's dead."

"Yeah."

"What else did you find out?"

"The old man apparently had a late night."

"Oh?"

"He fell asleep. I guess I'm not the most exciting company to be around." He waited for her response. There wasn't any. "All right, I'll see you at 12:30."

"Mick. This goes a lot deeper than just a disappearance. I may be in over my head."

Sever studied the statement. "In more ways than one." He hesitated. It was such a remote hunch he thought twice, three times about even bringing it up. Finally, "Ginny. I think I may have an idea where Pike is."

"Where? Mick, this is getting critical."

"It's a remote possibility. Let me think about it before I say any more."

She was quiet. There was an unspoken pact between the two of them. When they worked on a story, a certain amount of thought was internalized. You wrestled with this idea, you fought with that idea, and when you had a semblance of organization in your mind, then you verbalized it. He wasn't ready to verbalize and she respected that.

"Lunch. 12:30."

He hung up and walked down the sidewalk, feeling the ache in his knee. Ginny and Biddle? Jesus. He'd bristled at the remote possibility, but now she was practically telling him she was falling for the guy. Had they already slept together? He remembered when she'd had an affair just for revenge. It nearly drove him crazy. He had absolutely no rights. None. But this felt wrong. Dead wrong.

CHAPTER THIRTY-SEVEN

Larios was named for the chef. A trendy Cuban restaurant, it was owned by singer Gloria Estefan and her husband. Tourists and business types crowded the rooms inside, sipping tropical drinks and sampling the ceviche — tangy, lime-soaked chunks of grouper seasoned with cilantro. Sever figured you could make an entire meal out of the appetizer.

Although it was early afternoon, they ordered three dirty martinis. Vodka, a hint of vermouth, and a splash of olive juice from the jar. Sever took a sip. A little bitter and salty, the drink was pleasantly refreshing. One of these and he'd be ready for just about anything.

"Do you come here often?" Sever's voice was flat. Discussing pleasantries with his ex's new boyfriend was not high on his list of favorite things to do.

Biddle tasted the martini. "Once in awhile. There are so many good places to eat down here. Gloria was the client of a good friend of mine and we'd meet here every week or so. Sometimes she'd serve the drinks."

Ginny watched the two men with an amused look on her face. Sever wondered if she was considering the contest. Who would win the heart of the fair maiden?

"Mick, I told Tom about last night."

Sever gave her a stern look.

"I mean about you talking to detective Haver. How they thought someone shot Spinatti from the condo complex."

He let the vodka lay on his tongue, ice cold. Finally he swallowed. "Yeah. Haver asked if Pike had a rifle."

"Damn. They're going to try to lay this on Gideon. Damn."

"Did Pike own a rifle."

Biddle stuck a fork in a piece of tender grouper and put it in his mouth. He chewed thoughtfully. Finally he looked up, staring into Sever's eyes. "Yes. A couple of years ago a bodyguard suggested he get a gun for protection. Of course the guy meant a handgun, but Gideon was never one to do things on a small scale. He figured that a big rifle was more protection than a handgun."

"He kept it in the condo?"

"He did. I don't think he ever thought about how cumbersome it was. It was big, it was powerful, and that's all he cared about."

"Did he know how to use it?"

Biddle smiled. "I doubt it, but who knows?"

"And Haver never talked to you?"

"I was out late last night. Didn't get in until —" he consulted his watch, "maybe four."

"Still, I would have thought he'd want to ask you some questions."

Ginny swirled her drink, her fingers gracefully holding the stem. "Tell him about Gideon's finances."

Biddle nodded. "Ginny asked me about Pike's finances. I'm not his financial manager, but what I'm about to tell you is a matter of public record. I would never say anything that is privileged information."

"Of course not."

"About four years ago, Gideon's record sales starting dropping off. He hadn't had a hit in a while. He had a new, four-record deal with White Sand Records, and the sales eventually dropped off, but his expenses hadn't."

Ginny jumped in. "He had two yachts, the *Hit King* and another one. He owned, how many houses, Tom?"

The way she said *Tom* aggravated him. Light, fluffy.

"Five. Aspen, Miami, Los Angeles, Antigua, and a flat in Paris."

"Five?" Sever knew there's been several, but five homes at the same time? He thought about his two-bedroom apartment in Chicago.

"So he borrowed some money from his record company. And — you tell him"

"As I said, it's public record. Pike needed a lot of money, and he didn't have it. Guy couldn't pay all of his taxes either. So, he had to come up with a large chunk of cash."

Sever drained his martini and felt the rush in his head. The bruised scalp tingled. "I know he lived well. I've been around him enough to see. But where is all this leading?"

"Well, he now owed White Sand Records and the IRS. Millions. At this point he didn't have a lot of options."

"What did he do?"

"Sold the publishing company."

"To Jim Shinn?"

"Exactly. Shinn gave him enough money to get out of the problem."

"And Gideon downsized?"

"He was forced to."

"The five houses? The yachts?"

"Sold them. Bought the condo, and that was it."

Sever signaled the waitress and ordered a Corona. No more martinis please. Pike always seemed to have more money than God. "It's hard to believe that someone with his wealth can get into such deep financial trouble."

"Only people with his wealth *can* get into that kind of financial trouble."

"Who set up the sale? His attorney, Lou Frey?"

"No. His partner, Rusty."

"So Rusty helped him out of a jam."

A long-legged girl in a tube top, tan legs, and short skirt approached the table. "Excuse me."

Sever braced himself.

"Are you someone famous?" She looked Ginny in the face.

Ginny grinned and glanced at Sever. "No. No, I'm not the famous one here. But chances are if you look hard enough, someone here is."

The girl gave her a disappointed look and ambled off.

Biddle watched her go, her rear swinging as she disappeared from sight. Finally he looked back at Sever. "Pike didn't see it like *help*. He didn't want Shinn to have any part of it."

"So how did he see it?"

"He never faced up to the problem. It's hard for me to say this, because I work for the guy, but Gideon blames a lot of other people for his troubles. Never himself."

"Who does he blame?"

"Rusty."

"Did he fire Rusty?"

"Some people think he did."

Sever gave him a questioning look.

"I told you, Rusty washed up on shore, his head bashed in. There's been a rumor that Gideon may have had something to do with that."

"Jesus."

Ginny leaned over the table. "Mick, you're telling me that the cops think Gideon may have shot Larry Spinatti. Is it out of the realm of possibility that he would have Rusty killed?"

"What good would it do him?"

"People thought it was revenge."

"What do you think?"

Biddle paused and surveyed the room. "I don't know. He's changed. No, I don't think that he would kill someone, but he's different."

Sever's mind raced. He'd been over it and over it. Gideon Pike did *not* impress Sever as a killer. Detective Ray Haver insinuated that Pike was a suspect. Biddle wasn't sure, and it was obvious the suspect wasn't around to defend himself. And what about the threats? Pike felt he'd been threatened. Komack had mentioned the threats. "Tell me about Jim Shinn. How did he appear in this picture?"

"Jimmy owned a small publishing house. He owned a handful of songs and was looking to expand. When Pike's finances went south, when his record sales started tanking, Shinn took advantage of the situation. You know, Mick, as I said, it's no secret. Gideon lived way beyond his means."

"Did anyone else try to buy the catalog of songs?"

"Oh yeah. Pike's record company for one."

"They got outbid?"

"They —" he paused and tapped his index finger against his glass, "they went away. There may have been other bidders. I don't know. Rusty and Gideon kept that between themselves. All I know is that Shinn ended up with the songs. He kept the name Hit King, and that's the story."

"Is there any reason Jim Shinn would threaten Pike?"

"Threaten him? How?"

"I'm asking you."

Biddle shrugged his shoulders. "I think Shinn believes Pike owes him more money. As business deals go, he gave Pike one hell of a personal loan. Maybe he's talked to him about upping the payments."

"Upping the payments? And here Shinn is making millions every year with Gideon's publishing company?"

"There's a lot involved, Mick. A lot nobody understands."

"Like the recording rights? Pike and Komack getting back all the recording rights?"

Biddle gave him a cold stare. "You know, I'm not comfortable discussing intimate business dealings with you. I've shared the past with you. The recording rights are in the future. Okay?"

It wasn't okay. It didn't make any sense.

"Exactly what *do* you do for Pike?" Sever's volume was up a notch.

"I don't think this conversation needs to go any further. I deal with Gideon on a number of matters. At this point I don't care to share those matters with you."

Ginny pushed back her chair, her eyes darting between the two combatants. She brushed her hair back behind her ears and crossed her legs. "Tom, what else does Shinn do? You said he has several businesses."

"I don't know everything he's involved with. He's got a fruit distribution company, he imports Korean cars," he trailed off. "Where did you hear that Shinn was threatening Pike?"

Sever's head was starting to throb and he wished for some aspirin. Maybe the beer would help, or maybe it was part of the problem. He took a long swallow. "Ed Komack told me that Pike felt threatened by Shinn."

Ginny's eyes opened wide, and she coughed as if choking.

"When did you talk to Komack? Recently?" Biddle was sitting straight up, studying Sever's face.

Oh, yeah. *They weren't supposed to have been in the condo last night.* The talk with Komack never happened. Now he had to back out of this. Sever took another swallow of Corona and let it slowly slide down his throat.

"I thought he was in New York." Biddle looked puzzled. "Have you seen him?"

Sever recovered. "That's where I talked to him. In New York. On the phone."

"He said that? That Pike was threatened by Shinn?"

"He did." Sever watched Ginny relax.

"So that's what this is all about?" Biddle eased out of his chair and stood up. "This is really hard for me to say. Gideon isn't just a client, but a good friend, and a neighbor. Look, the guy pays the bills." He swept his gaze between Sever and Ginny. "However, since he lost the publishing company he's changed. A lot. He's hostile about a lot of things. If anyone should feel threatened, it's Jimmy Shinn." Biddle turned and walked toward the restroom.

CHAPTER THIRTY-EIGHT

She'd driven the Porsche, and Biddle had come with her. He thought about suggesting Biddle get his own damned ride, but knew that wouldn't go over well, so unless Sever wanted to ride under the hood or in the trunk, it was time for a taxi. He flipped through the pay phone directory and found the address for Hit King publishing. The address was buried in a section of Miami called "Little Havana."

It took ten minutes to get a cab. Sever wondered what was going on back at the Grand. Just because she'd asked him to fly to Miami and help her, and just because she and Sever had had a romantic encounter in the last forty-eight hours, didn't mean she was obligated. Hell, he'd been in the same position many times, and if he felt good about some girl, he went for it. He'd never found a mature way to handle a relationship, especially the one with Ginny. He always ended up feeling like he was still in high school.

The cab crossed the causeway and headed toward Little Havana. Miami sprawled everywhere, like a fat lady with no foundation garments. Founded in 1896, greater Miami was made up of thirty-one cities, and seventy percent of the two and a half million people in those cities were Spanish.

"Little Havana? Not like the real Havana." The cab driver seemed to sulk.

"You're from Cuba?"

"Many years ago. Before Fidel. Fuck Fidel!"

"When did you come over?"

The cab driver seemed to grip the steering wheel tighter. "1956. Fuck Fidel."

Sever grasped the message. The man was a boy when he left his homeland, but the feelings remained the same.

The last time he'd been down here had been in March, maybe five years ago. The entire town had been celebrating Cayo Ocho, the longest street party in the world. Spirited Latin music, drunken brawls, wild dancing, drunken brawls, spicy Cuban food, drunken brawls — everything you could want.

As they crossed Cayo Ocho Avenue, Sever could see a group of old men dressed in brightly colored short-sleeve shirts, playing dominos in a little park. The driver, now somewhat subdued, drove slowly, the traffic heavier than before. A black Cuban lady, hair up in a mango-colored bandana, wandered the street, coffee cup in hand, yelling in Spanish at everyone.

"Shut up you old bag!" The driver turned for a brief moment and looked at Sever in the backseat. "We should rightfully be in Havana. Fidel has destroyed hundreds of thousands of families." He straightened up and stared straight ahead. "It is time we went home."

They passed the eternal flame, burning in honor of the Cubans who lost their lives in the Bay of Pigs invasion. The driver waved his hand. "Fuck Fidel!"

He pulled off onto a side street, past several restaurants, the smell of grilled meat wafting in the air. Hit King was sandwiched between a dry cleaner and an empty building, its windows covered from the inside with brown wrapping paper.

Sever paid the driver, tipped him fifteen dollars, and left him with a "Fuck Fidel." He thought the man actually smiled.

He crossed to the sidewalk, admiring the olive-green Lexus convertible with the license plate reading JIMMY SAYS.

He entered the glass door and was immediately taken back by the shabby interior. The red, threadbare carpet and worn gold couch and chairs gave the impression the business had fallen on hard times. The office area was behind a thick, sliding-glass window. Sever assumed it was bullet proof. After all, this was part of greater Miami.

He tapped on the glass, and the girl working at her desk looked up with a bored expression. Slowly she stood and opened the windows. She was young, slender, with streaked blond hair and pouty lips. She had the body of a stripper and Sever tried to remember he was there on business. Gideon's disappearance had something to do with Hit King Publishing.

"Can I help you?"

"I'm looking for Jimmy Shinn."

"Oh, I'm sorry." She licked her lips. A very sexy move. "He's not in at the moment."

Sever smiled. "Well, I noticed the car outside. Isn't that Jim's Lexus?"

She glanced at the door. "Oh. Yes. But he's not here. I'm sorry."

No further information. She stood there waiting for him to fold. He hadn't noticed it before, but she was chewing gum. Slowly, methodically chewing gum.

"Well how about you tell me where he is."

The lights went on in her eyes. "Oh. Sure. He's at lunch." She finally smiled, and Sever understood that it took her awhile to grasp the situation.

"Any idea where?"

She pouted. "I don't know if he wants to be disturbed. He's having a meeting."

"I won't be more than a minute. I just need to check on some information. Is it within walking distance?" He prayed that it was.

"Well, I guess it won't hurt to tell you. Jimmy's at the Obispo Café."

"And that's where?"

"Exactly one block south and half a block east. It's where he goes almost every day, so I memorized the location."

Sever closed his eyes. Deliver him from the young dumb blondes. "Thank you. You've been a big help."

She grinned. "Good. I hope you have a pleasant day." She closed the window and walked back to her desk.

Walking distance. Good news. He walked down the sidewalk one block and turned on the next street. The neon sign stuck out from the stucco wall. OBISPO CAFÉ. OPEN FOR LUNCH. The curbside restaurant had a handful of tables on the sidewalk, but only one table was occupied. A spike-haired guy of about twenty-one and a dark-skinned girl sipped what appeared to be mojitos, the fresh mint leaves stuffed inside the glasses filled with rum, lime, and sugar. Sever walked by them and entered the café.

Small booths lined the walls, most of them empty. The lunch hour had come and gone, and the Obispo was almost empty. Two old men sat across from each other in the second booth, both smoking round, black cigars, and waving their hands in animated gestures. No women. Just men, older men discussing the state of the world. Fuck Fidel.

A pretty waitress in a black skirt carried a tray of sizzling grilled pork sandwiches on thick slices of Cuban bread. She smiled at Sever as she passed him.

Sever turned and watched her go by. He saw the big man in the ill-fitting sport coat walk in. Although the room was dimly lit, there was something familiar about his face. He studied it for a second, then turned, looking for any sign of Jim Shinn.

The outer room opened up into a series of smaller rooms, and Sever took a left. At the end of this long room was a table. At the end of the table was a man who looked Asian, olive skin and coal-dark hair. Sever had seen the face before. Clearly. Up close. He closed his eyes for a moment and focused.

The painting.

The canvas in Pike's closet. It was a portrait of Jimmy Shinn.

Shinn faced Sever, seemingly engrossed in conversation. Two other men had their backs to Sever. A Che Guevera poster hung on the back wall. Sever watched the man for several seconds. It had to be Shinn. Sever expected a high-powered meeting of publishing moguls would take place in a much fancier venue. He slid into a booth, catching just the glimpse of the man who followed him in, who also took a booth.

Sever ordered a Cuban coffee with cream, knowing he'd probably be up for two nights afterwards. He occasionally stuck his head out watching the meeting. When the waitress delivered the café-conleche, he leaned out one more time. One of the men was just rising from his chair. He turned to leave, and Sever saw his face. Lou Frey.

Frey turned, nodded at Shinn, and quickly walked back toward the exit. Sever pulled back and turned to look at the wall. Frey walked right by him without a glance.

Sever ignored the coffee. He leaned back out and saw the second man push back his chair. After a minute's worth of conversation the second man stood up. He turned, and Sever pulled back his head. He'd recognized this man too. There was absolutely no doubt who it was. Ed Komack.

CHAPTER THIRTY-NINE

Now it was a question of whether to go back, introduce himself and say, "Where is Gideon Pike?" or walk away. It shouldn't have surprised him that he knew two of the three players. It was perfectly logical that Pike's lawyer and his writing partner were meeting with his publisher. He debated whether or not to confront Shinn. No matter what he'd heard about him, the good and the bad, he played a large role in the singer's life. And Pike had gone on the record saying he felt threatened by the Korean business tycoon. It was time to see what all the talk was about.

An old man brushed by his booth, dressed in fashionable razor-sharp creased green slacks and a dark checked golf shirt. It all happened so fast that Sever didn't get a good look at his face. His shock of gray hair was set off by his dark skin, and Shinn hustled around the table to pull out a chair for the elderly gentleman.

Sever missed his opportunity. He watched as Shinn helped push the chair in, then signaled a waiter. There was a rush of activity as the waiter gestured to yet another server who double-timed it to another room. In just moments she reappeared with a bottle of San Pelegrino and two glasses. The waiter removed Shinn's glass of dark liquor and replaced it with a water glass. The young girl poured the sparkling water into both glasses then both servers left the room, one positioning himself in the doorway as if standing guard. It appeared to be almost a ritual. The two men toasted.

Sever stood up and made his decision. He walked back to the table. The younger man looked up, obviously surprised. He rose to his feet as if to gain the advantage. Sever was ten feet from the table, and he already felt tension in the air.

"Excuse me."

Shinn glared at him with what appeared to be coal-black eyes. "This is a private meeting."

The older man turned and frowned. Maybe seventy-five-to eighty-years-old, his thin face looked like someone had hung the skin carelessly, folds and wrinkles draped over the skull. His eyelids were droopy, but his eyes were focused. He stared intently at Sever. It didn't appear Mick was welcome.

"I won't take much time. I'm Mick Sever."

Something in the younger man's look told Sever that he knew who he was.

"You're Jim Shinn?"

No answer. The man stood his ground, moving out from the table.

"I'd like to make an appointment, when we could talk."

"About what?"

"Gideon Pike."

He smiled, his teeth clenched together. "Mr —?"

"Sever." The guy knew damned well who he was.

"Mr. Sever. I don't discuss clients. With anyone."

"If I ask you a question, and you don't want to answer, don't. This isn't going to take long."

"Mr. Sever. I'm involved in a meeting here. I don't have time to talk to you now, or in the future." Shinn nodded at a waiter, who was standing in the doorway.

"I'm a friend of Gideon's. The police apparently have reason to believe that he was involved in a shooting."

"You don't hear so good. I don't discuss clients!"

Out of the corner of his eye Sever saw the two Korean men, knit polo shirts with lightweight sport coats. They moved quietly into the

room, standing by the table between Sever and Shinn. It was awfully
hot for sport coats.

"Why don't you leave, Mr. Sever? This is a private area."

Sever watched one of the goons slip his hand inside his jacket.
There was no question what was under there.

"I was just about to go."

Sever turned and quickly walked out, dropping a five at his
booth for the untouched coffee. The last thing he needed was someone chasing him down the street for an unpaid bill. He glanced over
his shoulder, one final look at the two men. The old man was talking
loudly in his native tongue, his index finger pointing like a gun barrel at Jimmy Shinn.

Bodyguards? Guns? Miami was a tough town. Jimmy Shinn was
a tough businessman.

He didn't see the big man following behind him, but he sensed
him. He was still working on where he'd seen him before. In the hotel? Maybe it was a coincidence. Sever kept a quick pace, his knee
aching with every step. Turning around would signal the man that he
knew he was being followed. No taxi, and he didn't know the public transportation system well enough to grab a bus. If he even knew
where one was. He headed toward Hit King, just a block away now.
Stopping to look in a small bakery window, he watched for the reflection of the big man. There was no one behind him.

Sever opened the door to Hit King and tapped on the glass. The
young girl at her desk glanced up, frowned and continued to work.
He rapped on the glass with his knuckles. She kept her head buried
in her work. Already someone had given her a rough time about di-
vulging the boss's lunch plans.

"Hey." Sever shouted out. "I just want to use the phone for a
second. To call a taxi."

She looked up and shook her head.

He hated cell phones. Still, there were times —

They came through the front glass door like two pit bulls, slamming it open, and each one taking him by an arm. Sever caught a

glimpse of the young girl as she raised her head, a shocked look on her face. The two men in sport coats picked him up and hustled him through an open doorway at the rear of the reception area. They dropped him onto a red padded desk chair, and one took a stance by the door. The other planted himself on the desk and glared at Sever.

Sever's heart raced. His eyes darted around the room, looking for some way out. No windows, just four walls, two of them decorated with album art. Sever recognized several of Pike's albums.

"Where is Gideon Pike?"

Sever blinked. That was *his* line.

The Asian man was short, on the heavy side. His legs barely reached the floor. He slipped out of his sport coat, and Sever's suspicions were confirmed. A shoulder holster hung under his left arm. The gun stayed holstered.

"Where is Gideon Pike?"

"And that's the question I was going to ask your boss."

"I'm not playing games. We want to know where he is."

Why did this pushy son of a bitch think he knew where Pike was? He'd been asking the same question all over town. Now someone thought he knew? He actually did have a vague idea, but —

"Whoever told you I have that information is wrong. I'm looking for him too."

The man took a deep breath, then exhaled. "I have an anger management issue. When I get angry, I don't manage very well. You see this?" He pointed to the handgun.

"I see it."

"For show. When I get really angry, these are what you need to watch out for." He held up his hands, open.

"Look, I don't want a fight. There is nothing I can tell you about Pike that you don't already know."

Komack's words came back. Pike felt his life was being threatened. Sever understood the feeling.

The Korean slid off the desk, and Sever tensed up.

"We want to know where Mr. Pike is. It's my understanding you know. If you hear from him, if you see him, you contact us immediately. At this office. Do you understand?"

Sever let out his breath. "Who do I ask for?"

"Harry, the guy who almost beat the shit out of you."

CHAPTER FORTY

In most relationships you find that there's a certain part of a person that remains private. Obviously there was a private side to Pike. Sever didn't know Gideon Pike as well as he thought he did. And he only had a vague idea of where he might be. No specifics. But it made sense. Pike was with someone he loved. Very possibly his sister. And how the hell did those two henchmen know that he had an idea? The one positive note was that Shinn's two goons thought Pike was alive. That was great news. The downside was that they were looking for him too, and seemed hell-bent on finding him.

He wished he knew Pike better, because he needed more information about how he worked. As close as they had been, he still wasn't sure what made him tick. Now he wished he could crawl into his skin and feel what Pike felt. Where did the singer go when he wanted to become invisible?

They'd developed a closeness over the years through the entertainment business. When Pike was still a new phenomenon, before he'd announced to the world that he was gay, he'd talked to Sever about the difficulty of admitting his sexual preference. Pike was afraid that one slip could ruin his career. His record company agreed, and had even suggested he develop a romantic interest with the female singer of a rock band called Cocky. Tammi Catrel was a cute, vivacious little package of energy who would have made an interesting partner, and she was determined to network her way to the top, even if it meant dating a guy who wasn't a serious candidate for a long-term relationship. After one album, and a couple of high profile dates with Pike, she and Cocky had disappeared. The last thing Sever had heard was that she was trying for a comeback, and dating a hard-core rocker named Sheryl Byrd.

Over the years, Pike had hit after hit, and Sever followed his career with story after story. There were occasions when the songwriter called Sever just to touch base and talk off-the-record about his problems. His friendship with the singer was the reason Ginny had asked him to come to Miami, but he still didn't know enough. If he was to find Pike, Sever would apparently need a lot more information. He could remember maybe twelve different times he'd done a story on Pike, and he thought he was getting to the core of the man, but then Pike had shut off like a faucet. There was a private side to Gideon Pike, an invisible side that no one saw. And now, with the story of his waning fortune, the idea that he may have shot Spinatti, and the implied threats from his publisher, Sever had to admit he didn't know much about his old friend at all. He hadn't seen or talked to him in the last three years.

It was a freezing January when Pike had played Chicago the last time they'd met. After the show he and Sever visited a downstairs piano bar called the Redhead where the regular keyboard player had relinquished his seat to let Pike regale the crowd with his hits. The basement bar crowd was in awe, squeezing next to the piano, pushing and shoving to be close to the icon. Pike had a smile for everyone, an autograph for most of them, and tried to accommodate as many requests as possible. Men and women reached out, just to touch his arm as he worked his magic on the keyboard.

As word reached the street, a steady stream of people lined up on the four steps to the entrance, and spilled out onto the sidewalk. And even though it was the middle of winter with the temperature hovering around thirteen degrees that night, Pike's heat seemed to permeate the block, and for an hour and a half he played, sang, hugged an occasional fan, and led them in several rousing sing-alongs.

With their glasses raised on high, they sang "You Knew What I

Needed." Swaying, the piano-man banging out the chords, they cho-
rused in drunken revelry the lyrics that could have been written
about Chicago.

> Lights bright city, a town so loud
> Just a faceless man, in a great big crowd
> Don't fall down and don't get lost
> Get your mind together but what a cost
> But someone saw right through my soul
> looked right through like there was a hole
> You knew what I needed
> You saw what was there
> You knew what I needed
> Someone near who cared.

They screamed and cried and yelled for more and everyone, including Sever, was exhausted at the end. The intimate performance
had been infinitely more satisfying than his concert two hours be-
forehand.

Sever knew of the man's insecurities. He knew of his doubts and
fear that the whole fame thing would dry up and blow away. And he
also knew that Pike often hoped the fame *would* evaporate. He'd
shared with Sever the pressure he felt to constantly top himself. Sever
knew secrets about Pike that no one else in the world knew. But the
singer/songwriter was a phenom. He felt his fame and popularity
were fleeting, and as popular as Pike was, the man never believed that
his songs were anything more than little novelties that simply captured a moment in time.

Sever knew some of Pike's secrets, but apparently not all of
them. He knew how uncomfortable the man was with entourages, or
bodyguards. He was comfortable with just the occasional friend or
lover. Women loved him, and most men felt no threat from him, finding him a simple, charming man. But Gideon Pike had held sway over
a musical generation for more than four decades.

Financial trouble? Possibly. Pike's lifestyle was legendary. While he seemed to move through the world of entertainment with little baggage, he never lacked for creature comforts. And his gift giving was notorious. Sever glanced at the solid-gold Rolex on his wrist. A gift from Pike. And there were stories that he'd bought several lovers a Mercedes or Rolls Royce. At one time he'd owned a jet, several restaurants that had failed, plus all the houses, and at least two yachts. Now he'd fallen on hard times and had disappeared. All in the last three years.

Did he live beyond his means? Biddle thought so. Or did this accident he kept referring to in the diary have something to do with his financial woes? Did Jimmy Shinn bail him out of a financial nightmare or did Shinn cause the trouble?

What the hell did Jimmy Shinn have on Gideon Pike? For Pike to sell his songs, give away his future, he either owed more money than God had, or something else was terribly wrong.

The new cab driver was silent as they cruised through Little Havana. No condemnations against the ruling regime in Cuba, no obscene comments to passersby.

Somebody thought Sever knew where Pike was. And he'd only *just* thought of the possibility. The two thugs who had threatened him at Hit King were almost like Mafia hit men. There seemed to be a *Godfather* mentality at the publishing company. Then there was the boat incident, and getting mugged at Platinum.

Sever closed his eyes and pictured the singer. On stage, he wore his glittered wide-lapeled suit and performed his Jerry Lee Lewis impression, where he stood on the piano bench and played over-the-top solos, finally jumping down and kicking over the piano bench. His gut wrenching ballads brought the audience to tears, and when he wound up for a soulful finish, he would stand in a pin spot, sweat running down his face as he slowly got down on his knees. Sever'd seen the close a dozen times, but it never failed to move him.

"Ladies and gentlemen, boys and girls. My world is my music. If I've brought some passion to your world, if I've in any small way brought you joy, then my music, my life, has been worth the pain and suffering, the joy and sorrow that has brought it to light. Thank you for making my music, my life, worthwhile."

There would be thirty seconds of silence. Stone-cold silence from the stage. The lights would fade to dark. Everything turned black. The crowd would be subdued, then you could hear the beginning of the roar. From the grass seats, the upper levels, the clamor would start. The noise would build, shaking the foundation of the performance center, louder and louder with the crack of hands clapping together in explosive percussion, shrill whistling in a multitude of keys, and raucous shouting. The momentum would build to a thunderous roar, and Pike would reappear, the blinding white lights exploding on the stage.

His spangled James Brown cape, tossed carelessly over his shoulders, fluttered and sparkled in a fan-driven wind from offstage. His band would bow gracefully, in deference to the star of the show.

With a nod to the assembled, Pike would sit on the piano bench, study the keys, then hit a full chord, jumping up and never sitting down again.

> If there ever was a time and place
> If there ever was a place in space
> It would be the time I spent with you
> We've done something no one else can do
> We've got it on —
> Made the miracle of love
> We've got it on —
> It's pure passion from now on
> We've got it on.

CHAPTER FORTY-ONE

Ginny wasn't in her room. He needed to tell her about the goons from Little Havana, but she was gone. Sever thought about calling Biddle's room, but decided it would be poor form. His head still hurt, so he took three aspirin and washed them down with a Scotch from the mini-bar. He walked down to the pier, noticing the Brazilian girl getting some late afternoon sun on the deck of her boat. He waved, and she motioned to him.

He met her halfway up the plank. Her miniscule bikini consisted of a creamy white top that barely covered her nipples and a tiny triangle over her pubic area.

"Mr. Sever." Her accent only helped make her sexier. "I've watched you with the beautiful blond. She is very gorgeous. Even though she is an older woman, I would be interested." She flirted with him with her exotic eyes, waiting to see what his reaction would be. "I'm certain she and I could learn a lot about each other."

Sever stared into those brown eyes. "I'll pass the word on."

"I think maybe I should tell Mr. Biddle. He seems to have captured her fancy for the moment." She flashed her bright smile and turned her perfect butt to him, with nothing more than a thin piece of white cloth between the cheeks. Over her shoulder she said "But I would also entertain the idea of you and I learning about each other. If you're ever interested, let me know." She walked back onto the boat.

Sever stood there for a moment, his cool totally blown.

"Wait a minute."

She turned, a smile on her face.

"You think Biddle and the blonde are interested in each other?"

"They were down here an hour ago, holding hands, walking and talking. I would say there is a strong possibility."

Sever took a deep breath and kept his concentration on the beautiful girl. "What else do you notice down here? Did you see Gideon Pike in the past week?"

She nodded. "I did."

"With anyone?"

She nodded again. "A beautiful woman, with deep green eyes. We spoke for a moment. I don't think he wanted to be recognized."

"Was this woman his sister."

"His sister?"

"Yeah. His sister. She has a young son and —"

"Would he kiss his sister on the lips?"

"Gideon?"

"They seemed too interested in each other." She flipped her hair back, and walked into the cabin.

He turned and walked down to Brady's boat, passing an old fisherman with a rod and tackle box, and a small man with large sunglasses and a stocking cap pulled low. They both nodded at Sever. Friendly marina. The dock was quiet and the old man wasn't home. He considered the invitation from his exotic friend, and thought about extending the conversation. It would wait. He'd decided on another plan of action. He just hoped to hell he didn't get beat up on this one.

The rental car was a Pontiac Grand Prix, nothing fancy, but he only needed it for one night. He took a short nap and woke up at 2 A.M., splashing water on his face to wash the cobwebs away.

Sever drove the Pontiac to the Platinum and parked across the street at Cap'n Rod's Carryout. He'd called, and April was dancing tonight. Until 3 A.M. So if she left by the rear door, by herself, he'd possibly have a chance to ask her questions without the club's bruiser busting his chops. If she came out with someone, or if someone picked her up, he'd go back to the hotel and try again later. April had information. He was certain of it.

Somewhere on the street he could hear Latin music, horns and guitars blaring from a doorway. A hip-hop sound, maybe Ludicrous, boomed out of a second-story window, and a car in the parking lot across the street shook with the back-beat from a 50 Cent song. Miami was alive at 2:45 A.M.

He watched the doors. A couple of girls straggled in, jeans and tee shirts. After makeup and a costume change, they would go through a transformation that would make them hundreds of dollars for the early morning shift.

Nobody came out. Three girls went in. Two bright halogen lights flooded the lot so he could see all the activity. He watched two girls share a joint before going inside. Then the late-shift dancers started leaving. Jeans and tee shirts. He hoped he'd recognize April with her clothes on.

Sever smelled fried food. The odor wafted through the open windows of the Grand Prix and he glanced around, looking for a fast food restaurant. He hadn't had anything to eat since lunch, and he suddenly realized he was hungry.

She came out by herself, stopping, looking both ways as if she expected someone. Then she walked quickly to a red Toyota. Sever started the engine and eased out of the carry-out lot onto the street. As April approached the exit he pulled in front of her and saw the anger on her face.

He jumped out and walked up to her window.

"What the hell is this all about?"

She didn't recognize him.

"April, I'm Mick Sever. You got some guy to beat me up the other night."

Her mouth flew open in surprise. "Oh, my God."

"I'm not here for paybacks. I'm here because I'm very concerned about a friend of mine."

"Gideon?"

"Gideon. And you've got some information. I know you do."

"Oh, God. I could be in so much trouble."

"If something's happened to Gideon, and you keep quiet, you could be in more trouble."

"You don't know, Mr. Sever."

"Look, give me ten minutes and a cup of coffee."

She seemed to study the proposal. "Shit. He's with Misty tonight. What the hell. Ten minutes?"

"Ten minutes. You tell me where." His eyes caught the backseat, a box of diapers and a child's car seat strapped into the seat belt.

"I can only stay for ten, fifteen minutes tops. I've got obligations at home."

He nodded. "Lead the way."

She pulled out onto the street and drove for about three miles. Traffic was light, and Sever half expected her to try to lose him. Instead, she drove slowly, making sure he was behind her the entire time.

The red Toyota pulled into an all-night diner with a chrome finish on the outside and a blinking blue neon sign that simply said ED's.

She surveyed the parking lot, then glanced through the windows, seeming somewhat apprehensive about going in.

"I really shouldn't be with you."

"Would you rather go someplace more private?"

She gave him a frown.

"Who are we looking for?" Sever studied her.

She motioned to him with her hand, and walked up the steps to the landing. Opening the door, Sever could smell the burgers and fries, grilled cheese, and maybe pork chops along with some grilled peppers and onions. His stomach growled.

Three old men and a woman shared the counter and a handful of booths were occupied. One young couple played touchy feely, cuddling on one side of their booth, oblivious to the other patrons. April moved quickly to a corner booth, and sat facing the door.

"What do you want?"

Sever looked closely at her features. Without the makeup she was older. Fine lines feathered out under her eyes and she had a pale, drawn quality about her.

"What's your real name?"

"That's why you wanted to talk?"

"No. I just thought it might be nice to know who I'm talking to."

"Martha. Do you believe that? Isn't that a plain, nothing name?"

"I had an Aunt Martha."

"Mr. Sever, we're not going to be friends here. We're not going to bond. Why don't you ask your ten minutes worth of questions, and let me get out of here?"

The waitress in black shorts and a white, stained blouse approached the booth.

"Just a black coffee please," April said.

"Bring me a burger — mustard, pickle and onion — an order of fries, and a Coke."

She walked away, tucking her pencil behind her ear.

"I'm not sticking around long enough for you to eat."

"You've got your own car out there. You can leave any time you want."

"Okay. What?"

"Who are you afraid of?"

"Jimmy."

"Jimmy?"

"Come on. You know who I'm talking about. He didn't like you snooping around and asking questions. You almost got me in trouble."

"April, Martha, I don't know who you're talking about."

"The guy who owns Platinum. Jimmy Shinn."

Sever's mouth dropped. "Jimmy Shinn owns the strip club?"

"The last time I looked."

"No shit?"

She laughed. "No shit."

✱　✱　✱

Half an hour later she was still there. They'd talked about the club, and April's interest in Shinn, Sever slowly working into the dicey stuff that got him beat up before.

Sever glanced at his watch. "What about your kid?"

"The baby sitter will sleep over. She knows some nights I don't make it home."

"So, Jimmy lives over on Star Island?"

"In the house that Gideon owned. It's really cool. Gideon had a wrought iron staircase that goes up to the master bedroom, and it's designed to look like the keyboard on a piano. It is so neat."

"So this was part of the payback? The house was to help pay off the money Gideon owes Shinn?"

She gave him a blank stare.

"Supposedly Pike borrowed a lot of money from Shinn to help pay off some debt and maybe some back taxes. I got the impression it was common knowledge in this area."

April twirled her hair with an index finger. "I really don't know anything about a payback. I know that just after I started at Platinum, Jimmy moved in and Gideon moved to the condo."

"Big come down."

"Oh, this is one beautiful house. The swimming pool is shaped like a grand piano and the hot tub is a musical note. There used to be a lot of nude paintings on the walls, but Jimmy had them all taken out. Now the walls are bare. He's not much of a decorator."

"April, who is Bridgette?"

She froze. The same question that got him in trouble the last time.

"I've got to go."

"Look, you've come this far. I need to know who she is, and what her relationship to Gideon is."

"Bridgette is my best friend."

"Good. Then if she's in trouble, you'd want to help her."

She looked at him warily. "Who said she was in trouble?"

"You seem to go out of your way to avoid talking about your best friend."

She was silent.

Sever chewed slowly on the remains of his sandwich and sipped a cup of lukewarm coffee. "I'm here to help Gideon. That's it. If you tell me who she is, I may be able to help her."

She brushed her hair off of her forehead, and Sever studied the face, no makeup, looking for all the world like a young mother who'd had a long day. "April, who is she?"

"You know Jimmy is looking for Gideon. He wants to find him real bad."

"I know. And I want to find him before Shinn does."

She was quiet again. She stared out the window as the occasional car drove by.

"He wants Gideon to sign a contract, and —"

"And what?"

"Jimmy is afraid that Gideon is going to tell."

"Tell what?"

She placed her hands flat on the table and leaned into Sever's face. "Tell your ex-wife that he's being blackmailed."

Sever decided to drop the Bridgette questions for the moment. "Can you tell me what Shinn has over Gideon?"

She squinted, as if focusing on the question. "I'm not sure. It started about three years ago. I was just part-time then. Gideon was coming into the club with a guy named Rusty, I think, and Jimmy was talking to him about buying into his publishing company."

"You heard them talk about this?"

"I hear a lot of things at Platinum. I'd sit down with Gideon and his friend and they'd laugh about it. This Rusty kept saying how Jimmy was a small-time player, a hood, and there was no way they were going to do business with someone like him. They made fun of him."

"And?"

"A dancer was killed in the parking lot."

Sever shook his head. "April, are we still talking about Rusty and Gideon?"

"I don't know how it all ties in. A dancer was run over in the parking lot outside the club. This Rusty was a lawyer or detective or something, and I think he kind of helped smooth things over and —"

"Smooth what over?"

"I shouldn't have brought it up. I really don't know. I know that the next couple of times they came into Platinum things were very strained, and Rusty would go down to Jimmy's office and talk for several hours. It was my job to kind of stay upstairs and entertain Gideon."

"And you think all this has something to do with Shinn blackmailing Gideon?"

"I don't know." She turned the palms of her hands up on the table. "Please, don't ask me any more questions. I don't have any more answers. All I know is that soon after that Jimmy took control of the publishing company."

"And Pike and Rusty?"

"Rusty didn't come in much after that. He died in a drowning accident a couple of weeks later. I know Gideon was really broken up about it."

He was pushing hard, but he didn't want to lose her. "So you think Jimmy Shinn was concerned that Gideon would talk — about the blackmail scheme."

"I heard him on the phone talking to his father and Sam. Sam is this big guy who works for Jimmy. Anyway, Jimmy said he can't let that story be told."

"Was it a threat on Gideon's life?"

"I'm telling you what he said. Jimmy could not allow Gideon to tell your wife that he was blackmailing him." She paused, watching something over Sever's shoulder. She seemed lost in thought. "Mr. Sever, do you know how much I can make on a good night at Platinum?"

He shook his head. No idea.

"$1500. Sometimes more."

His eyes widened.

"I've got to get a little creative, but I can do it."

"You're going somewhere with this."

"We had this dancer who wore thigh-high boots. It was her trademark. And she had yellow boots and red boots and suede boots and black boots. Every night a different color. And do you know how much she could make?"

Sever gave her the lead. Eventually she'd get to the point.

"Sometimes twice that. $3000. Guys went crazy. She's this beautiful girl, naked except for thigh-high boots. She actually wore more than any of us, and just sucked up the money."

"This was Bridgette?"

"Yeah."

"Your best friend."

"Uh huh."

"Who is she?"

"Kyle's mother."

"And Kyle is?"

"My Godson. Kick. That's his nickname. He really kicked when Bridgette was pregnant, so they nicknamed him Kick."

"They?"

"Bridgette and Gideon. Kyle is Gideon Pike's six-year-old son. Bridgette is Gideon's wife."

CHAPTER FORTY-TWO

The figures didn't lie. Not when you knew what the numbers were. And Jimmy Shinn knew the art of keeping two sets of books. One that showed him his not-so-small fortune and one that he showed to other interested parties, like the IRS. He had to hand it to his father. If nothing else, he'd taught his son how to work the angles.

And Jimmy Shinn knew enough about figures to know when someone was running a scam on him. Hell, he'd run scams on everyone else. If Jimmy was responsible for the two-book system, that was one thing. When someone else tried to run a two-book system on Jimmy, it was time to bring it to a screeching halt.

Shinn strolled through the crowded club, nodding to the doorman who was taking the stiff cover charge from a line of men. Platinum was a cash business. Cash and credit cards. And loads of cash passed through the business every night. A cop on the take had found him two armed guards just to stand by the bar each night to make sure no one got any bright ideas.

And not only did the cover charge make him money, along with the extensive list of expensive drinks, but each girl paid him twenty dollars an hour for the privilege of dancing. They paid him! This was the amazing part of the plan. So when he had thirty girls on a shift, he was making $600 an hour. Then, if they used the private lap dance room, they paid another $20. Shinn was making more in one twenty-four-hour period than most small companies made in a month. And everybody paid him.

He motioned to the new accountant as he walked downstairs, making sure the young man was behind him. The books were light. And in a cash business, the books shouldn't look light. He knew the bar help was straight with him. The managers who collected from the girls? They'd been with him for a long time and he paid them well, plus a commission when they hit their numbers.

Shinn opened the door to his basement office, one flight down from the club, and took a seat behind his desk. The accountant stood.

"Tony. You've been here six months. Do we treat you right?"

The young man squinted through his thick glasses. "Sure. I got no complaints, Mr. Shinn. A lot of guys would be jealous, with all the girls around and everything."

"Come over here." The young man approached the gunmetal gray desk. It matched the cold cement walls in the small office. "Look at these figures." Shinn pointed to the numbers neatly displayed in Quicken format with impressive graphs, but Shinn liked to see it all handwritten in a ledger book. It's the way his father kept his books. It all seemed more personal that way.

The young man with the dark, wavy black hair leaned over and studied the numbers.

"You see here, Tony, this is where a couple of my managers say we were doing some record numbers of clients. These numbers just don't seem to reflect that. So I checked the upstairs figures, and they just don't jibe." Shinn stood up.

Tony squinted, adjusting his glasses.

"Well, Mr. Shinn. I can only go by the cash that's given to me every night and —"

Shinn's right arm shot across the desk, grabbing the man's black-framed glasses. He ripped them from his face, threw them on the desktop and picked up the desk phone, slamming it down on the glasses, crushing the lenses.

In a controlled, level speaking voice he continued. "You see,

Tony, or maybe now you *don't* see, these figures don't add up. I need an accountant that can see the big picture. With an eye toward the future."

Tony Ciminillo froze. Tears welled up in his eyes, and he shook. Shinn thought he might have a seizure right there.

"Somebody is taking my money."

"Oh, God, Mr. Shinn. Oh, God."

The office door opened, and a Korean man in a sport coat walked in. Shinn walked to the door and left, closing it behind him. His father would be proud. Don't ever let someone take advantage of you. Don't ever let anyone get the upper hand. It was one lesson he'd learned well.

Even with the door shut, halfway down the hall he heard the explosion. He hoped Harry had remembered to wear earplugs, and he hoped he did a good job of wiping up the blood from the concrete.

CHAPTER FORTY-THREE

"Honest to God, Mr. Sever, I don't know where she is. She calls and tells me she's all right, but I don't know where she is."

"Take a guess. Your best friend. Where would she go?"

"Her mother owned a little house in Coconut Grove. She only mentioned it to me in passing, telling me her mom rented it out from time to time when she needed money. I don't think it was anything fancy, but it's the only place I can think of."

"And how would I find this place?"

"Mr. Sever, I told you, I don't know where she is. And even if I did, I couldn't tell anyone."

"Shinn is trying to force Gideon to sign a contract. He needs Gideon alive. And I assume he knows that Gideon and Bridgette —"

"Have a son? I made the mistake of telling him." She bowed her head and stared at the table. "Oh, God. This little boy is so precious."

"I've seen him."

"When? Where?"

"Gideon has a painting of him in his condo. It's rolled up in a closet."

The clatter of dishes in the kitchen drifted through the diner, and an old drunk in a dirty gray tee shirt and Bermuda shorts argued with the cashier over his check. Sever noticed that the smell of greasy burgers and onions had lost much of its appeal.

"Jimmy doesn't know where she is. He's looking, but he doesn't know."

"April," Sever leaned across the table, "he'll find her. He'll put pressure on her, and she and the boy can force Gideon's hand."

"I never should have told him."

"Who's looking? Who has he put on Gideon's trail?"

"He's got Sam. He's a really big guy, not too smart, but scary as hell. And there's Tweedle Dee and Tweedle Dum."

"Tweedle Dee and Tweedle Dum?"

"One of the guys is named Harry. I don't know the other one. That's what we call them at the club. Two Korean guys that work for Jimmy. Once in awhile he rewards them with a girl from Platinum." She made a face. "They both wear guns and they can get real rough. And then there's his father. He never comes in, but I know he's out there. He calls and threatens Jimmy two or three times a day."

Sever pictured the old man at the restaurant. And the big guy who followed him in.

"Who else?"

"I don't know. He's got a bunch of other guys who work for him, but those are the closest. I could be in a lot of trouble for telling you this."

"I'm not telling anyone."

"Probably not as much trouble as Bridgette, though. I think Gideon is with her."

The phone message from Gideon. The woman in the background warning him that someone could trace the call. Bridgette.

"Look, if there's anything else, anything at all that you remember, call me at the Double Tree."

"I can't. I can't do this anymore. This conversation never happened, Mr. Sever. I've got a little girl at home. I can't take that chance."

"Think about it. I need to know why Gideon's being blackmailed, and I need to know where he is."

She rose from the booth, glancing about nervously, and without looking back at him, walked out of the diner. Sever watched her through the smudged window, disappearing into the red Toyota in the dimly lit parking lot. He saw the Lincoln follow her out as she turned onto the street. He was being paranoid. Just another customer leaving at the same time.

Four-thirty in the morning was a little early to be calling someone. but he ignored the blinking message light and called Ginny's room. It rang seven times and he hung up. She wasn't there.

Sever pushed the in-house message button on the phone and the automated voice answered. "You have two unplayed messages. Message number one." There was a click, then silence. "End of message. Message number two: "Mick Sever, this is Charley Strict. We met in Lou Frey's office. I'd like to talk to you about Gideon Pike. I may have some information I could share." There was a pause. Sever waited, hoping there was more. "I'd rather not meet in the office, but there's a little area down by the marina near your hotel. A couple of tables and benches overlooking the harbor. I'll be down there about 5:30 A.M. I know it's early, but I start my workday around 6:30 A.M. so if you could meet me —"

Sever hung up and walked to the window. The sky was black, with faint pinpoints of light from a handful of stars. The lights from the causeway were bright and he could see South Beach lit up like a carnival. There were people just getting started on their evening activities over there. Sever made out the *Hit King* and *Old Man and the Sea*. He wondered if Brady was in for the evening. Leaving the curtains open, he lay on the bedspread, and picked up the receiver again. He punched in Biddle's number, then hung up before it rang. He had no right, and he knew it. He wished he knew who had called and hung up.

Five-thirty A.M.? Strict said he had information. Sever just wished he could talk to Ginny. 5:30 A.M.? The guy was out of his mind.

He made a mental note of the time, and let his mind start to close down. He saw the big guy bustling into the Cuban restaurant. The guy with the ill-fitting sport coat. Sam. April said he was scary.

And he saw the face, knowing he'd seen it before. The boat. The speedboat was coming at him, and the big guy with the ugly face was grinning as he bore down on them. It was Sam. Damn! Sam worked for Jimmy Shinn. There was no question about it, Jimmy Shinn had tried to have him killed. He stood up and went back to the window.

Five minutes later he called Ginny's room. Voice mail answered.

"Gin, it's Mick. I got a strange call from Charlie Strict. Remember him? From Frey's office? He wants to meet me by the marina at 5:30 this morning to talk about Gideon. That's all the information he would give me, but I thought you should know." He hung up, and lay back down.

Half an hour later he left the room and went downstairs to the dock. The burger from Ed's still lay heavy in his stomach.

CHAPTER FORTY-FOUR

His cell phone rang just as he was about to explode. He had to make a snap decision. That moment of pleasure? Or a phone call that could shape his future? He rolled off of Misty as she let out a deep sigh.

"Yeah. This had better be good."

"Mr. Shinn, it's Sam."

Mr. Muscle. Always make time for Mr. Muscle. "Yeah, Sam."

"I think I know where he is."

"You do?" He tried to keep the excitement out of his voice. There was silence.

"Sam?"

"Yeah, Mr. Shinn. You know our friend told you that Sever thought he knew where Mr. Pike was?"

He hated talking business on a cell phone, but this sounded promising. "Right. Our friend. He said Sever seemed to think he knew where Pike was staying."

"Sever apparently only had an idea. He needed to get a little more information. And he got it tonight."

"He did? So he knows where Pike is?"

"So do I." Sam chuckled, a flat, lifeless laugh. "See, your dancer spent some time at a restaurant with Sever and I just hung out, waiting, you know? I figured she must be telling him some stuff that she wasn't telling us."

Shinn smiled. "You figured this out, huh?"

"I did. Why else would she talk to him for an hour? So I followed her home."

"And?"

Misty got up and headed for the bathroom, her cute butt wiggling as she walked.

"Let's say we had a talk. Kind of like the talk she had with Sever."

"You were persuasive?"

"I got your answer."

"And how is she?"

"Well, sir, it took a lot out of her if you know what I mean. She didn't feel much like having another conversation, but I convinced her. Mr. Shinn, you told me to use any means necessary."

"Yes, I did."

"Well, sir, you'll probably have to hire another dancer. I don't think she'd do you much good any more."

Shinn shuddered. "Sam, if you've got the answer, then we don't need the two writers any more."

"I was thinking the same thing, sir."

"You handle situations well."

"Yes sir, I do."

"So, I assume the situation will be taken care of."

"I'll see to it."

"And we won't be hearing from the dancer?"

"Don't see how we could, sir. Don't see how we could."

CHAPTER FORTY-FIVE

Everything was damp to the touch. White nylon ropes that reached from the boats to the dock dripped with moisture, and he felt the dampness cling to his deck shoes as he walked down the cement walk. Hell, he couldn't sleep. May as well be a little early for this strange rendezvous.

He passed the Brazilian girl's boat, and the others down to Brady's. The *Hit King* rolled gently on the water, the yellow tape no longer evident. Sever looked around, then walked the wooden plank up to the deck of Spinatti's final residence. The lights from the harbor were enough to see his way around. The sun would start its slow climb in the sky in about an hour, lighting up the bay and burning off the early morning dew. The door to the galley was open and he walked in, remembering this was where he'd found the Platinum matchbook. It was tidy. No dishes or glasses out. Everything put away in the cupboards. He walked out and stared up at the wall of windows in the distance, counting down and across until he saw Biddle's condo. There was a light on. He tried to leave the thought that she might be there, but it stuck with him. He counted over two windows to Gideon's condo. Right next door. Everything was dark.

He heard a crack, like someone snapping a whip in the distance. There was a brief movement on Gideon's balcony, a fleeting shadow. At this distance he couldn't be sure. He *was* sure of the thud and the wood chips flying up three feet from where he stood. A splinter hit his cheek and he jerked his head, trying to figure out what had just happened when he heard the crack again. This time he heard the whine as a bullet crashed into wood behind him, biting the frame of the galley inches from his head.

Sever ducked, bending over and running hard as he heard the whine of a third bullet. This was more like an angry buzz. He didn't even want to know where this one hit. With brief hesitation he leaped over the railing into the inky dark water. He hit the briny bay with a splash, letting himself go deep, feeling the weight of his clothing dragging him down.

Chilly. He hadn't been swimming in the ocean in years, and he'd forgotten how cold it could be. His clothes clung to his skin, adding weight and texture. It was a most unpleasant sensation, clammy and cloying, and he kept sinking deeper. He wanted to stay there for as long as possible, but he hadn't taken much air. He counted to twenty and felt the aching in his lungs. They were burning. Another ten seconds and he struggled for the surface. Only jeans, a tee shirt, and canvas deck shoes, but they felt like a lead weight. It was slower on the way up, like dragging another body or two with him.

He was about to burst. Breaking the surface, he gasped for air, ragged sounds resonating from his throat as he sucked in gulps of oxygen. He was on the far side of the boat, unable to see the condos or the hotel. He worked his arms and legs, trying to stay afloat and paddled to the rear of the boat, grabbing a taut rope and hanging on as he peered around the *Hit King*, looking up at the condo.

More air. He took short, shallow breaths, trying to replenish the starving capillaries in his lungs.

Nothing. No motion, no sign of anything. The light in Biddle's condo still burned. Most of the units were dark, several with dim lights behind gauze curtains. Sever knew nothing about firearms. Nothing. Could someone see him with a night-vision scope? He wished he were invisible. Staying close to the yacht, he hugged the rope. His muscles were weak, his arms ached, still he waited five minutes. Ten minutes. The Rolex worked like a charm. He felt himself slipping, giving in to the strain, as he shivered in the early morning air. He pushed away from the boat and swam hard to the dock, letting fear for his life supply the adrenaline, finally grabbing at the first pylon he saw.

Slowly he pulled himself out of the water and sat on the edge of the concrete, catching his breath. Total exhaustion. The boat blocked his view of the condo. He couldn't see it. Could someone in the condo see him?

He waited, glancing at his watch. Almost 6 A.M. There was no sign of Charles Strict. Sever wasn't surprised. He waited. His arms and legs were numb. His brain wasn't far behind. Early birds chattered, calling back and forth across the water. He heard a generator start, and smelled coffee coming from a nearby boat.

"Mick?"

He brushed the wet hair from his forehead and glanced down the dock. No one.

"Mick? What the hell?"

He looked up. Brady was standing on his deck, white shorts and a dark blue knit shirt. He held a cup of coffee in one hand, steam rising from the china mug.

"It's a little early for a swim, my boy. Come on up and I'll get you a cup of coffee."

"Brady. It's been a hell of a morning."

"In that case I'll put something in the coffee."

Sever slowly stood up, water draining from his pants and shirts. He pulled off his shoes and slowly walked up the plank to the yacht. He couldn't remember ever being this tired.

"Hell of a morning, Brady. Hell of a morning."

"You've got to call the cops."

Sever studied the murky brown coffee in the oversized mug. "Give me your cell phone."

Brady handed him the flip phone, and Sever punched in the

hotel number. He connected to her room and she answered on the third ring.

"I'm on Brady's boat. Someone tried to kill me."

He heard her take a deep breath.

"Let me get dressed. Five minutes, and I'll be down."

CHAPTER FORTY-SIX

Biddle was with her. The casual familiarity, the looks at each other and the light conversation seemed as if they'd been a team for years rather than a day.

"Tom knows everything that we know. He's got a stake in this too, Mick."

Biddle nodded. "Ginny says you think you may know where Gideon is."

Sever looked at Brady. The old man sat stoically, sipping his third cup of coffee. He wasn't going to fall asleep this morning. He looked back at Ginny and Biddle. Fucking Biddle.

"I got the idea yesterday. He has a sister, and I thought he might be staying with her."

"Did you tell anyone?" Ginny watched him intently.

Sever thought. "I told Brady that I thought I *might* know where he was," he nodded at the old man, "and you."

"I told Tom you had an idea where she might be."

Tom closed his eyes, rubbing them with his thumb and index finger. "And I told Frey when I talked to him yesterday."

"Frey's assistant wanted to see me down here this morning. And now they're shooting at me."

"Jesus, Mick. I'm so sorry. Frey —" he trailed off.

Sever glanced at Ginny. "You want the whole story?"

"I think we all need the full story."

"It's not his sister. The paintings we saw in his condo, they were . . ." He hesitated.

"Mick. I told him we broke in. Tom needs to know."

Tom *needs* to know. All right.

"It's not his sister. Tom, do you know about Bridgette?"

Biddle shook his head. "No."

"She was a dancer at Platinum. She's apparently married to Pike."

"Married?" Ginny sat up in her deck chair. "I thought —"

"Not only married, but they have a six-year-old boy."

"Jesus." Biddle fumbled with his cup, setting it down on a plastic end table. "You'd think I'd know about that. I'm his god-damned neighbor!"

"Apparently he kept it a secret, a double life. But Bridgette's friend at the club spilled the beans to Shinn."

"Shinn?" Ginny looked puzzled.

"Tom, you didn't tell her? Shinn owns Platinum."

Ginny looked puzzled, the crease in her brow deepening. "Jimmy Shinn? The guy who owns the publishing company?"

"The same."

"Did you know?" She looked at Biddle.

"Yeah. I didn't know it was important."

Brady stood and walked to the galley, pouring himself another cup of strong black brew. No wonder he wanted to stay awake. This was just getting good.

"I told you that Mick got beat up by the bouncer!"

"Ginny, I didn't put it together. Let's get back to where Gideon is. Mick got shot at this morning and he thinks it came from Gideon's condo. Gideon has a rifle, capable of hitting a target at this range. Is Gideon trying to kill Mick?"

"If he's the one who killed Spinatti, then he might be trying to kill me. But I doubt it.

I don't think he's got a thing to do with this."

"Then who does?" Ginny turned her attention to Sever.

"Shinn." He paused, still not comfortable with Biddle's presence.

"Here's a scenario. Gideon says 'no' to signing the contract, and threatens to tell you that Shinn is blackmailing him."

"There's no proof that he's —"

"This is my little fantasy. Let me tell it."

"Okay."

"Gideon is ready to tell you everything. It may have something to do with a hit-and-run killing in Platinum's parking lot. But the bottom line is, if you publish the story about his being blackmailed, he figures it neutralizes Shinn's power."

Biddle put his hand on Ginny's shoulder. "But if Gideon implicates Shinn — if Shinn is really blackmailing him, then Gideon has to say why he's being blackmailed. What if that involves a serious crime? For instance, hit-and-run?"

Sever studied the man, wondering how much he knew, and how much he kept inside.

"Tom, are you and Gideon friends?"

"Sure, we —"

"No! I mean solid friends."

"We are. Gideon took a chance on me. I watch his back and he watches mine. We've been through a lot, and no matter what I've said in the last couple of days, I don't seriously believe that Gideon is capable of killing someone. Not Rusty, not Spinatti, and not you."

"All right, I have it on good authority that Jimmy Shinn wants to find Gideon in the worst way, and I mean the worst way."

Ginny frowned again. "He wants to kill him?"

"Well, that's one option. The other is to threaten his wife and kid."

Biddle walked to the galley and poured himself a cup of Brady's coffee. "And I'll ask the question again. Do you know where Gideon is? Can we find him, protect him, get him to go to the cops?"

"April thinks he may be in Coconut Grove."

They were all silent for a moment. A Boston Whaler sputtered to life in the water across the dock and two young men opened the throttle, heading out of the bay. Finally Brady spoke up.

"You know, if the man wants to become invisible, why don't you let him? We all need to walk away once in awhile. Maybe your friend just needs a little time alone."

"Brady, I agree with you. One hundred percent. However, if Shinn finds him, he may kill him. And I believe Gideon wants to live. He's obviously got something very important to live *for*. A wife and a kid. We'd better pray we find him first." Sever glanced at Ginny. "I think the first thing we need to do is visit Lou Frey's office. This time, I'm not calling ahead for an appointment."

Brady shook his head. "The first thing we do is call the cops. Somebody took a couple of shots at you and —"

Sever smiled. "And you're looking out for me?"

"Hell no! Those shots were less than thirty feet from my boat. I want to stop this guy before he shoots up my boat too."

CHAPTER FORTY-SEVEN

Detective Haver motioned to the uniformed officer, who slowly dug the slug out of the wood work.

"I'll bet we have the same caliber and bore that was used to kill Spinatti. Is there a reason Pike would want to kill you?"

Sever glared at him. "Pike didn't want to kill me. Just because it came from up there," he pointed to the condo, "doesn't mean it was Pike."

"We've got a dead lawyer, a dead lover, and an almost dead writer. It's Pike. If it's not Pike, who is it?"

Sever was quiet. The rest of the story could wait. Haver didn't need all the other information. Not yet.

"Well, Mr. Sever, you be careful. If it was me, I'd get the hell out of Dodge."

"But it's not."

"Not what?'

"It's not you. It's me, and I think I'll stick around and see how this story ends."

"It's funny," Haver wasn't laughing, "but you keep showing up. Let's see, there was the incident with the blood on the boat, then you were on Mr. White's boat shortly after they found Spinatti's body, and you just happened to be hanging around the condo lobby when we went up to check Pike's condo, and now you're on the Spinatti yacht and in the line of fire."

Sever watched his eyes, piercing and perceptive. "And your point is?"

"I wonder if you're involved in this a little deeper than you're admitting."

Ginny walked over to the detective. "I asked Mick to come down here to help me with a story. We're sitting around here with our mouths hanging open, pretty much amazed at what's happening. We have no idea what's going on, and the fact that we're curious doesn't mean you have the right to accuse Mick. Jesus Christ, someone tried to kill him this morning. And all you can do is point your finger?" She'd gotten a full head of steam, and Sever knew what that was like.

"Mrs. Sever, I don't believe in coincidences. When there's a pattern, there's a specific reason."

"And the fact that Mick happened to be in the same vicinity —"

"Sets up a pattern."

"Bullshit. You don't think he's involved, and you can't be serious about Gideon Pike being a killer."

"As far as I'm concerned, Pike is the main suspect. As far as the department is concerned, he's a person of interest. And as far as your ex-husband is concerned, the pattern repeats itself just a little too often." Haver turned to Sever. "Call me if you decide to leave town."

"I thought you said to get the hell out of Dodge."

"I said that's what I would do if I were you." The detective was plainly irritated. "However, I'm not you, remember? And as a law enforcement officer, I'm telling you to stay in town. I may want to contact you at a later date."

"Detective," Ginny was an inch from his face. "Your veiled threats are crap. Why don't you leave Mick alone, and find Gideon Pike? With the entire Miami Police at your disposal, I'd think you'd have a much better chance of solving these shootings than making your bullshit accusations down here. My hus —" she paused, "My *ex*-husband was almost killed this morning. Why don't you do something about it?"

Detective Haver spun around and walked down the plank to the concrete dock, turning back one last time. "Sever, keep your head down. There's enough murders in this town as it is. I don't need a famous writer getting killed."

CHAPTER FORTY-EIGHT

That pesky green light. Message number one: "Mick, I got your call. I was taking a shower. Call me when you get this."

Ginny *had* been in her room the first time he'd called this morning. Maybe.

Sever sat on the edge of the bed, holding his head in his hands. The shooting this morning had left him shaken, and more than a little mad. That, coupled with two cups of Brady's Cuban black coffee and no sleep had him keyed up. He took slow, deep breaths, his lungs still burning. He didn't often feel he needed someone, but right now he really needed Ginny. And she was somewhere else — with someone else.

Pissed him off.

He could feel his heart rate slowing down, slowing down. He pictured a calm beach, the water slowly lapping at the sand. Palm trees blowing gently, their fronds waving in the breeze like giant fans, cooling him off.

Fuck this shit. He wanted to kill somebody. It was only fair. Someone had tried to kill him. He jumped off the bed and stormed out of the room. It was time to find Charley Strict and get to the bottom of this.

Ginny was expecting him. She'd asked to go along, as had Biddle. Well, they could either find their own way, or not go at all. This thing had become somewhat personal, and Sever wanted to confront Strict on his own.

He'd dropped the rental off, so cabs were the transportation of necessity. The driver let him off in front of the building, and Sever walked in, only now considering that the doors might be locked. It was not yet 8 A.M. Attorneys probably opened their doors at 9:00? 10:00? But Strict said he started his day at 6:30. Sever figured he'd find out for himself.

The elevator took him up and opened at Frey's floor. Everything was quiet. No bustle of people, no office activity, just an 8 A.M. hush.

Sever felt his fingertips tingle. He was wired, and that probably wasn't a good thing. He walked to the outer door, turning the handle, expecting it to be locked. It wasn't. The door swung open effortlessly. The lobby was dimly lit with recessed ceiling lights casting an ominous pall over the room. He stepped in and let the door shut behind him.

Thick hunter-green carpets, green and brown fabric wallpaper, and an acoustic tile ceiling swallowed every essence of sound. It was as if a vacuum had surrounded the room. Sever walked the few steps to the hallway and glanced down the long narrow corridor to the offices. A light spilled into the hall from the office at the far end. Sever silently walked across the heavy, green carpet. Reaching the doorway he hesitated, trying to orchestrate his timing. He took a deep breath, then entered the room.

A green-domed desk light shone brightly on the glass top of the antique oak desk. It's reflection bounced light into the hallway. The glow of a computer screen added to the room's shadowy brilliance.

No one was there. The soft sound of a jazz station filtered through the room, and Sever's eyes caught the shelves of books on the far wall. He hesitated, sticking his head through the doorway and looking down the hall. He heard the lobby door click shut, and he pulled his head back in.

He could picture the person walking down the hall, coming back to this room. He stepped behind the door, immediately feeling silly. What was he going to do? Step out and —

He stepped out as the person entered.

"Jesus! You scared the hell out of me! I mean — I was down the hall to get a drink of water and — Jesus!" Ed Komack looked as if he'd seen a ghost.

"At least I didn't hit you over the head with a bottle of sparkling wine."

The humor had little effect on the man. He seemed to be trying to catch his breath and his composure. "What are you doing here?"

"I was about to ask you the same thing. We keep running into each other under strange circumstances."

"Look, Sever, you're the one who shows up unannounced. Lou Frey is my attorney. He's making copies in the conference room. What the hell are you doing here this early in the morning?"

"Looking for Charley Strict."

"Charles isn't here." The voice of Lou Frey was deep and sobering. "And the question is well put, Mr. Sever. What the hell are you doing here? We're not open yet." Sever watched from the corner of his eye as Frey walked into the room, white sleeves rolled up and red and gray tie loosely knotted around his neck.

Sever's blood was racing through his veins, his heart beating strongly. He spun around and confronted Frey, staring straight into the man's eyes. "Strict set me up this morning."

"Set you up?"

"To be shot."

The corners of Lou Frey's mouth turned up. "To be shot? You mean killed? Mr. Sever, that's some imagination you have! You should write fiction." The smirk turned to a full-blown grin.

"Where is he, Frey?"

"I don't know. But I'm certain that Charles Strict has never set anyone up in his relatively short life."

"Charley Strict told me he had information on Gideon Pike. He asked me to meet him at 5:30 A.M. on the dock outside my hotel. At about 5:15 someone started shooting at me from Gideon Pike's condo. Now you explain that, you son of a bitch."

Frey cocked his head to the side, studying Sever like a clinical psychologist. "There's no reason to be vulgar."

Sever wanted to throttle him right there. Vulgar? He pictured his hands around the pompous man's throat, squeezing until the vain lawyer spilled his guts. "Someone tried to tear me apart with a speedboat, I've been beat up in a strip club, smacked over the head with a bottle of champagne, and this morning someone tried to put a bullet in my brain. I somehow suspect you know a lot about this, and calling you a son of a bitch is probably much too mild a term."

"You're accusing me? You'd better get some damned good proof!"

"Right now, I'm accusing your assistant."

"He's not here to defend himself."

"Oh, I'll even bet he doesn't show up today! In fact, since I wasn't killed, maybe he won't show up at all. Was that his job? To see that I went away?"

"Mr. Sever, I seriously have no idea what you're referring to."

"And Mr. Frey, I think you're full of shit. Rusty washed up on shore, his head bashed in. Spinatti gets shot on his boat. It seems that anyone who gets involved with Gideon's situation —"

Frey held up his hand. "What *situation* are you referring too?"

Sever paused, calming down and collecting his thoughts. Hell, he wasn't even clear on what the situation was, but this guy knew. "Jimmy Shinn wants more than he's entitled too. Apparently he has a stranglehold on Pike, and," he motioned with his arm toward Komack, quietly standing with his arms folded, "and I have no idea how Komack is connected. But if Pike is being blackmailed, that story is going to get out. I promise you I'll see to it, and take you down at the same time."

Frey seemed somewhat amused. "What leads you to this assumption? Not that Gideon may be obligated to Mr. Shinn, but that I'm involved?"

"For starters, a meeting you had at a restaurant with Komack and Shinn."

Frey looked at Komack. "We're in business together, Mr. Sever. Mr. Shinn owns the Hit King publishing company. Mr. Komack, Gideon, and myself often have meetings to discuss the business of publishing."

"Someone tried to kill me this morning, Frey. Have you ever been shot at? It gets your heart going. I swear to God, if I can prove that you had —"

"I believe you're being much too dramatic, Mr. Sever. You've overstayed your welcome."

Komack's eyes darted between them. Finally he spoke. "Mr. Sever, I may have overstepped my bounds the other night. I told you that Gideon was concerned about some things. He's somewhat over dramatic about the way he looks at business decisions, but he *does* make most of the decisions for our team effort. And just to make sure things are balanced, we have Lou Frey's firm to represent our interests."

"Someone tried to kill me this morning, Komack."

The soft electronic trill of a telephone caught Sever's ear. He glanced back at the desk and watched the amber light flashing. Frey ignored him for a moment and walked over to pick up the phone.

"Yes?"

He was silent for a minute or longer, his face expressionless.

Finally, "Yes. And you're sure?" He frowned now, pursing his lips. "I can be there in," he glanced at his gold watch, "fifteen minutes. Thank you."

Frey hung up and worked his shirt sleeves down, buttoning them in silence. Then he buttoned the top button of his shirt, and pulled the silk necktie tight. He finally looked at Sever, seeming to measure his words.

"They found Charlie Strict in the shallow water near the marina by your hotel. Mr. Sever, I believe it's time for you to leave." He gave Sever a hard look, then motioned for him to start walking toward the door.

"Jesus!" Sever stood still, rooted to the spot on the floor. "How? What —"

"Shot in the head. They believe the shot was from the same place and possibly the same caliber as they dug out of Spinatti's boat."

Sever thought about the third shot, and maybe another while he was under water. Was Strict walking on the dock as the gunman started firing? And what if the intended victim was Strict all along, and not him?

He turned to Komack. "The shots came from Gideon's condo."

Sever watched Komack's expression, deer in the headlights.

"Do you remember that you told me Gideon asked you to find something up there for him? Do you?"

Komack shook his head, his face losing color by the minute.

"It was a rifle, wasn't it? It had been wrapped up in that blanket in the closet. Did you find it? Is your business partner shooting people in the marina? Did he shoot Spinatti? Did he shoot your attorney's associate, Charley Strict?" Sever's voice was louder. "Did Gideon take a couple shots at me this morning?"

Komack shook his head frantically. "It's not true. You don't know —"

"Mr. Sever, it's time for you to leave." Frey grabbed him by the elbow and tried to push him down the hall, but Sever shook him off.

"Who shot at me this morning?"

"Whoever it was, apparently they killed the wrong man." Frey stepped into the elevator as the other two followed.

They reached the bottom floor and exited together.

"You're driving to the hotel?"

Frey nodded. He and Komack started walking toward a parking garage on the corner of the street.

"Can I ride along?"

"Mr. Sever, I suppose I should admire your nerve in asking, but having you along is the last thing I want. Get your own god-damned ride." He stared hard at Sever.

"Mr. Frey, there's no reason to be vulgar." Sever turned and hailed a cab. He stuck by his statement. The man was a son of a bitch.

CHAPTER FORTY-NINE

"It was easy, Mr. Shinn." Shinn shuffled a pile of financials on his ornate, white desk, listening on the speakerphone as Sam debriefed. "I
went through your personnel files at Platinum. Bridgette's last name
is Stockhardt. I figured that was her mother's name too. I found one
Stockhardt in Coconut Grove. She keeps a phone at that address
listed in her name. A C. Stockhardt. Hell, everybody knows when
there's an initial before the last name, it's some lady. Probably Carol."

Shinn blew a cloud of smoke toward the ceiling, reveling in the
information and the Caribbean spice from his Cuban Cohiba. Sam to
the rescue. The big guy was often mistaken for just brawn, but he was
sharp as a tack. Shinn thought for a moment, then spoke into the
phone.

"O.K. Sam. I want you to have someone check the place out.
No more than twelve hours. If they're in there, we should see some
activity in the next twelve hours. Take one of the boys with you, and
you stay back. You do tend to be a little conspicuous, and I don't want
Pike spotting you. Got it?"

"Got it, boss." The big man hung up the phone.

Shinn pushed two numbers, and the phone went through a series of beeps, automatically dialing his next location.

"Hello."

"I think we've found him."

"Where?"

"I'll let you know soon. It *appears* he not only shot Spinatti, but now he's killed the kid from the attorney's office."

"I know. Appearances are important."

"So the assumption is he could be dangerous?"

"We can make that assumption."

Shinn took another drag on the cigar. "And if the police get an anonymous tip, and there is any shooting, I suppose Gideon could end up getting hurt, or killed."

The voice on the other end was clipped. "Could happen."

"Because if he were to die, it could actually solve some problems. There would only be one partner to deal with."

"Call me when you find out for sure."

"Stand by. You'll be the first to know."

Shinn hung up the phone and sucked on the cigar, exhaled, and studied the stream of gray-white smoke that spiraled to the ceiling. He pushed back the leather chair and put his feet up on the gold-trimmed white desk. Gideon Pike would have never allowed cigars in this room when he owned the house. And he definitely would not have allowed feet on the desk.

Fuck him. He didn't own the house. There wasn't much the guy owned at all, and interest on his sizable loan was constantly mounting. That was the nice thing about blackmail. Shinn found he could keep raising the stakes. If you don't give me this, I'll expose you. If you don't give me that, I'll expose you. If you don't start paying me twenty-five percent, thirty percent on everything you make, I'll expose you. Forty percent and no, forty-five. But the son of a bitch had finally decided he'd had enough. He had refused to sign over the recording rights. He'd threatened to go public with the blackmail story.

Well, there was mounting evidence that Pike had killed Spinatti, Charley Strict, maybe Rusty, and there was evidence he'd tried to take out Sever. And Shinn had the original story. The hit-and-run killing in Platinum's parking lot. Oh, Pike was in so much shit. If Gideon Pike wanted to fuck with Jimmy Shinn, be prepared. If Gideon got the message, if he realized how much trouble he was in, maybe the damage could be repaired. If he didn't get the message, fuck him. A dead Gideon Pike meant that Shinn would deal with Bridgette and Komack. Both of them pussycats. The more he thought about it, the more he realized that Gideon Pike had outlived his usefulness. Bridgette and Komack would be a piece of cake.

He punched in one more code.

"Hello?"

"You've got the rifle?"

There was a hesitation on the other end.

"Yes or no?"

"Yes."

"You've got to get it back where it belongs."

"Tonight."

"In the meantime, we've got the address in Coconut Grove."

"I heard that's where he's staying."

Shinn thought for a moment. "Am I the last one to find out?"

"I heard. That's all."

"All right. Listen, Charley Strict was a nice addition, but Sever would have been ideal."

"I thought so. It would have been perfect if Sever'd been nailed too. It just didn't work."

"Sam is checking out Coconut Grove." The cigar was dangerously close to burning his fingers. He always smoked them to the nub. Aside from the first puff, a good cigar seemed sweeter the closer you got to the end. Maybe life situations were like that. Sweeter the closer you got to the end.

"I'm sure Sever is going to try to find Pike."

"Yeah." Shinn closed his eyes, picturing the pushy writer in the restaurant when he'd confronted him. "You know, if guns are involved, and I'm pretty sure they will be, it would be interesting if Sever were there. Maybe there's a chance that he and his wife could get caught in the shooting. Maybe that's the way to go. Maybe we'll get another chance."

"Are you asking, or suggesting."

"Can you make it happen?"

"I'll work on it. What's the time frame?"

"As soon as Sam confirms that Bridgette and Gideon are staying at the house."

"What about the kid?"

Shinn paused, stubbing out the cigar. What about the kid? "Whatever happens, happens. Don't worry about the kid. I want this handled."

"You're a heartless fuck."

"I am. But I don't hear you complaining."

"No."

Shinn stood up, shaking out the wrinkles in his gray trousers. "I'll call you as soon as we have confirmation."

"You do that. In the meantime, I have to pay my respects to Charles Strict. Wish to hell I could pay them to Mr. Mick Sever too."

CHAPTER FIFTY

The words on the daily log were written in thick, indigo blue ink. The pen was different than the one that had been used in the two-volume diary in the library back on Biscayne Bay.

Jesus Christ. Now they are accusing me of murdering Larry Spinatti. It's all over the news. Jimmy Shinn is too smart to be very close to all these things. I'm certain he's maintaining some distance. And Sam is too dumb to do more than the muscle work. Somebody else is setting me up. And if they can set me up so that there is a case against me, accusing me of this murder, then it's obvious they don't need me anymore.

So, are they figuring out a way to kill me? They've got to find me first. And obviously I can't keep hiding forever. I've got to get help, and I don't trust anyone. Even the cops.

Maybe Mick. Sever can't be involved in all this deception. Who the hell else can I trust? He's got nothing to gain, nothing to lose, so I'll call Mick. And I pray that if he agrees to help get me out of this mess, nothing will happen to him. I can't have anything

happen to Mick Sever. I already owe him. Now I may
be putting him in danger. Maybe he does have something to lose.

I may be over dramatizing things, which I'm
prone to do, but Sever saved my life years ago. So I
should leave him out of this. But I won't. My first ob-
ligation is to Boots and Kick, and if Mick can come to
the rescue, then I'm going to involve him.

Pike put down the pen and studied the words he'd just written.
He ran his hand through his thinning hair, and pulled the wire-rim
glasses from his face. Sever was at the Doubletree. He knew that. With
his stocking cap on and his dark sunglasses, Pike had taken several ex-
cursions into the real world. Even back to the condo. He had passed
Sever by the dock just yesterday, unobtrusive, undistinguished. Invisible. No one paid him any attention. It couldn't last forever, but for a
brief time it was a blessing.

As if I were invisible, you pass right by my world.
I try to make you notice me, like a flag that flies unfurled.
But you walk by, your head up, a look that's in your eyes,
and I stand there unnoticed, a man in thin disguise.

It was funny how the words to some of his biggest hits came
back to haunt him. In the song "Disguise" he was devastated that he
went unnoticed. Now he was elated that the disguise worked. Maybe
he could pull it off for the rest of his life. Take Bridgette and Kyle to
Costa Rica, and forget he'd ever had a career.

Somewhere, sometime, somehow it would catch up with him. It
would. He'd be having coffee in a restaurant in Costa Rica, and
someone would walk in and say "Oh, my God!" and the word would
hit the street, and Shinn would hear about it instantly because the son
of a bitch knew everything. He reminded Pike of a fly, with multiple
lenses in his eyes. The man could see everything. You never knew who
was watching you and reporting back to Shinn. Someone would rat

him out, and the simple life in Costa Rica, or wherever the hell he decided to live, would be blown.

Call Sever. Lay it all out. If he didn't want a piece of it, he could hang up and walk away. There was no one else to trust. Rusty was gone, and even Rusty was suspect in the end. He'd been a friend, a lover, and still Pike couldn't totally believe in him. Maybe Bridgette. He had to have faith in someone. He'd called Sever and left a brief, abbreviated message. Now it was time to give him some detail. Hell, he couldn't just hide forever. It was time to take some action. Lives were at stake.

He thought about that for a moment. Real lives were at stake. People had been killed because of him. Jesus! Rusty and Larry Spinnatti. Shinn would stop at nothing. He closed his eyes.

Dear God, I don't believe. I've never really considered an omnipotent being. But if you are real, if you are all knowing, all seeing, all forgiving, please spare my wife and child.

Did God approve of gays? Did God believe in protecting innocent women and children? He could only hope. He could only pray, and call Sever.

Pike picked up the pen and started writing.

> If God helps those who help themselves, then it's time I start making plans. It's time I start putting together a plan to save and protect the people who are dear to me. My sister, Marie, my nephew, Jonathon. My wife, Bridgette, and my son, Kyle.

He pulled the thick yellow-page directory from a drawer in the kitchen and thumbed through the hotel section. Hotels. Doubletree.

Pike dialed the number, finally taking some action. Finally trusting someone to give him advice. His support group was down to one, and he prayed. A man who didn't believe in God, prayed that this one person would make all the difference.

CHAPTER FIFTY-ONE

Sever called the hotel just before he grabbed a taxi. They connected him to his messages, and he hoped there wasn't one from Ginny telling him that she and Biddle were moving in together, but then he felt like he was back in school. Jealousy had never suited him well.

"Mick, this is Brady White. I've got an idea I wanted to run by you. Come on down to the boat."

That was it. The only message.

Sever had been somewhat leery about showing up on the dock where they'd found Charles Strict's body. There was no question that Ray Haver would be there, and of course he'd harken back to his idea about patterns. Sever did seem to show up at the worst times. Call it reporters' instinct. Call it sticking his nose in other people's business, but he was always there. He'd always felt it was a good thing, but with the Miami homicide division watching him, now he wasn't so sure.

When the cab driver let him off, he walked around to the rear of the hotel. Uniformed officers were still working the scene, along with two divers garbed in black scuba gear who were searching the calm waters in front of the marina.

Sever walked up to a policeman who was manning the temporary ropes that surrounded the area.

"Hi, I'm Mick Sever. I have some information for Detective Haver."

Haver saw him, and immediately broke off a conversation with a young woman and strode with purpose over to Sever.

"Well, I wouldn't have expected any less. You showing up. This Strict character, he's the one who set up the appointment this morning?"

"The same." Five seagulls hovered overhead, squealling, apparently waiting for the gathering crowd of people to throw them some food.

"Damn. It's a pattern, Sever. Whether you know it or not, you're involved."

Sever looked the crime scene over, failing to see the body of Charles Strict.

As if anticipating his question, Haver followed his gaze. "We had the body removed."

"All right, detective. Maybe I am involved. Charles Strict called, and told me to meet him down here at 5:30 A.M. I showed up, and somebody tried to kill me. I visited his office just about an hour ago and he wasn't there."

"I have a pretty good idea where he was."

Sever frowned and pushed his hair off his forehead. His life was in danger, and all this cop could do was make smart-ass remarks. "The point is, I sincerely believe that Lou Frey and Charles Strict are involved. I was out here this morning for one reason. Charles Strict."

Haver took a deep breath. "Well, I certainly can't ask him any questions."

"Then ask *him*." Sever pointed to Lou Frey and Ed Komack as they walked up to a uniformed officer. "That's Lou Frey."

Haver looked, then walked away from Sever and approached the attorney. Sever would have given anything to listen to the conversation, but he held back. Ginny should have heard about this by now, so where was she? Maybe she was occupied. He glanced around for a pay phone, but there wasn't one. Some day he'd break down and join the cell phone generation. It seemed more and more like a time that had come.

"Mick." The voice broke into his thoughts. "There's a lot you don't understand. I'm asking you to leave this alone. If you don't, more people are going to get killed. People that I'm very close to." Ed Komack looked up at him, fear in his eyes.

"Who?"

"Gideon, Bridgette, and Kyle."

"You know?"

"Yeah."

"The diaries we took from the condo — he kept referring to Boots and Kick. But what about the mention of an accident? Do I get an answer? Or are you part of this? Are you working for Shinn?"

"Leave it alone, man. I'm asking you. Please." Komack spun around and walked away, disappearing into the growing crowd of people who were straining at the ropes, trying to make some sense of it all.

He was on the marina side of the ropes, so he walked down to the *Old Man and the Sea*.

"Brady?"

No answer.

"Brady, it's Mick Sever."

Still no answer.

Sever walked up the plank to the deck. He studied the busy scene by the hotel, watching the divers once again go into the water. Maybe they were looking for a weapon.

"Brady?"

Nothing.

Sever walked down the stairs, reaching the bottom where there were two staterooms and a head. Head. It still amused him. John — head, restroom, bathroom — but there was no bath. He did see a shower stall in one of the staterooms. Small but efficient, the rooms were designed with wood paneling, and each one had a queen-sized bed that took up two thirds of the room itself. He chose the one on the left and walked in, all the time expecting the white-haired gentleman to suddenly appear and ask what he was doing.

He opened a closet and saw the neatly hung clothes. On the far end of the clothing rod was a tuxedo. Brady White, ready for any occasion.

Except for clothing, the closet was empty. Sever was surprised. The limited storage space on any boat was usually packed with all sorts of things.

He walked into the second state room and glanced around, admiring a picture on the wall. A splash of red, with feathering pastels of pink, orange, and blue spreading to the edges. Sever inspected it close up. Gideon Pike. Brady had an original.

He studied the room with renewed interest, wanting to open drawers, and see what made this man tick. For no reason he could think of, he leaned down and looked under the bed.

There it was. No covering, no case. A rifle with what looked like a walnut stock.

Sever shuddered. He stood up, his eyes darting around the small room. It was then he heard the footsteps on the deck and froze.

CHAPTER FIFTY-TWO

"It's him, boss. He came out to grab a newspaper up in the yard. Got a stocking cap and sun glasses on, but it's him."

Shinn let out a sigh. "Good work, Sam. You've got our boy."

"Now what do I do with him?"

"Wait. I think the police may want to know about this. After all, Pike is a suspect in a couple of murders."

"Yeah, there's that."

"Stay there. You've got Harry with you, so you guys just watch the place. Make sure Pike doesn't go anywhere. And Sam —"

"Yeah, boss?"

"Be careful. He may have a rifle."

Sam laughed, and the line went dead.

Shinn punched in another number. "Take down this address. 1209 Villa Avenue."

"There's no mistake?"

"None. We know where he is."

"Who else?"

"Bridgette and the kid. Kyle."

"I'll go. I'll just tell the brass it was an anonymous tip. But you're sure you don't care how it plays out?"

"It works either way. I'd prefer to be done with it, but you work it out however you have to."

"I'm on it."

Shinn hung up, and made a final call.

"Yeah."

"We know where Pike is." He recited the address.

"And you need everyone to be there, right?"

"I do. Everyone. Sever and his ex. Can you arrange it?

"I think so."

"You get paid enough to make it happen." Shinn frowned, thinking of the money he paid for favors. Favors and results. This time he'd better see results. "Call me. You let me know if you can get them there."

"Where are you going to be?"

"Platinum, the basement office probably. Call me."

Shinn put the phone in its cradle, and studied the sparkling water from his home-office view. A couple of sailboats dotted the blue bay, and he could faintly hear the gardener running his mower over the well-manicured lawn. Life could be good. And it was about to become better. His father would finally be off his back. He would prove to his father that all the trust he'd given him had been well placed. Maybe his father would finally treat him with respect, just as he expected — demanded — it from his son, and Jimmy could control the situation hands-on. And if it all worked out according to plan, there would be no more threats about going public with the blackmail. He wouldn't have to play his trump card.

He rose from the white desk and walked to the wine refrigerator, hidden behind wall panels under a bookshelf. He opened the door and pulled out a bottle of white. Perfectly chilled. He knew nothing of wines, but there was a wine cellar in the basement where Pike had collected over 2,000 bottles, and it seemed a shame to waste all of Gideon's expensive treasures. Now, it seemed even more appropriate to have a glass and toast the piano player.

To Gideon, who is about to be rediscovered. To Gideon. Without him, none of this would be possible.

Shinn twisted in a corkscrew and popped the cork, pouring the fruity beverage into a wineglass. He took a sip, swilling it around in his mouth. What the hell did he know. He tilted the glass and drained it, wondering what the hell people got so excited about.

He picked up the keys to the Lexus and walked to the garage, starting up the quiet engine and opening the garage door with the push of a button. He glided out onto the tiled driveway and headed toward the island gate. Time to play nightclub owner, maybe buy a couple drinks for some regulars, flirt with some of the new girls, and make it with one of them in the back room.

Life was good. *To Gideon Pike, who had a fabulous career. To Gideon, who couldn't hold onto it. And most of all, to the man who took it all away.*

Shinn waved at the gatekeeper.

"Evening, Mr. Shinn, sir."

There was respect. The poor fucker understood the stations in life. He realized his was the bottom of the rung. A pathetic loser. Shinn couldn't help but be reminded that his own father treated *him* like the gatekeeper. That was all going to change. Things were about to turn around.

He accelerated onto the causeway. Around the Mercedes, on the ass of the lumbering Bentley, in between the Mustang and Pontiac GTO, then back into the right lane. Life was good. Damn.

CHAPTER FIFTY-THREE

Footsteps on the stairs and nowhere to hide. Sever stood still, waiting.

"What the hell?" Ginny grabbed the railing. "God, Sever, you scared the hell out of me."

"I wasn't exactly expecting you."

"What are you doing here? Is Brady here?"

"No. I don't know where he is. You saw the commotion up there?"

Ginny nodded. "We're in this so deep."

"I think we're just in the way. They've been trying to get Gideon to sign over the contract on his recording rights, and they've threatened him by killing Rusty and Spinatti. We just came along at the wrong time."

"We came along at the same time Gideon decided to go public with the blackmailing. And we still have no idea why he's being blackmailed."

Ginny sat on the edge of the bed.

"It had something to do with the death of a dancer at Platinum. I get the impression that Gideon may have had something to do with it."

"Gideon killed this girl?"

"Maybe. Remember the reference in the diary? He keeps blaming an accident for his troubles. I've been thinking about it and this could be the accident. It happened in the parking lot. She was hit by a car, and apparently no one has ever been convicted."

"Wow. Hiding a killing for three years. And maybe Shinn has the proof that could tie Gideon to the killing?"

"But now they've found out he's got a wife and kid. April told Shinn. So they've got *that* to hang over his head." Sever looked back up the stairway, wondering where Brady was and when he'd be back. "With those kinds of threats, they've been taking his assets one by one."

"I hope you're wrong, but if you're not we're just in the way. And if we get in their way —" She trailed off. "So you were waiting for Brady?"

Sever hesitated. There could be a number of excuses for the rifle. But it was here, right under the bed she was sitting on. "Gin, I want you to look under the bed. Don't touch anything, just look."

She slowly stood up. "This is nothing gross is it? A dead animal?"

"Just look."

She knelt down. "Oh, my God." She stayed there, hypnotized by the weapon. "Is it the same one?"

"I have no clue."

"Brady? Not Brady." She stood up, brushing the knees of her tight jeans. "Do we tell Detective Haver?"

"What? That a man has a rifle on his own boat? I don't think we're there yet. I think we talk to Brady first."

"If he tried to kill you this morning, you may not want to talk to him."

"There's something else." He pointed to the painting on the wall.

She studied it for a moment. "It doesn't prove anything. He has good taste in art."

Sever took her by the arm. "Why would he have an original Pike painting? None of it makes sense, but I think it's time we get off this boat." They walked up the steps to the deck. There was no sign of Brady, and down the pier they could see one of the police cars driving off. The crowd had dispersed.

"What were you doing on Brady's boat?" Sever stopped and stared at Ginny.

"Looking for you." She looked like a sad puppy dog. "I lost you this morning, and —"

"I thought you had better things to do."

"Well," she stretched out the word, "I'll just say it's been interesting. Are you upset?"

Sever thought about it for several seconds. "Yeah. Sure I'm upset. You and Biddle, but on the other hand I'm not sure about what. What you do with your life is up to you."

"Always has been."

Sever was silent.

"I told you, Mick. I will never go through with you what we went through before. Never. Too much grief. This, the way *this* is, it's a lot easier."

He didn't understand what *this* was, and he didn't want to.

They walked the pier to the hotel, up the steps into the condo lobby.

"I'm going to check the phone for messages. I really need to talk with Brady." Sever headed for the hotel side of the lobby.

"Yeah. I'll see you later?" She gave him a questioning look.

Sever nodded, not knowing what to say.

He took the elevator up to the room, slipped the card into the door and walked in. The green light was blinking.

Message one: "Mick, it's Brady. I made a little trip to a hangout of yours. Platinum. Did a little talking, bought a couple of girls drinks, and I think I've solved the Gideon Pike puzzle. I got Bridgette's maiden name. It's Stockhardt." He chuckled, obviously amused at his cleverness. "I checked with information and sure enough, there's someone with that name at 1209 Villa Avenue in Coconut Grove. The only one in the book."

Sever looked out the window, seeing the shimmering water by the marina. He should have thought of that himself. But then again, he wasn't exactly welcome in Platinum.

Message two: "Mick, it's Gideon."

A long pause, and Sever was glad because it took him a couple of seconds to catch his breath. Gideon,

"I need some help, friend. You know what's going on, but as Paul Harvey would say, *you don't know the rest of the story*. First of all, I didn't kill Larry Spinatti. It may be my rifle that killed him, but I didn't do it. Second of all, you may not know it, but I'm married. To a woman, Mick. It's all very strange, even to me, but I've got a son, too. It's a strange relationship. This woman, she's different than anyone I've ever been with. Someday when we've had a couple of drinks, I'll try to explain it. Okay? Who'd believe it? Me, a dad." There was silence on the line.

"I've got some problems that I think maybe you can help me with. Hell, I don't know what you can do, but you've got a pretty good head on your shoulders. Mick, going back a few years, I may have accidentally —" Again he was quiet. Sever could hear Pike's breath catch in his throat. "I may have killed someone. I was drunk, Mick. Rusty and I — you remember Rusty — Rusty and I had been drinking pretty heavily at this club called Platinum, and when we left I guess I got behind the wheel of that Jag I used to own, remember, and — Mick, I need to talk to you.

"I'd rather not tell you where I am, but I'll call back maybe tonight. Can you be in about seven? Got to talk to you, man. Got to. See, Jimmy Shinn has been trying to use this against me. And, I think he had Rusty killed, and Spinatti too. Shit, I'm in so fucking deep, Mick, it's about ready to drown me. Listen, man, I remember the last time you were there for me. You saved my life and it's probably not fair to ask you to do it again, but this time it's more than me. If Shinn finds out where I am, he'll come after my wife and son. He wants everything I have, and I can't let him take them."

He stopped. There was a radio playing in the background and Sever could make out a commercial for a beach-side restaurant. There was a good thirty seconds of silence. Then Pike's voice was back.

"I thought I saw someone I know on the sidewalk outside my house." Sever heard Pike's heavy breathing. "Big guy, named Sam. Just for a second. I'm watching out the kitchen window. He works for

Shinn. Have they found me, Mick? Do they know where I am? Because Bridgette and Kyle are here too. I'll call you back, man. I may
have to make some new plans." The line went dead.

Sever didn't know if Shinn had the address or not, but Sever did.
It was time to visit Gideon Pike and have a sit-down meeting. It was
time to get to the bottom of this story.

CHAPTER FIFTY-FOUR

In the sixties and seventies, you didn't hang with musicians unless you drank copious amounts of alcohol and did drugs. That's what hanging was all about. And wild sex. Jesus, there had been some moments. Powders and pills, colored liquids, and long shiny needles filled with God knows what. Crazy, mind-altering chemicals soaked into sugar cubes, wrapped in cigarette paper, or baked into brownies. It was all about the next high. It was all about working a crowd into a frenzy until they were on their feet, screaming and rushing the stage, then trying to top that spectacular sensation with drugs, booze, and women. And it was going from one high to the next, until they all blurred together into an orgy of excess. But once in awhile, the excess was meant to be a final escape.

Sever half remembered the party. It was at some movie star's mansion in Beverly Hills and he'd been surrounded by musicians from two or three bands, a handful of porn stars and strippers with gigantic artificial tits. The host was passing out silver spoons and guiding guests to the dining room table where you could choose from grape LSD punch; bowls of purple, red, and green tablets; or lines of pure white cocaine.

The guitar player for Rosemary's Baby saw human-sized black widow spiders and ran, crashing through a large picture window and slicing through every blood vessel and nerve in his right hand. Two teenaged girls who had come along with the band, Rugged, drank

Jim Beam from a bottle, had their clothes ripped off, and in a drunken comatose state were busy pulling a train for any interested party guests.

Gideon Pike sat in a corner, drinking vodka, and nursing a bad case of depression. Sever tried to talk to him but the piano player remained silent, watching the debauchery around him.

An hour later Sever couldn't find him, and he'd been taught that you always left with the one who brought you. Sometimes he followed that rule. Searching through the mansion, he stumbled on orgies of all sexes, and passed-out party goers, who paid no attention to his intrusion. In his own altered state, he was worried for his friend. He'd been in a foul mood, and Sever was concerned about what he might do. Finally, in a third-floor room he found Pike. The singer was sprawled out on a canopied bed, his skin cold and clammy to the touch. A handful of pills were still clasped in his fist, and his breathing was shallow.

Sever wasn't at his most coherent, but he remembered shaking Pike, trying to get a response. When there was none, he picked him up, wrapped his arms around his waist and squeezed. Pike gagged, then vomited all over the lamb's wool comforter. The doctor who later pumped his stomach told Sever that if he hadn't caused the singer to vomit, he would have died in a matter of minutes. And that was his desire. To end the pressure and the pain of his demanding life and lifestyle. Sever had taken away that opportunity, and although Pike thanked him repeatedly, he asked that he keep that deep, dark secret from everyone. He'd wanted to die that night with no help from anyone. But Sever had saved his life.

Now, Sever had heard the message. Gideon Pike wanted to *live*. And this time, he was asking for help.

CHAPTER FIFTY-FIVE

There was no time to rent a car. A taxi would have to do. The door-man waved the cab to the curb, and Mick got in.

"Mick!"

He looked out from the backseat. Brady was power walking, surprisingly fast for a man his age.

"Did you get my message?"

Sever stepped out, the driver glancing back at him. "Yeah. I'm going there now."

"How about if I ride along?"

Sever hesitated. "I think this may be something I want to do on my own."

"I think you need someone on this trip."

"All right."

Brady walked to the far side of the cab and stepped inside.

"But you've got to answer one question."

"I've got one for you too. Where is Ginny?"

"I don't know. But this is something I have to do without her."

Sever gave the driver the address, and he pulled out onto the street.

"Brady, I came down to the boat."

"Yeah. I told you. I went to Platinum. What a place. Jesus, Jimmy Shinn's pussy palace."

"I looked for you."

"You said that."

"No. I said I went to the boat. Now I'm telling you I scoured the boat. I saw you had an original Gideon Pike painting."

White looked puzzled. "Yeah. In the bedroom. I was on the *Hit King* for a party about a year ago, and I told Spinatti I liked it. The next day he walked over and gave it to me. Told me that Pike liked to give people his paintings."

Sever looked out the window, watching the people passing by. Weathered old men and women, their skin dark and creased from the sun, some of them bent over carrying lunch pails. Others in loose cotton pants and shirts, balding or gray-haired immigrants, looking out of place in the fun and sun capital of the United States. This was their Miami too.

It wasn't just the beautiful South Beach people, but the working class. The people who scraped by to make ends meet, even in this electric city full of the high life.

"Brady. There's a rifle under your bed."

Brady squinted in the afternoon sun. He looked at Sever, then smiled and looked away, at the same people Sever had studied a moment ago.

"And?"

"There's a rifle under your bed."

"Yes, there is."

"Do you want to tell me about it?"

"I have half a mind to tell the driver to let me out."

"What the hell is the rifle doing under your bed?"

"Are you accusing me of something?"

"Why the hell would you have a rifle under your bed?"

"Not that I owe you an explanation —"

"But?"

"Pirates."

"Pirates?" Sever frowned.

"Pirates. Don't tell me you're that naïve. You get ten miles out on a boat like mine and there are pirates who would just as soon shoot you and take your boat as spit at you."

"Pirates."

Brady looked out the window. "If this is an issue with you, let me out. If not, I think you could use some help. You don't know what you're going to run in to when you get to Pike's place."

"All right. It's not an issue. You can't blame me for asking. Jesus, pirates."

"Pirates."

"Have you actually seen any?"

"They tried to board one time, Mick. I fired a couple of shots, and they took off."

Sever lapsed into silence, looking out of the window. The old man had balls.

Four boys played stickball in front of a block of crumbling white stucco tenements.

On the corner a white-haired man sold meat on a stick from a portable wagon grill, the pungent odor of grilled pork drifting through the taxi's open windows. Sever thought back to South Beach, with it's J-Lo and Mark Magraths, it's Nicky Beaches, Mangos, News Cafés, and topless sun worshipers. Miami was a constantly changing panorama of fascinating lifestyles and scenery.

"Gideon called."

"You talked to him?"

"No. Answering machine. He hung up half way through the call. He thought he saw one of Shinn's goons outside his house."

"Oh, shit. That's why you're in such a rush?"

"Yeah."

"And if Shinn's boys are there, just what are you and I going to do?"

"Well, I haven't thought that far ahead."

Brady grinned, the lines around his eyes crinkling. "When I had the fishing business, we'd lay out a day's ration of food, water, beer, and mixed drinks. We'd have several different rods and reels and a variety of bait, depending on what we were fishing for that day. When our customer got on board —"

Sever smiled. "Yeah, yeah. I know. I don't plan. Life for me seems to be live for the moment."

"We could be in for one hell of a moment."

The cab driver turned to them. "We're on Villa Avenue."

"Let us off a block away." Sever reached in his pocket for cash. "We're about to find out, Brady. We're about to find out."

CHAPTER FIFTY-SIX

Pike looked out the window. It could have been anyone. Anyone 350 pounds, with a marine-style haircut, and an ill-fitting sport coat. Could have been anyone.

Bridgette was in the back bedroom, playing some computer game with Kyle. The Dodge wagon was in the garage. A blue Dodge wagon from six or seven years ago. At the time it seemed like the ideal disguise. Now he'd settle for a powerful Jag or Corvette. Something he could climb into and speed away. Sam. Damn.

Pike walked to the kitchen cupboard and pulled out a pair of binoculars. He scanned the street. The houses were stucco and wood, the yards dotted with small palms and palmetto shrubs. Colorful crotons and lush, thick-leafed rubber trees were scattered in the mix. Villa Avenue wasn't a main road and the traffic was light. He wasn't sure what vehicle to look for. The only one he knew for sure was Shinn's olive-green Lexus convertible. There was little chance Jimmy Shinn would show up when he had people like Sam to do his dirty work. Sam, and, oh shit, was that Harry? He swung the glasses back again, double-checking, down to the corner where the stop sign was. A twenty-foot tall banyan tree hovered over the street, and the Korean man standing in its shadows looked for all the world like Harry Coy, one of Jimmy Shinn's boys.

So now there were two. Maybe more. Pike felt a cold chill pass through him. No one else knew where he was. They could walk right in and kill him. They could kidnap Bridgette and Kyle. Hell, they could do whatever they wanted, and no one would ever know.

He went to the master bedroom. Pike had owned houses with master bedrooms as big as this house, but those days were gone. He opened a dresser drawer and pulled out a nickel-plated revolver. He knew it was loaded. Six shots.

He'd never fired it. He wasn't sure he could hold it steady enough to hit anything, even with two hands, but it felt good. Good, safe, and reliable.

"Gideon?"

He jumped.

"Gideon?"

"Jesus. Don't sneak up on me like that."

"What in God's name are you doing with a gun?"

"Bridgette, go back with Kyle. There are some men outside —"

She squinted her eyes, a puzzling look on her face. "Men?" Then she shuddered. "Oh, my God. They found us." She took a deep breath and he saw the tears form in her eyes. Those deep green, emerald-pool eyes. He shuddered. This beautiful woman was in jeopardy because of his selfish desires.

"Go. Kyle needs you."

"Call someone. Call the police. We'll deal with whatever happens. It's better than getting hurt, or killed."

"Bridgette, please."

She stood there, a pleading look on her face. Her hair pulled back, no makeup, jeans, and a sweatshirt, it was hard for Gideon to remember she'd stripped for a living. And maybe that was the safest thing she could have done. Pike certainly hadn't provided much of a life for her, and for Kyle. Boots and Kick. They were in danger, and it was all because of him.

He motioned to her and she spun around and walked back down the hallway. He could hear Kyle in the bedroom, the door open, saying "I want to see Daddy. Let me see Daddy." There was nothing more important in the world than that little boy.

Pike scanned the street again, his eyes lingering on the corner. No one was there. Not Sam, not Harry. No telling where they were, but it was a good bet they were getting closer.

He sat in a plastic kitchen chair, facing the doorway, the gun in his right hand resting in his lap. There was nothing else to do but wait.

CHAPTER FIFTY-SEVEN

"You have no plan."

"I have no plan. Brady, we need to assess the situation. If we can just walk up to the house —"

"We probably shouldn't. It would be too easy."

He'd never felt so out of sync. Pike had said that Sam was outside the house, and Sever felt fairly certain the big man was armed. The two Korean henchmen that worked for Shinn had guns under their sport coats so it was probable that Sam had one too. And what the hell were he and Brady White going to do to an armed 350-pound gorilla. And then it hit him again. It had been easy to accept what Brady White said, but the truth was that Brady had a rifle under the bed. There was absolutely no guarantee that Brady wasn't involved with Shinn. Sever was on his own, and he didn't like the odds.

1201 Villa Avenue. The house was almost hidden by the trees and brush that grew in front. Wild bushes and trees that had never been trimmed back.

1203 Villa Avenue. The path that led from the sidewalk to the front door was made of crushed shells.

1205 Villa Avenue. Sever looked up and down the street, wondering where the enemy was. For all he knew they could have been to the house and gone. A mint green Volkswagen Beetle drove by with license plates from Ohio. He hesitated, noticing the alley that ran between 1205 and 1207. If they approached from the rear, it might be safer.

He gazed up the stone alley, then back at the street. A police cruiser drove slowly up the street. Sever wanted to run after it, asking for assistance. He watched as it turned the corner in the next block and headed right on the cross street.

"Let's take the back alley."

Brady frowned. "We get back in there and anything can happen. Out here, it's in the open."

"Fine. You stay out front." Brady was a wild card. Sever wasn't sure whether it was better to have the old man with him, or head off on his own.

"No, I'll stay with you. I'm too old to be playing the Lone Ranger."

They walked back to the alley, along the tall wooden fence that hid 1207 Villa Avenue. The alley crossed a back street, running behind the homes. Scrub shrubs grew four- and five-feet high on either side of the drive and Sever and Brady walked slowly, seeing 1209 just beyond the shrubbery.

Now there was a break in the shrubs and Sever could see the road between 1207 and 1209. He paused, wondering what to do next. A Chevy pickup truck went barreling down the street, its muffler either missing or badly cracked. The loud roar echoed through the neighborhood for several seconds. Sever nodded at Brady, and they started toward the house.

He glanced again at the street, and a police cruiser was easing up the street. Two in a matter of a minute. Brady hadn't seemed to notice.

The rear of the house featured a small wooden screened-in porch. There was no sign of any activity, no one sitting on the porch or out in the back tending the sparse flower garden. It was a nondescript house, finished with stucco and an orange tiled roof. No pool, no wet bar outside, just a middle-class home.

"Mick," Brady was looking beside the house, out at the street.

"There's a cop car again." The third one in less than a minute and a half. Maybe the same one.

"So maybe we should just go out to the street and stop one."

"I'd agree," the old man said, "except that according to you and everyone involved, your friend doesn't want to be found. Especially by the law."

"Better found than dead."

Brady nodded, looking him in the eyes. "I've got something that might interest you."

Slowly kneeling down, he motioned to Sever to do the same. Now they were behind shrubs. No one could see. Brady reached into his pocket, keeping his eyes locked on Sever's.

He slowly pulled out his hand, a small derringer clutched in his grasp. "Surprise. The rifle isn't the only weapon I've got, Mick." He smiled.

CHAPTER FIFTY-EIGHT

He picked up the receiver. No dial tone. That had never happened before. He pushed the button and got no response. Fuck it. He still had two cell phones. Call the cops. Save the family. If it was that easy, he'd have done it years ago.

Maybe the phone thing was just a psychological ploy to put him on edge. Something straight out of a '60s movie. Another cop car drove by. God, but he wanted to run out and flag it down. Tell them he was afraid for his entire family, but he couldn't do it. Couldn't trust anyone.

Pike could hear Kyle in the back room, laughing with his mother, playing a game, while Bridgette kept a brave face. She had to be scared to death. Bridgette knew what Jimmy Shinn could do.

He leaped from the chair when he heard the crash. Scared the hell out of him. A shattering sound of broken glass. He dashed into the living room, stopping short of the jagged pieces of pane glass window that were strewn over the carpet. A rock the size of his fist was lying in the center of the room, and what remained of the picture window was cracked with spider web veins reaching into all corners.

Pike froze for a moment, not believing what he saw. It was the middle of the day, and they were attacking the house. He held the re-volver in front of him, and like a zombie walked to the window.

There was no one outside. He kept the revolver pointed toward the window, and stepped back.

The second crash came from the window down the hall. Pike hesitated. They were messing with him, trying to throw him off. He quietly stepped to the hall and froze.

"Hi, Gideon."

It was Harry, Shinn's Asian goon. His Colt .38 was pointing at Gideon's stomach.

"There isn't a doubt that I'll pull this trigger. Not a doubt. I think there's a doubt about you. Ever shoot someone, Gideon?"

"What do you want?"

"Oh, it's too late for that. Jimmy wanted you to sign a contract. Jimmy wanted you to keep your mouth shut. You refused on both counts. Too late. That's over. Put the revolver down."

Pike laid the gun on the floor and stepped back. Harry picked up the revolver, studied it for a second then shoved it into the waistband of his pants.

Pike was shaking. The voices from the bedroom drifted down the hall.

Harry glanced at the closed door. "Do you want them to be safe, Gideon? Huh? Do you care if Bridgette and the kid are safe? Because if you do what I tell you, I'll guarantee that nothing will happen to them." The gunman smiled, trying for a reassuring look.

Pike was not reassured. Not in the least.

"Turn around and move." Pike walked to the kitchen, seeing the police car parked across the street, several houses down. "Sit down and keep quiet." Harry walked to the window, keeping the Colt trained on Pike. "See that cop car out there?"

Pike nodded.

Harry pulled out Gideon's revolver with his other hand. He flipped open the cylinder, spun it once then closed it. He pointed the barrel at the window and fired two shots, the explosions deafening in the small kitchen.

"Jesus! What the hell are you doing. What the hell?"

"Gideon?" Bridgette shouted.

"Stay in the room, please. Stay in the room!" Pike was screaming.

"Easy, Gideon. Easy. We're just provoking the cops."

"And they'll start shooting back. What the hell are you —"

Harry turned and fired again, the revolver sounding like thunder.

Pike sat with his mouth open wide. His ears were ringing and buzzing at the same time. He started to get up.

"No, no. You stay right there."

Pike sat back down, seeing the second squad car pulling up, its lights flashing. How long had they known he was there? He couldn't see any officers. They were probably behind the cars or coming in the back.

"Gideon Pike!" The amplified voice boomed across the street. "We know you're in there."

Harry looked at him and smiled. "No shit. You can't put anything over on these Miami cops."

"Throw your gun out and come out, Gideon."

Harry fired one more shot through the window.

"Daddy. Daddy." Kyle was sobbing in the bedroom, his voice shaking with fear.

"Shut the kid up. Seriously, tell him to shut the fuck up." Harry's eyes hardened, and he again pointed his pistol at Pike. As if on cue, Kyle was silent.

Pike could see just a small portion of the street. No one was out. No cars whizzed by. They had probably blocked off the street. They weren't talking anymore. Probably convinced that he was going to shoot it out. What was the purpose? What was the point? What was Harry trying to do? Get him killed? He closed his eyes and took a deep breath. That was it. They had to have a reason to kill him. He was a suspect in the shooting of Larry Spinatti, and now he was holed up in a house like one of those '30s gangsters, shooting it out with the cops. Only *he* wasn't doing the shooting. Still, it was his revolver.

"Stand up!" Harry motioned to him with the gun.

Pike slowly rose to his feet.

"Get over by the window. Now."

He stepped forward, just to the side of the window.

Pike heard the explosion and could swear he felt the heat from the bullet as it whizzed by, a million miles an hour, embedding itself in the refrigerator behind him.

Bridgette and Kyle. What the hell was he going to do with Bridgette and Kyle? A bullet could whip through the thin walls of this cheap house and cut them down in a second.

Pike screamed out, "Bridgette, get on the floor, under the bed. Now!"

Harry gave him a grim smile. "Don't worry about them. I told you, nothing will happen to Bridgette and the kid. Now you listen to me. You shot your boyfriend from your condo while he partied on the yacht. You tried to kill Mick Sever this morning, and succeeded in killing your lawyer's assistant."

"What?"

"Charlie somebody. It's not important."

"Oh, Jeeze. Charlie Strict? You killed him too?"

"They'll have the rifle by tomorrow, Gideon. With your fingerprints. Do you understand? And now you've fired, let's see, one, two, three, four, five shots at the police."

Pike sat back down, his head slumped, his chin resting on his chest. "What the hell have you done?"

"Pretty much made you dispensable."

"Why?" There was resignation in his voice.

"I told you, you refused to be a team player. Your salvation just isn't in the cards, Gideon."

"So what happens now?"

"I'm going to put this revolver in your hand."

Pike sighed. What the hell was he supposed to do? Shoot at the cops with the last bullet? Shoot Harry?"

"Then I'm going to put my hand around yours and we're going to pull the trigger."

"At who?"

"You."

Harry put the revolver in Pike's hand, and pressed the barrel into his temple.

"It will be easy, Gideon. You couldn't handle all of this. The pressure was just too much."

"God, no." He'd thought the pressure was too much once before. He'd tried to end it all with pills. Now, when the pressure was unbearable, he wanted to live. God, he wanted to live.

"God, yes. Take a deep breath, man."

The back door exploded like a cannon had been fired through it. Harry spun around, and watched Sever rounding the arched entry-way to the kitchen, a derringer in his hand.

There was one shot left in Pike's pistol. Harry raised the revolver and aimed squarely at Sever's head.

"Aahhhhh! Daddy! Daddy!" A bundle of three-foot energy came hurtling from the hallway into the kitchen as Kyle streaked into the room and leaped into his father's arms.

The crack of a gunshot from across the street reverberated off the surrounding houses and the bullet smashed through the window with a sickening thunk as it pierced flesh and bone.

CHAPTER FIFTY-NINE

The phone rang and rang and rang. Shinn stared at it, willing it to be picked up on the other end. Either Sam was occupied, or he chose not to answer it. He hung up and dialed again.

"Hello."

"Sam."

"Hey, boss."

"Tell me, what the hell is going on?"

"We got Harry in there fine. The cops are shooting it out right now."

"Either the cops get him, or Harry sets up the suicide. I want the fucker dead."

"It's too early to call it, boss."

The girl on the stage, Doreen the Machine, gyrated and pushed her pelvis at the leering men. Shinn had never seen her before. The turnover in this business was unbelievable. Almost every night there was a new selection of pussy.

"You call me when it's over."

"You'll be the first, I promise."

Shinn bought the three men at the bar a round. Three guys who paid a $15 cover to sit at the bar instead of staring at the snatch on stage deserved a free drink. It was the least he could do.

His cell phone rang. He stepped outside to answer it, away from the ear shattering music with the throbbing bass. The uniformed parking lot attendant nodded at him.

"Hello."

"Jimmy, how soon can we proceed with our plans? You need to get those contracts signed. We're talking millions of dollars here, son."

The old man refused to let up. "Give me an hour, Father. One hour. It should all be over by then."

"Jimmy," the tiny voice with the stilted English sounded almost cartoonish. "Make sure when it is done, it is done. We will have the grand prize, but there can't be any loose ends."

Shinn drew a deep breath, the humid Miami air filling his lungs. How long before he could be his own man? How long before Richard Shinn trusted him. Only after the old man died. "Yes, Father. Everything is in place."

"Call me."

His father mocked his business ventures, *then* deeply involved himself in them. Christ, the recording business alone was pulling in millions every year. Millions. Wasn't it time for his father to give it a fucking rest? Admit that Jimmy Shinn was a success, and could handle the affairs of the family.

"Don't I always call you?"

"Don't be insolent with me, Son. Call me."

Shinn folded the phone and shoved it into the holster on his belt. He turned and looked up at the pink block building with the eight-foot-high polished aluminum sign that said PLATINUM.

Underneath was the flashing red sign that screamed LIVE GIRLS 24 HOURS A DAY. He thought back to April. Gone. And maybe later on this afternoon, Bridgette. He thought about the girl who had been run over in the parking lot three years ago. Live girls, dead girls, it didn't seem to make any difference. You used people until they were no longer of any use, then, like his father had suggested, you make sure there are no loose ends.

CHAPTER SIXTY

The force of the bullet knocked him off the chair, plowing through his shoulder and out his upper back. Pike sprawled on the floor, looking up in bewilderment as his son lay crying next to him.

Sever pulled the trigger, the sharp blast surprising him from the tiny derringer. At this close range he'd missed. Harry raised his Colt, and Sever fired again. Only two shots, that's what Brady had said. This one had better do the trick. The gun jumped in his hand and a small, red spot appeared under Harry's left eye. The Korean man stood there for a moment, trying to comprehend what had happened, a bullet buried in his brain. Then he dropped his pistol, put a hand to his face and crumpled to the floor.

"Brady!" Sever called to the old man. He came in from the back, surveying the damage.

"You're a dangerous man, Mick Sever." He bent over Pike and examined the wound. "He's breathing, but not very well. I'll get the cops to call an ambulance."

Sever picked up the screaming boy, and headed toward the bedrooms. "Bridgette? Bridgette? It's Mick Sever. Everything is all right."

She came bursting out of he door, a wild look in her eyes. "Oh, Jesus am I glad to see you. Kyle, Kyle, Kyle. He ran from me —" She grabbed him and squeezed the boy to her, saying over and over again "Thank you God, thank you God, thank you God."

Sever heard Brady's voice, yelling to the police on the other side of the street. "Police? We've got two wounded men in here. We need an ambulance."

Sever walked back into the kitchen as a bullet screamed past him.

"Damn. Get down Brady."

The old man fell to the floor and crawled over to Sever. "Did they hear me?"

"I don't know how they couldn't." Sever raised up and shouted out the window. "Please, we need an ambulance."

There was no sound. An eerie silence permeated the neighborhood. No traffic, no birds, no children playing in sprinklers. The only sound Sever could hear was Kyle sniffling in his mother's arms somewhere in the rear of the house, and the rasping of Gideon's breath as he lay on the kitchen floor.

He crawled to Harry and picked up the Colt .38 where the man had dropped it. Someday he was going to have to take a firearms course. Rifles, derringers, pistols, it was all foreign to him. And he may have just killed a man. Probably should take some safety lessons so he didn't accidentally shoot himself.

"Mick," the old man was whispering now as if he felt the silence was something to be respected. "I swear I heard glass crunch down the hall. I saw a broken window down there on my way in."

Sever shoved Brady's derringer into his pocket and held on to the Colt. He got to his knees, crawling to the entrance to the hallway. He took a deep breath and eased his head out.

"Mick." Ray Haver stood in the corridor, holding his gun with two hands. "I am so glad to see you."

"Jesus. You scared the hell out of me. We need an ambulance. Gideon's been shot, and there's a guy who works for Jimmy Shinn who may or may not need medical attention." Sever stood up as Haver walked into the kitchen.

"Ah, Brady White. And where's Mrs. Sever?"

Sever ignored the question. "Did you hear me? We need to get an ambulance."

"Put the gun down on the table, Mick."

Sever laid Harry's Colt down.

"I told you, you're involved. You're always around when there's trouble. I'm truly sorry about this, Sever, but when there's a lot of gunplay, innocent people get hurt." Haver nodded his head and pointed the gun at Sever.

"What the hell are you thinking?"

Haver smiled. "That I probably would have liked you if I ever got to know you."

"Oh, shit. You work for Shinn. You son of a —"

Sever heard the explosion, and waited for the pain. Nothing. He saw the dark red splotch spread on Haver's starched white shirt just before the detective toppled over.

"Man's got to protect his family and friends, Mick." Gideon Pike lay face up, the spent revolver in his hand. He coughed and flecks of red drooled from his mouth.

Sever kneeled down. "You saved my life."

"We're even."

"Quiet. We'll get you out of here."

"Wait." He coughed again. "Two things, man." His voice was weak and shaky. "Shinn was going to tell the cops that I killed a girl in his parking lot about three years ago. I was drunk, never should have been driving, and I don't remember a damned thing about it. I'm sorry for it, Mick. They've used it against me every day of my life, and it's the sorriest thing I ever did. I was a coward, man. Should have confessed a long time ago." His breathing was ragged, congestion rattling in his chest. "Second thing, you tell Kyle that his dad loved him. A lot."

"Just keep quiet. We'll get an ambulance."

"Tell him, Mick. I may be a lot of things, but I love that kid. More than life."

CHAPTER SIXTY-ONE

He called Ginny's room on Brady's cell phone. No answer. Sever kept one hand on the steering wheel, one on the cell phone, breaking traffic laws left and right, whipping Pike's old blue Dodge wagon at breakneck speeds around sharp corners, through stop signs, and just now running through a Publix parking lot to avoid a light at the intersection.

Next he tried the cell number, keeping his eyes on the road the whole time. Punching in the numbers, he prayed that the *good* cops were on the scene back at Pike's house. He'd handed off the detectives' gun to Brady, and peeled out of the back alley, fully expecting a hail of gunfire.

Taking the cops by surprise, to Sever's amazement, he'd left without a shot being fired.

Sever kept a wary eye on the rearview mirror knowing some cop car was going to come screaming up his tail.

It rang twice and she picked up. "Mick!"

"Ginny, are you all right?" Sever winced as he pushed the station wagon through a yellow light.

"Listen to me. I was supposed to meet Tom here at his condo, and —"

"Ginny, I've got to tell you what happened."

"Mick! Listen. He's not here. But I think I found the rifle."

"*The* rifle?"

"It's on his bed, wrapped up in that blanket."

"Oh, Christ. Get the hell out of there. Now. Get —"

"Someone's just opened the door. I've got to go, Mick."

"Ginny?" No answer.

Oh, God, don't let Biddle do anything. Please. He thought back to the house. They'd called an ambulance using Brady's cell phone, and the old man had literally pushed him out the door.

"I can hold down the fort, Mick. You've got to see about Ginny. Go. Go!"

The ambulance was pulling in as he pulled out. He didn't want to leave, but there was no choice. Brady was in charge. And if Shinn was paying off the entire force, Brady, Bridgette, Kyle, and Gideon were all screwed.

Flying around a corner, Sever clenched his teeth as he narrowly missed hitting the curb. His hands squeezed the steering wheel, his knuckles white. Right now Ginny was the most important thing in his life.

It was then he heard the siren wailing, faint, then louder, all in a matter of seconds. Sever checked the rearview mirror. Nothing.

The high-pitched whine was closer, cutting through the sound of traffic and Sever saw cars pulling off to the right.

He kept going. By the time he explained this to the cops, Ginny could be dead.

Sever picked up speed as the rest of the traffic pulled to the curb. The siren was blaring now, the sound shooting through his ears. He spun around, and finally saw the vehicle.

The ambulance went screaming by him, lights flashing, and disappeared in the distance.

He breathed a deep sigh of relief. They could have been taking Gideon to the hospital. He *hoped* they were taking the piano man to the hospital.

He whizzed past houses. Sever slammed on the brakes to avoid hitting an old lady pushing a shopping cart across the street. The brakes squealed and the smell of burning rubber filled the car.

"Shit!" He didn't need to kill anyone else today.

* ★ ★

"You can't park that car there." The doorman waved his arms at him as he ran for the entrance. "You can't just leave that car and —"

"Keys are in it," Sever shouted. He sprinted for the building's glass entrance doors.

"Hey!" One of the guards stepped out from the small desk. "You can't go in there. This is a private —"

The sliding glass doors opened as a young man walked out with an Airedale on a leash. Sever ran through the doors as they closed and stepped into an elevator. The guard stood helplessly as the elevator doors slid shut. Sever pushed twenty-three, and let out a sigh.

He massaged his knee, studying the lights as they raced through the numbers of floors. God, let her be safe. 19, 20, 21, 22, 23.

The door slid open. He wished he had two more bullets for that derringer.

CHAPTER SIXTY-TWO

The phone's chirping scared him. He'd been waiting, concentrating, and then when it finally happened, it scared the crap out of him. Shinn pushed the talk button.

"Yeah?"

"Boss, it's Sam."

"All right. So how are things?"

"Not good."

"Not good meaning —?"

"Harry's dead. The detective's dead. And the last I heard, Pike was still alive."

Shinn was stunned. His father was going to be so pissed. "Fuck! Well, if Harry and Haver are dead, they won't talk. How the hell did this thing get so screwed up?"

"Sever."

"Sever messed it up?"

"He broke in, and everything went crazy."

"Where is he now?"

"Don't know. Pike had a blue Dodge wagon in the garage and Sever went peeling out in that."

"And his ex?"

"Never saw her."

"Biddle?"

"He never showed up either, boss."

"Sam, get over to Biddle's. If the girl is there, pick her up. I mean now." Shinn slammed the phone shut, and stared at the cold, gray wall. Father wasn't going to be happy. Not at all.

He dialed the second number.

"Hello."

"Where the hell is Mrs. Sever?"

"I've got her."

"Do you have any idea what has happened?"

"At first I couldn't locate her, so whatever happened went down without her. But she's here now, and I'll take care of it. What happened?"

"Biddle, I pay you to baby-sit Pike, and he skips. I've got to find out he's married from one of the fucking *dancers*. Then I ask you to manage the Severs. Mick Sever screwed up the entire Coconut Grove plan, and you don't even show up with his ex-wife. And now two of my men are dead."

Shinn was breathing hard. He could feel the heat in his face, and the more he talked, the hotter he got. "Harry's dead. Haver is dead. Sever walked away. Do you think you're doing your job? Do you?"

"Jesus, Jimmy. Harry and the cop?"

"What about your job? A simple baby-sitting job is all it was. Watch Pike, watch the Severs. You, Biddle, are a useless piece of shit. Swear to God. I am going to have to clean up this entire mess because you can't even wipe your own ass."

"Jimmy, I'm sorry. I can't be everywhere at the same time. And let's not forget what the rest of the job was. Is Spinatti still around? Didn't I take care of that?"

"Sever's still around, and he's busting my ass. And the last I heard was that Pike might be alive too. It seems to me you were asked to take care of those problems."

"I've got the wife. What do you want me to do with her?"

Shinn simmered for a moment. It was a sure bet that Sever was headed back to the Grand Condominiums. They'd have to use the Mrs. to get to Sever.

"Okay, I've already sent Sam over there and here's what you do. And damn it, Biddle, don't fuck this up."

CHAPTER SIXTY-THREE

His eyes wandered seventeen stories to the pool far below. He called her once more. Thank God for Brady's cell phone.

Nothing. If there was nothing wrong, she would answer.

Sever sprinted down the hall, breathing heavily as he reached the door.

Measuring one foot in front of the other, his knee throbbing, he walked the final fifteen feet. Ginny was on the other side of Biddle's condo and he couldn't let that go.

He knocked. As if he'd been waiting, Biddle opened the door.

"Mick. Good to see you."

He brushed by him, his eyes darting left, then right.

"Where is she?"

"You see, Jimmy thought you might be this way. All full of bluster and attitude. She's not here, Mick."

"Then where the fuck is she?"

Biddle smiled. "Don't get tough with me. I may be the only person who can put you in —"

Sever hit him in the stomach. The guy seemed to be in shape but it felt like his fist drove through to the spine. Biddle doubled over like a file folder, and heaved his guts on the floor.

"Where is she?"

Biddle gasped, trying to straighten up. "And what do you think this is going to do to help you —"

Sever hit him with a left cross. His fist caught the man's nose, snapping the cartilage as blood spurted out. Biddle hit the tile floor in the kitchen and his head bounced.

"Where is she?"

"Platinum." He mumbled, gingerly touching his broken nose, wincing at the sight of all the blood.

"Get up."

"You're going to hit me again."

Sever gazed at the broken man lying on the floor. "No, but I might kill you." He pulled the empty derringer out of his pocket and pointed it at Biddle.

"I'm getting up. I'm getting up."

Sever tossed him a dish towel, and Biddle pressed it to his nose, stemming the bleeding. They marched into the hallway.

"She'd better be all right, Biddle, because if there's one scratch on her — one scratch, I promise you I'll kill you. Do you believe me? Do you?"

CHAPTER SIXTY-FOUR

Sever weaved in and out of traffic like a NASCAR driver, getting the finger from pissed-off motorists.

"You tried to kill me this morning. It was you, wasn't it?"

Biddle was silent.

"I hate to go back on my word, Tom, but I may hit you again."

"Yeah. It was me."

"And Spinatti?"

"Yeah. Him too. Look, Sever," he sounded nasal, his busted nose filled with blood, "Shinn's got Ginny. So none of this is going to do you any good. There's nothing you're going to be able to do."

"Call him."

"Oh, he knows we're coming. He wants to talk to you both."

"Call him." Firm, controlled, Sever was impressed with his own outward demeanor. Inside he felt like a raging lunatic. He was here because of Ginny, and he wasn't going to leave until she was safe.

"All right." Biddle fumbled for his phone and punched in two numbers.

"Jimmy? Yeah." Sever listened, but couldn't make out the voice on the other end. "No, Jimmy. He's here."

Sever grabbed the phone from Biddle's hand. "Shinn, we'll be there in a couple of minutes. I swear to God if you've so much as touched her —"

"You'll what?" Shinn's voice was pitched high. It sounded like the man had a bad case of nerves. "I've got her, Mr. Sever. I don't think you're in much of a bargaining position."

"The cops are on their way." Sever's bluff sounded hollow.

"I'd know if they were. Trust me, I'd know. No, let's just calm down, Mr. Sever. We'll work this out when you get here. And Sever, no guns. No weapons. You try to be a hero, and you'll both end up dead." He hung up.

Sever hit the brakes, bouncing his passenger. "Get out of the way!" He yanked on the wheel, swerving to avoid a small delivery truck, then resumed his speed.

He stared out the window. "Do you know about the hit-and-run accident in the Platinum parking lot?"

Biddle's eyes opened wider. "What do you know?"

"That Shinn has been using that accident to blackmail Gideon."

"I don't know anything about that."

One hand on the wheel, Sever pushed the derringer into Biddle's side. "Biddle, I'd just as soon pull the trigger right now." He hoped the guy wouldn't call his bluff. Actually, he'd kill the man without any compunction, but there was the case of no more bullets.

"Okay. Damn. Chill a little." Biddle's eyes were open wide and perspiration dotted his face. "Shinn's been blackmailing him. Nobody else knows. Just Jimmy, Sam, me, and —" he screwed his face up, pressing the towel tighter to his nose. "Well, Rusty's not around any more."

"Rusty knew?"

"Rusty was with Pike in the car the night the girl was run over."

"Anybody else in the car?"

"I wasn't there."

"But you know what happened."

Sever pulled into Platinum's parking lot, spun the wheel, and shot into a handicapped parking spot in front. He saw the white outline of a wheelchair. Handicapped people had to see strippers too.

He thought about kicking Biddle a couple more times to qualify for the handicapped spot. He didn't. Instead he dragged the man out of the car.

They entered the club, the man staggering beside him. Biddle held the dish towel pressed tightly to his face. The doorman stepped back.

"Mr. Biddle. Are you okay?"

Biddle kept moving, now leading Sever toward the back. A thin, black beauty with tiny breasts squatted on stage, a beer bottle strategically placed just below her shaved crotch. Sever saw the crowd of men straining to get a better view.

"Through that door."

They walked down the concrete staircase, Biddle grasping the railing with his free hand.

The muffled sound of music and loud cheering filtered into the narrow hallway as they neared the open office door. Biddle stepped aside as Sever entered.

Jimmy Shinn sat behind the desk, chewing on an olive from the open jar in front of him. Massive Sam stood to the right, arms folded, looking like a commercial for the World Wrestling Federation. Remembering the boat crash just a couple of days ago, Sever memorized the face.

"Put your arms out." Shinn's voice was calm. He was back in control. "Sam, pat him down."

Sever felt the big guy's hands lightly skim down his tee shirt and jeans, paying special attention to his ankles and waist.

"Nothing."

"Good. That means you listen." He noticed Biddle and did a double take. "What happened to you?"

Sever spoke up. "Ran into a door. He probably should have that nose set."

Biddle stood silent.

"Mr. Sever, you've gotten involved where you shouldn't have. You've caused some problems, which, by the way, can be fixed. But, you've made things unnecessarily difficult, and I am not happy." He smiled, his teeth clenched. "Sam, what happens when I'm not happy?"

The gigantic man grinned. "Nobody is happy, Mr. Shinn. Nobody."

"Where is she, Shinn?"

"Sever, let me have my fun. After all, you screwed up a lot of plans. It's the least you can do for me." He pulled a pistol from his drawer and laid it on the desk. "Sam, bring in our friend."

Sever breathed easier. She was all right. Now he'd get to see her and decide for himself if she'd been harmed in any way. Sam walked out the door and except for the faint music, there was silence. Shinn spit a pit into his palm.

"Boss, I've got your guest." Sam walked in, and motioned for the person in the hall to follow.

Looking smaller and more diminutive than ever, Ed Komack stepped into the room.

CHAPTER SIXTY-FIVE

"I believe you know each other?" Shinn let his eyes wander between Sever and Komack, as if watching their reactions. "Mr. Komack has been in negotiations with me regarding taking over the partnership of PK Records should something happen to Mr. Pike. Something did happen to Mr. Pike today, although I understand he's still in critical condition. My guess is that he won't make it."

"Are you going to make sure of that?" Sever asked.

"Even if he does make it, he's in a lot of trouble. Killing his partner Rusty, killing Spinatti, killing Charlie Strict, and trying to take out a couple of squad cars just an hour ago."

Sever still couldn't figure it out. Komack as one of the bad guys. It didn't make sense. "Where's Ginny?"

"We'll get to that. Don't worry, Sever, it's all going to be one happy reunion."

Komack was strangely silent. Not one word from him.

"You see, Ed walked in at a bad time. He wanted to discuss some business just as Sam was bringing in your former wife."

Komack's face was pale. He trembled as he stood next to Sam.

"I'm afraid we weren't as gentle to your ex as we might have been, and Ed happened to see and hear some things that he probably shouldn't have. Do you want to tell them what you heard?" He nodded to Komack.

The man shook his head.

"Oh, come on. Tell them."

Sam put his hand on Komack's shoulder and squeezed.

"Okay, okay."

The big man let his pressure ease up.

"I heard that Gideon had been shot. That the detective, Ray Haver, was working for you, and he got shot. What else do you want me to say?"

"There was one more thing that came up in my conversation with Sam. I want you to tell Sever what it was. Now."

Komack grabbed the desk, supporting himself. Sever noticed the bruise on his cheek as if someone had backhanded him recently.

"No."

Sam reached over and slapped him. Then he slapped him again, kicking his legs out from under him as the small man toppled, his chin catching the metal desk. He ended up sprawled out on the floor, spitting red blood from a cut inside his mouth.

"Get up, you pathetic piece of shit."

Komack struggled to his feet.

"Tell them!"

Komack rubbed his jaw. "You told Sam that with Rusty gone, and with Gideon dead, no one would ever have to know what really happened the night the girl was killed in your parking lot."

"I did. I said that, not knowing you were hanging around outside the door. But what did happen that night?"

Komack's color was gone. He was white as a sheet, and Sever could see the perspiration running down his face. Possibly it was mixed with tears. "You told Gideon *he* killed the girl. You told him *he* ran her down, then took off. You had pictures of the car's damage and evidence to prove that his car was the weapon. And you threatened him. You told him that you'd go to the cops if he didn't turn over his publishing, his property, and everything else he owned."

"Tell us what *you* think happened, Ed." Shinn was using his most condescending attitude.

"You drove the car that night."

"Me?" He chuckled.

"You. Rusty and Gideon were higher than kites. You drove the car, and you hit the girl. When you got out to Star Island, you drove Rusty and Gideon to the house, then you pulled Gideon into the driver's side to make it look like he'd driven home. You walked off the island, had someone pick you up, and the next day you told him he'd killed the girl. You took pictures of the car, you took hair and skin samples, and God knows where you've hidden them, but you convinced Rusty and Gideon to sign over the publishing business to you or else you'd turn all the evidence over to the cops. And Gideon believed he killed that dancer. That's what happened."

"You tell a remarkable story, Ed. Please, go on."

"Rusty knew. He told me that he had vague recollections of you being in the driver's seat. And I believe when he tried to talk to you about it, you had him killed."

Shinn stared at him. "Pretty strong accusations."

Komack seemed to get his courage back. "Oh, they're more than accusations. I know what happened."

"And how can you be sure? No one's ever been arrested for the girl's death. There's never been any evidence." His voice rose a couple of notches. Shinn reached into his olive jar and grabbed a couple, popping them into his mouth.

"Someone will find the evidence that you've hidden. Then all they have to do is prove you drove the car."

"And how the hell are they going to do that?" Shinn shrugged his shoulders, looking up at Sever. All of this was supposed to be behind him. The players were all supposed to be dead. He'd see to it that they were dead in a matter of minutes.

"There's an eye witness."

"What?" Shinn was suddenly very serious. He spit out the pits. "Bullshit!"

"He came forward two days ago. Trust me, this person remembers."

"After three years? You're full of crap. Who? Who?"

"The gatekeeper out at Star Island. He remembers the night vividly, and remembers you driving Gideon's car."

Shinn's jaw dropped. "The gatekeeper? That little shit that lets people on and off the island? That pathetic scumbag who drools when an expensive car rolls through his gate? You're out of your fucking mind."

"The same. Even though it was three years ago, he said it was the only time he'd ever seen Gideon let *anyone* drive his blue Jag."

Shinn's eyes darted to Sam. "Take them up the back stairs. Now! If I can take care of you assholes, I can certainly take care of the little prick at the gate." Jimmy picked up his pistol, and Sam reached inside his jacket for his gun.

Shinn's phone chirped. He grabbed it off the desk, and flipped it open. "Not now."

Sever could almost see the steam coming out of his ears. Obviously, the gatekeeper story was news to him. Komack was full of surprises.

"I said not now, old man! I would appreciate it if you would leave me alone until I call you and tell you that it's all handled. Do you understand?" He listened for a second, then screamed into the mouthpiece. "I don't give a shit what you think. I'm the one on the firing line here, and I'll make the god-damned decisions!" He slammed the phone shut and threw it against the wall, the chrome case shattering on the concrete block. So much for fucking respect.

Shinn followed as they walked down the concrete hallway, steps echoing out of time with the muffled rhythm of the music up above. The metal door at the end of the hall swung open and Shinn motioned for Sever, Biddle, Sam, and Komack to go up. He held the gun at his side. Sam and Biddle went first, Sam meeting them at the top with his pistol pointed at Sever.

"There's a Chevy van over there. You three get in."

Thirty feet to the van. Sever moved slowly, trying to figure out something he could do. Still no sign of Ginny. He wasn't going to get into that van until he knew she was safe.

"Move it, Sever."

A Lincoln Town Car swung in ahead of them, parking in the first available spot. The driver's door opened and a well-dressed man stepped out.

"Ed. Sever." Lou Frey shouted to them.

Sever stared at the man as he reached back into the black car. "Frey, they've got guns!"

"Get down." Frey's voice was commanding.

Sever dropped to the blacktop. Glancing up he saw a pistol in Frey's hand jump and Sam let out a scream. A second shot rang out and there was glass breaking.

Sam lay on the ground, clutching his thigh and moaning. There was no sign of Shinn or Frey. Lying on his stomach, Komack nodded. And where was Biddle? He hadn't seen him since they got to the top of the stairs.

An explosion rang out and more glass shattered. From his position Sever could see Frey crouched on the driver's side of the Lincoln. Shinn was somewhere on the other side of the lot. Sever and Komack were right in the middle, sitting, or in this case, lying ducks.

"Shinn, the cops are on their way." Frey stayed behind the car.

"I own the fucking cops." His voice came from behind a light blue Ford Focus.

"Not this time, Jimmy."

"Stand up where I can see you, Lou. Come on." Another shot fired at the Lincoln. It pierced the heavy steel door.

Sever rolled to his right and reached out. Sam's pistol lay just out of reach. The large man lay moaning, hands trying to stem the flow of blood from his leg.

Another shot and the side window of the Lincoln blew out. Sever scooted forward and stretched his arm as far as he could. He could feel the trigger guard with his little finger. Snagging it, he pulled the pistol close. God, he wished he knew something about guns.

Was the safety on or off? How much kick did the pistol have? He rolled on top of the weapon, keeping it hidden underneath him.

A shot was fired from behind the Lincoln, and they heard a scream.

"I'm coming out, Frey. Don't shoot." Shinn tossed his pistol onto the blacktop and crawled out from behind the Focus. He stayed down, crouched close to the vehicle.

Sever let out a sigh of relief as Frey moved out from cover and walked to Shinn.

"Get up. I called the cops from my car. They should be here any minute. In the meantime —"

"Mick!" Ginny shouted as the door of the Chevy van swung open. The van they were supposed to be in. She tumbled out, head first, sprawling on the pavement. Biddle stepped down from the driver's side, a gun in his hand. He roughly grabbed her by the shoulder and pulled her up, keeping the gun against her back the entire time.

"Jimmy or his goons left a gun in the van, but Sam's got the keys." Biddle smiled, a trickle of blood running from his nose. "Mick, if you'll be so kind as to toss them here, the lady and I will be on our way. They're in his pocket."

"Get them yourself."

"Don't get cocky with me. I'll blow her head off, and you know I'll do it."

Sever inched across the parking lot, staying low and keeping the gun under him. He could feel it digging into his stomach. He reached Sam, and put his hand down in the man's pocket.

"Come on. Quit stalling." Biddle was shaking.

He felt the ring of keys and pulled them out of Sam's pocket. Sam lay there, writhing in pain.

Sever cocked his arm and tossed the keys.

"Cute, Sever." He pulled Ginny with him. Sever noticed for the first time that her hands were tied behind her back.

"Gin." He motioned to her with his hand, and she dropped to the ground. In the middle of reaching for the keys, Biddle jerked upright and Sever rolled, pulling the heavy pistol from under his stomach.

He prayed and squeezed.

The gun erupted in his hand with a kick-ass explosion and he pulled the trigger again, watching his confused target spin around and bounce off the side of the van. He pulled the trigger again, and again, keeping his eye on the target as Biddle slid down the steel panel.

He thought he heard sirens in the distance, but the damn noise from the gun had been so loud he figured it was probably just the ringing in his ears.

CHAPTER SIXTY-SIX

The *Old Man and the Sea* was shined up, the teak deck gleaming, and the brass and chrome newly shined.

"Here's to Gideon." Sever held his glass high.

"To Gideon." Brady, Ginny, and Komack toasted.

"Mick, again, I'm sorry for not giving you more information. In retrospect, you and I should have shared what we knew." Komack took a sip of the champagne.

"*We* did share, with Biddle, and look where that got us."

Ginny nodded. "I was a real ass, getting interested in somebody like that. Hopefully I've learned my lesson. Stay away from people in the business. It can be very dangerous, right, Mick?" She glanced at Sever.

Brady stood up and walked to the railing. He gazed at the *Hit King*. "So Shinn was paying Spinatti to keep Gideon in line?"

Komack nodded. "Yeah. Lou and I didn't know Spinatti was in on it, but we've been working on this for two years. We knew what Shinn had, how he was blackmailing Gideon, but we couldn't get Gideon to go public with it. He was scared. He couldn't believe that he'd killed someone. He was in denial, yet he didn't want the story to get out, even if it wasn't true. It turns out Biddle, his manager, and Spinatti, his boyfriend, were paid to keep tabs on Gideon. When Gideon finally agreed to tell his story to Ginny, Shinn wanted to send him a message. First of all he threatened Gideon. When Gideon disappeared, he threatened Spinatti. Sam and Harry went down and beat him up."

"That's when we found the blood on the deck," Sever said.

"Yeah. They came down and cleaned it up the next night. And when Gideon didn't come out of hiding, they had Biddle use Gideon's rifle to kill Spinatti. Biddle was a sharpshooter in the army."

"Apparently Spinatti had outlived his usefulness." Brady walked back to the deck chair. "So now they made it look like Gideon killed the boyfriend."

"As far as Jimmy Shinn was concerned, Gideon had about out-lived *his* usefulness. He was finally going public with the story, even if it meant jail time. And, he refused to give up our recording rights."

"Gideon talked a lot about the publishing business. Made a big deal out of it," Ginny said as she took another sip of bubbly. "He was trying to get me to understand how much he'd given up. I just couldn't figure it out. Then Mick and I saw the value of the pub-lishing company in his diary. Two hundred forty million. Remember, Mick?"

"How much *we'd* given up." Komack looked at her. "Although I was working some side projects, and I was able to survive pretty well, they were bleeding Gideon dry."

"And Rusty?"

"You knew him, didn't you, Mick? Rusty thought there was something strange about the hit-and-run story, and he confronted Shinn. Well, Shinn didn't want anyone messing up his lucrative deal. So we're guessing that two weeks later, he forced Rusty to draw up papers for transfer of the publishing company by threatening to go public with the accident in Platinum's parking lot. Even though he was suspicious, Rusty didn't have enough information to prove Shinn wrong, so he signed the papers. Then they bashed Rusty's head in and threw him in the water."

"Outlived his usefulness." Brady poured more champagne for everyone.

"So why did Frey's associate, Charlie Strict, set up a meeting with me? And why did Biddle shoot him?"

"I know why Charlie Strict wanted to talk to you. He was pushing Frey and me to start sharing some information. Trouble is, we didn't know if we could trust you and Ginny. So Strict was going to talk to you and try to get a feel for just how much you could be trusted."

"And Biddle shot him."

"He tried to kill you. He heard your message in Ginny's room, and knew you'd be on the dock. I guess he wanted to put one more nail in Gideon's coffin. Now they had three murders to hang on Gideon. The dancer who was run over, Spinatti, and Strict. You were the target, Strict was a secondary target."

"And Frey? What's his story?"

"He's a very talented attorney. He takes his job pretty seriously and he looks out for his clients. He and I talked about this for a long time, and we pieced it together."

Sever waited for more. Komack shut down.

"Ed, the guy showed up with guns blazing, for Christ's sake. He's a little more than a talented attorney."

"Oh. I got a phone call off to his voice mail telling him I was coming to Platinum. Lou tells me that he had a premonition that something bad was about to happen, so on a whim he drove over. Personally, I think it was luck. He always carries the gun, and when he saw us parading out of the building he figured it out. Thank God he carries."

Ginny stood up and walked to the railing, stroking the smooth polished brass. She leaned back on the metal and the breeze played with her hair. "And what is the story with the gatekeeper over at Star Island?"

Komack chuckled. "Blind luck. I had to go over there the other day to get some papers from Shinn. I talked to the gatekeeper and when I told him where I was going, he just told me."

"Told you?"

"He said, 'Oh, you're going to see Mr. Shinn. You know, he's the only man I know that ever was allowed to drive Gideon Pike's Jag.' "

Sever smiled. "He said that?"

"Out of the clear blue, swear to God." Komack nodded his head. "He still remembered. So I pushed him, and he said it was about three years ago and Pike, Rusty, and Shinn had pulled onto the island drunk as hell. Shinn was driving. I got the impression this gatekeeper was not a Jimmy Shinn fan."

"What about Shinn's old man?"

"Hard to say. Frey says they've got to do some digging to prove that he was in on the blackmailing. I'm sure they'll get him eventually. This guy has been involved in organized crime for over fifty years." Komack looked out over the water back to Pike's condo. "You know, Jimmy and his father just about took us down. All the way."

Sever studied the man. He'd been a lot more involved than anyone knew, and the stress was finally starting to lift. "Ed, what do you know about Ray Haver, the homicide cop?"

"With the millions that Shinn had, he was paying off more cops than just Haver. When the payments dry up, and they certainly will now, the loyalty stops. Internal Affairs will try to find out who was on the payroll, but chances are those cops will crawl back into their hole until the next offer comes along." Komack stood up. "I've got to go. I promised Frey that I'd sit down with him and go over some paperwork. There are contracts to sign, and I'm all of a sudden a full partner. Gideon had to almost die for me to get my dues. Life's full of ironies."

"If it hadn't been for Frey, we might all be history," Sever said.

Ginny took Sever's hand. "I . . . I . . ." she stammered, "I just want to say that what *you* did . . . I mean, it's been a couple of days but I still can't . . ." She shuddered. "If it hadn't been for *you* . . . I wouldn't be here right now. Mick, I . . ."

He squeezed her fingers. "I know." Sever looked out over the water. "The worst part of this whole thing was what happened to April — Martha."

They were all silent for a moment.

"She helped us make sense of the diary. Boots and Kick, the accident —" Ginny put her hand over his. "I'm not sure she ever put the entire thing together, but she was trying to protect Bridgette and Kyle."

"If she hadn't talked to me, she'd still be alive. How do I reconcile that fact?"

Brady walked over to them, putting his hand on top of Ginny's. "You saved Pike's life, Ginny's life, Kick's life, and Ed's life. I think Shinn would have killed them all."

"Honest to God, she was a sweet girl. And she wanted to do something to save Gideon and Bridgette and their son." Sever closed his eyes for just a moment.

"She did, Mick. She did." Ginny squeezed his hand.

Komack frowned. "Hey. Sam strangled April. You can't blame yourself for that. Don't beat yourself up."

Sever turned to Komack. "What about April's little girl?"

"Bridgette is going to watch the little girl, and maybe apply for adoption. April was Kick's godmother, and Bridgette is the little girl's godmother. They were looking out for each other. Considering she was a stripper, her chances with the court may not be that good, but hey, it's possible."

The chirping started on Komack's belt. He snapped open his phone. "Hello?"

He listened for thirty seconds. "I'll tell them. And you take it easy. I'll see you later today." He shoved the phone back in its holster. "Gideon. He's recovering nicely and he wants you to know that he and Bridgette more than appreciate everything you've done."

"And the story? The Diary of Gideon Pike?" Ginny looked at him inquisitively.

"He said you've got the exclusive on everything. You should be able to see him early next week. Should be a hell of a story."

"Should put you and Pike right back on top of the charts."

Komack smiled. "Can't hurt."

Sever and Ginny walked down the plank to the dock, looking straight ahead. He glanced up at the Grand Condominiums, watching the sun's blinding orange ball bounce off Pike's sliding glass door.

"I'm sorry, Mick. God, what you've been through. You know I'd never have asked you down here if I'd had a clue how bad this was going to be."

He looked into her eyes and saw his past. "I wouldn't have missed it. Even the three hours with the cops after they picked us up."

"And, I didn't mean to mislead you." Just the hint of a smile on her full lips.

"Maybe we'll do it again."

"Maybe. You know, we still seem to work together pretty well."

It was Sever's turn to smile. "But *we* don't work."

"No. Are you okay with that?"

Sever gazed back at the condo complex, then across the water to South Beach. The causeway was filling up with cars, eager locals and tourists heading out to the restaurants and bars, getting an early start on the nightlife.

"No. But I'll get over it." He wouldn't. But what the hell could you do?

"And maybe another project will come along."

"You never know."

"Actually, I've got one. You and I need to write some songs. Really. That's where the money is, Mick. That's where the money is. And I know this publishing company —"

CHAPTER SIXTY-SEVEN

February had been cool, some days not getting out of the sixties. Today was different. Highs in the eighties, and the locals in South Beach had shed their coats and jackets for short-sleeved shirts, shorts, short skirts, and sandals. Ocean Drive and the News Café were bustling as the old man sat down at the one outside table still open, laying the still folded newspaper on the empty chair next to him. He ordered a salad and a bottle of San Pellegrino water, his eyes surveying the assembled diners as if searching for someone that he knew. Finally he leaned back and closed those eyes, slowly taking measured breaths as if in a trance.

"Sir? Your salad is ready."

He opened his eyes, glancing up only for a second. Taking a long drink from the bottle of sparkling water, he gently unfolded the paper exposing the front page. The young handsome man in the picture looked back at him, a frown on his unblemished face. His arms were behind him as two men in suits walked on either side. The bold headlines told the story.

JIMMY SHINN CONVICTED
EXTORTION, MURDER, AND MORE TO FOLLOW

He studied the picture for a minute more, then slowly folded the paper and lay it back on the chair. Pushing the chair back and dropping a ten-dollar bill on the table, the old man stood up and walked away. No one noticed. It was as if he were invisible. If anyone had seen him, if anyone had cared, they would have seen an elderly Asian gentleman, his head hanging low, the tears streaming down his face.